Advance Praise

"A raw and unvarnished portrait of friendships, dreams, heartbreak, and growth. A nostalgic dance through the 1970s Mid-Atlantic region that will bring back so many memories of forgotten places and hidden treasures!"

— Kate Danley, *USA Today* Bestselling Author, *Maggie MacKay: Maggie Tracker Series*

"Not all young women were bra-burning feminists in the 70s, including Margie, the protagonist of *That Summer She Found Her Voice* by Jean Burgess. Margie's passage from a naïve recent college graduate to a woman who lives her values poignantly reflects the path of so many young women who came of age in the wake of the Second Wave of feminism. While traveling cross-country as a vocalist in a swing band, Margie also takes an inward journey, leading her to a place where she no longer defines her self-worth by her relationship with a man—be it her father, her boyfriend, or her boss. Burgess's meticulous attention to historical detail captures the flavor of the 70s, enhancing her engaging plot and compassionate characterization in a way that sheds light on the trajectory of feminism's influence on American pop culture."

— Barbara Van Aken, Ph.D. Department of English, Case Western Reserve University

"Being from a family of Maryland musicians, I found Jean Burgess' novel a well-written and engaging story of living with a band on the road. The protagonist is Margie, a young woman beginning her career as a musician and thrilled at the opportunity of playing with a traveling band. Her experiences and the characters she meets ring true."

— Eileen Haavik McIntire, author of the *90s Club* cozy mysteries

"*That Summer She Found Her Voice* is the story of a young woman, Margie, who finds her way out of a depression caused by a failed romantic relationship by touring as a singer with King Vido's Swing Band in the late 1970s. Burgess has curated a passionate first-person account of self-discovery. As an experienced theatrical director and playwright, she knows how to create sympathetic characters and compelling plots, using her considerable talent and craftsmanship to tell this story."

— Ira Domser, Professor Emeritus Dramatic Arts, McDaniel College

That Summer
She Found
Her Voice

That Summer She Found Her Voice

A Retro Novel

Jean Burgess

Apprentice
House Press
Loyola University Maryland

First Edition

Library of Congress Control Number: requested

Hardcover ISBN: 978-1-62720-484-2
Paperback ISBN: 978-1-62720-485-9
Ebook ISBN: 978-1-62720-486-6

Design by Apprentice House Press
Editorial Development by Evi Rizas
Cover photo by Yoel J. Gonzalez on Unsplash

Permission for Ram Dass quotations by ©Love Serve Remember Foundation, www.RamDass.org

Published by Apprentice House Press

Apprentice
House Press
Loyola University Maryland

Loyola University Maryland
4501 N. Charles Street, Baltimore, MD 21210
410.617.5265
www.ApprenticeHouse.com / info@ApprenticeHouse.com

For anyone whose voice is buried deep inside.
May you one day discover peace in its release.

1

A Miracle

Cambridge, Maryland – March, 1978

It was a miracle. A prayer answered. From the depths of personal despair, a possible solution loomed before me.

```
Audition Notice: King Vido's Swing Band.
```

Could this really be it? The answer? I'd been mentally spiraling for months, feeling trapped in this bummer of a town on the Eastern Shore. My hometown of Church Creek, population maybe 25, sat in the shadow of the nearest "big city," Cambridge, Maryland. While Cambridge was hardly a bustling metropolis, it was semi entertaining for this college graduate now one year passed with zero prospects for any sort of career, or marriage, as Dad kept reminding me. But there was more to my anguish than feeling trapped. I'd lost something vital to my survival.

It was my own damn fault. I was one of the lucky ones who even got to go to college. I mean, the options for most mid-1970s Cambridge High School grads were kinda bleak. But somehow, between grants, scholarships, loans, and working in the college cafeteria for four grueling years, I ended up attending and graduating from St. Angela College in Chestertown, Maryland. But, while the rest of my tiny 1977 graduating class had taken the disciplined steps to sharpen their skills, perfect their passions, and nail down a degree-related job or at the very least fall back on a teaching position during our final academic year, I did not. Did I have poor grades? Not at all. Did I lack a college major? Certainly not. The problem: Love knocked me on my ass!

Ah yes, the naïve belief in the promise of a true love derailed any future career plans I may have held. *And brother, did I fall freakin' hard.*

Between my junior and senior year of college I waitressed at Doris Mae's Diner in downtown Cambridge. It was there that I met my Adonis, my Romeo, my John Travolta. I'd spotted him at the counter once before, but we were slammed that day and I never had a free moment to say hello. The next time he came in, I was on the register, giving me the perfect opportunity to look him over. Tall and slim with amazing wavy blond hair pulled into a ponytail. When he came over to pay his tab, we chatted... well, mostly he chatted; I drooled.

"I'm David. I'm kinda new around here. Just started working over at Sid Johnson Marine Center on the docks."

"Uh-h, hi." I blubbered, trying to force myself to stop staring and form syllables into something intelligent. He smiled.

"Hey, if you like motorcycles, maybe you'd like to take a ride on my Harley someday." *Did I sense an instantaneous connection or was I so mesmerized by those gorgeous ocean-blue eyes I'd lost my mind?*

Gathering all the coolness genes I possessed, I strung a few words together. "Yeah, sure, I'd be down with that." *Right, that came out super cool, Margie.*

I watched him walk out the door, grooving on his casual, confident vibe: tight jeans, biker boots, striped button-down shirt with rolled up sleeves, and denim jacket slung over one shoulder. In other words, an off the hook and ultra-cool vibe.

But it was more than David's great looks and Harley. Once we started dating, his self-assured, spontaneous, enlightened personality knocked me for a loop. I loved how his aura filled the room. We spent hours talking about philosophy, religion, politics, world peace, current events…topics that were never discussed around my family dinner table. He opened my eyes to things I had never considered – Eastern religious practices, yoga, the teachings of spiritual leader Ram Dass, meditation. Mind-blowing stuff for a naïve only child raised in tiny Church Creek, Maryland by a commandeering father and quiet mother.

That first summer we spent a lot of time going for long walks along the breezy Choptank River and reading passages from David's favorite book, *Remember: Be Here Now.* "This book will change your life, Margie!"

"It's written by this psychologist Richard Alpert, at first about his experimentation with psychedelics. But later, Alpert goes to India and meets his guru, who names him 'Ram Dass,' and he dedicates his life to spreading spiritual inspiration. Isn't that freakin' radical?"

"It's way cool. His messages are really speaking to me, David."

He'd smile and push the hair from my face as we sat along the city pier dangling our feet in the water. I did find serenity sharing quotes like: "Emotions are like waves. Watch them disappear in the distance on the vast calm ocean." A single passage led to hours of dissecting Dass's idea. "I think the message is that you don't need to go to anywhere else to find what you are seeking," a tenet reinforced by David.

"Everything we need is right here, babe. We could be happy forever." His words transported me with images of the two of us, nestled together in a love cloud with no worries or concerns, away from my dingy childhood house. At the same time, I found myself journaling and writing less so that I could devote more time to reading and reflecting on David's recommended books.

With David's constant and strong encouragement, I embraced the idea that I needed to look no further than the present moment to begin to find peace and joy. "Be here now!" was the Ram Dass central message. Although I tried to express that I felt great joy when I sang or listened to inspired music or wrote a creative piece, David explained that those "externals" would never create lasting peace. He pushed me to accept his own interpretation of "being in the moment" to mean "letting go of all worldliness." While confused at times, I eventually became a willing voyager on this journey, as long as David was by my side.

Once the fall semester began again, David rode his Harley the fifty miles from Cambridge up to Chestertown to visit – just weekends at first, but then he started surprising me mid-week. We'd sneak off on his bike during the evenings to explore the charming streets of Chestertown or ride along the Chester River, picking up a pizza along the way to eat under a tree as we watched the moon's reflection in the calm river water. David seduced me with words. As a creative writer, I was a pushover.

"Do you feel it, babe? That energy, that electricity pulsating between us whenever our bodies are close?" I could only murmur in response, enraptured by his words and body.

"Margie, the way you radiate red auras of pure energy, it's amazing…and very sexy. I want you so bad, babe."

I didn't understand a word of it, but he drew me in. I became hypnotized by those deep azure eyes. I felt special, unique. I gave my virginity to him willingly on a knitted pink and brown granny square quilt spread out on the riverbank, while a chorus of crickets, croaking frogs, and quacking ducks provided a musical symphony in the background. He was my first. I fell for him hard and fast.

As the months flew by, David and I dabbled in talk of "What's next?" despite the "Be here now" philosophy. David had big dreams and painted a picture of his future.

"I want to buy a sailboat one day and cruise around the Chesapeake with my girl by my side." While it did cross my mind that a boat seemed a bit "worldly," I justified it as a "means to an end," the goal being a simpler life. *Talk about being naïve!*

"What about you, babe. You love the Chesapeake, right?" *Was he putting words in my mouth?*

Trying to remind him about my love of music, I said, "Well, my mom will tell you and anyone who will listen that from the moment I emerged from the womb I was singing and dancing…." I paused for a second, searching for a reaction on David's face but got nothing. "And you know how much I enjoy writing. That's the whole reason I'm majoring in music and minoring in creative writing at St. Angela's.

"Yeah, right." Little to no enthusiasm registered in David's response.

I tried to smooth over the ugly cloud that had so quickly developed. "I do love the Chesapeake and the water and all, but I thought that I might…someday…want to go to graduate school. You know, to learn more about music or writing."

At the mention of graduate school, David became mopey, and super quiet, as though the idea of grad school hurt his feelings. Initially, I took his reaction to mean that he wanted me to stay nearby because he loved me so much. That was what I told myself. Rather than summon the courage to ask him directly, I stopped talking about grad school, putting my plans on the back burner. *The reality is I stopped talking about grad school to avoid confrontation. Not speaking up is my specialty!*

While bike rides and midnight pizza and lovemaking on random weekdays did distract me from my course work, my grades remained solid. *Embrace the present moment, right? Or so I keep convincing myself.* But looking back, that final year of college wasn't supposed to be solely about solid grades. That was a time to master focus and artistic discipline and plan next steps. From those pursuits, my concentration waned. Even more damaging was the effect this had on my spirit, my love of music and writing. I strayed from my vocal work, practiced less, stopped auditioning for musicals at the local community theatre. My Senior Recital at St. Angela's was not my best work. I pretended I didn't care that David was a "no-show," telling myself that he wouldn't have enjoyed the classical music pieces I performed anyway. Instead of growing in my craft, my passion for music and writing became displaced by David's interests. But I was in love, so it was all worth it, right?

Graduation came and went. I stayed on at the greasy spoon in Cambridge, waiting on watermen, farmers, and locals, and seeing David whenever our schedules permitted. The bright sunshine of summer dissolved into the golden haze of early fall – the perfect backdrop for love to flourish on Maryland's Eastern Shore. Throughout the summer, we took bike rides exploring miles of back roads leading to tiny inlets along the coastline and saltwater outlets. In the evenings, we visited marinas packed tight with sailboats, their masts appearing as dark silhouettes against orange, pink, and magenta skies. We picnicked in secluded spots along the salt marshes watching egrets, herons, and osprey hunt for their own dinner, read books from David's suggested list in the sunshine together, and, of course, had incredible sex. By this time, I'd completely given up daily writing entries in my journal or any musical pursuits, focusing all my spare time on David.

How could I fritter away weeks rehearsing for a community theatre production of *My Fair Lady* when I preferred to spend my time at a secluded spot, gazing into David's eyes, listening to him talk after we made passionate love?

But as the weather turned colder in late November, a coolness developed in David as well. I didn't understand it. When I asked him to talk to me about the chill between us, he responded with something obscure from Ram Dass.

"It's only when caterpillarness is done that one becomes a butterfly." *What the hell did that mean?*

"David, I'm sorry but…I kinda don't get it."

"What I'm trying to say is that you can be such a sensitive, naïve chick sometimes, Margie." Just like that, insecurity slithered into my psyche like a toxic viper.

"But you still love me, right?" I whined, hating myself for the way I sounded.

"Love is love is love." Then he continued with more meaningless drivel. "I love all the universe's creatures, Margie. You really need to keep up with the teachings." That level of cryptic communication endured for several months, eating away at my confidence, my self-esteem, and mostly, my heart and soul. *I'm sure Gloria Steinem is cringing at my lack of self-awareness.*

Then the thunderbolt struck. One Thursday evening in mid-February, my shift at Doris Mae's Diner was wrapping up. The place was empty. As I sat around refilling catsup bottles and pepper shakers, a nifty idea popped into my head. I decided to surprise David when his shift ended.

"Hey Doris, it's so slow this evening. Do you mind if I knock off a bit early?"

"Not a problem, sweetie. Got a date with that nice looking boy, David?" she asked.

I laughed at Doris Mae's curiosity. A bit of a legend in town, she knew everyone's comings and goings, but she was discreet.

"Well, if you must know, even though I smell like greasy hamburgers and fried fish, I thought I'd surprise him with a romantic winter picnic under a warm blanket along the river. What do you think?"

Doris jumped into action behind the counter. "I'm thinking two tuna subs, dill pickles, and chips!"

"Perfect. I'll pick up a bottle of wine on the way."

Visualizing a romantic car picnic for two under a warm blanket along the river, I drove over to the docks around five o'clock, David's usual quitting time. I parked my car on the street and walked down the long ramp toward the shed where he clocked out. As I turned the corner on the ramp, I spotted David walking into the arms of woman. He embraced her affectionately as her long, black hair blew freely in the wind. I watched, horrified, for what seemed like an eternity, as they passionately kissed. David looked up as they separated. Our eyes locked and, in that glance, my heart imploded, my world shattering.

In the next moment, I felt a huge pressure in my chest, like boulders piling on, crushing my lungs. I gasped for air. I couldn't breathe. I could not…get…enough…air! I began to panic. Dizziness set in. I turned and tried to run up the ramp, grabbing the railing to steady each step. Somehow, I was able to navigate myself to my car and slip into the driver's seat. I swallowed hard, fighting back tears, becoming more concerned about a heaviness in my chest that made each breath increasingly difficult to draw. *Breathe, Margie. Slowly through the nose. Follow the breath in, watch the breath go out.* Frantic, I tried to remember the breathing exercises from meditation practice – *deep breath in, slow breath out, watch each breath in and out.* After several attempts, the spasm in my chest began to let go. But the realization remained: In a flash, this magical relationship between David and me vanished.

Looking back, I admit the obvious buildup made the event predictable, but heartbreaking all the same. So much so that I became despondent. A downward spiral became fixed in my brain and heart and spirit, fueled by a cycle of both blame and shame, from which I truly began to believe I would never return. One moment, I blamed David for ripping a gaping hole in my heart, the next I chastised myself for relinquishing so much of my soul to this man. The same thoughts tormented me: *I'd given up so much, for what? A guy? Motorcycle rides and romantic picnics? Love? What kind of future did I think I'd have with him? Was I idiotic enough to think he was going to rescue me from my drab existence in Church Creek, from waitressing for the rest of my life, from working at Dad's general store till I marry some Choptank waterman?* Anger welled up at myself, even more so than at David. *What a naïve fool I am. Everyone you know is off making a future and you're left behind. You threw away your music, your writing, your time. It's too late to apply for grad school. Most of all, you gave up on yourself and all that's left is an empty shell.* I taunted myself, again and again, feeling myself sinking lower and lower into an abyss.

I began feeling angry at everything and everyone in my life: at my thriving classmates, my dull customers at the diner, but mostly me. I couldn't stop berating myself. I lost not only the good times with David and my plans for graduate school, but now I was losing mind and heart as well. Wasting so much time fawning over David and ignoring my creative muse had left a cavernous hole in me. Without music and writing, I felt rudderless, joyless, purposeless. I was spiraling fast.

Holed up in my dreary bedroom with its worn-out shag carpeting and faded floral curtains in my parents' tiny, rundown house in Church Creek, I wallowed in my personal darkness. Mom tried her feeble best to cheer me up. I knew she was concerned, but I wasn't in a mental place to acknowledge what she was saying.

"Margaret, dear. I'm so worried about you. You won't come out of your room, you haven't eaten…this is so unlike you. Can I bring you anything? What if I make a batch of Tollhouse bars?"

I remained silent. Eventually she fell back on worn-out slogans from my childhood that I'm sure saw her through her own tough times and were probably learned from her parents. Sayings like "Push the hurt aside and keep going," and "Let's not let em' see you down," and "A smile will get you through the day." But frankly, her platitudes annoyed me now. They couldn't begin to help ease the heartbreak or this failure that was my life. I was sinking so deep I couldn't heed any of her well-meant adages. In fact, I felt worse having her fuss over me.

Dad's response was no better. He couldn't understand my depression. He stuck his head into my bedroom door and asked, "Why are ya still carrying a torch for that hippy? You're better off without 'em. He was a bad influence on ya with all that crazy yoga meditation malarkey!"

A few days later Dad popped into my room and offered what I'm sure he thought were profound words of advice, guaranteed to snap me out of my malaise.

"Aren't ya being a bit oversensitive, Margaret? Here's what ya should do: Quit that silly diner job and come work at the general store full-time until a nice local guy marries ya. Then pop out a couple grandkids!" This was a proposition I fiercely resisted and didn't help cheer me up at all. Of course, his world would have been complete if I gave up both my "foolish" ideas of music or writing and especially graduate school.

To avoid my parents in the evenings, I locked myself away in my room, staring at black and white images on a 12" portable TV. A Sears' *Wish Book* special! While my brain rotted on episodes of *Three's Company*, *Laverne and Shirley*, and *The Love Boat*, my spirit continued to leech from my damaged core.

When I did pry myself away from the house, there was David riding around Cambridge with a new girl on the back of his Harley – a source of constant pain. Just as I felt I might be getting a grip on my life, there he'd be zooming by, ripping the newly formed scab off my barely healed emotional wounds. I imagined him sharing long walks and picnic lunches with her, conversing about philosophy and spiritual topics, which only made me feel ridiculous and angry. *Was he telling her, "Everything we need is right here? We could be happy forever, babe."? Agh! That chasm in my heart will never heal if I keep seeing them together!*

Beyond the self-pity and anger, a darkness beyond black consumed me. I started hating my family, our dilapidated house, the town, its people, myself. I could not see a way out. Too late to apply for graduate school, zero music or writing opportunities in Cambridge, a pittance of savings I'd earned at the diner. It all became stifling. The thought of striking out to New York or D.C. or even Baltimore for a fresh start – laughable. The worst was the feeling of soullessness. What was my purpose if I had no music in my heart? Why even get up in the morning if I had nothing to write about? These thoughts started closing in on me, suffocating me, blocking out any ray of light or hope. Numbness and paralysis set in.

I felt nothing. Nothing jogged me out of the downward cycle. Nothing reignited my passion for music, my desire to sing, or even to write. I wanted to find my voice, to express my emotions, excitement, love. What I needed was hope, opportunity, a life preserver, something of gigantic proportions, to pull me out of this sinking state of mind and soul.

Hence, the miracle!

Dragging myself through my waitressing shift on a Wednesday in mid-April, exhausted from pretending everything was hunky-dory, I grabbed a soda and the daily edition of *The Banner* and drove to a favorite quiet spot. Near the end of High Street, a rocky perch facing the Choptank River had become my personal refuge, a retreat from the world and place to connect to nature. My semi-secluded spot provided a perfect view for watching the sun's reflection create a shimmering pattern of diamonds on the water as it began its descent in the late afternoon. The hypnotic effect took away the numbness for a moment until…

Suddenly, thoughts of death flooded my brain. I was knocked off-balance as these mental images and feelings battled it out in my head. Nothingness. *This emptiness is too much. What's the point…?* David. *He was all I wanted in my life.* Dark water below. *But wait, I know I'm depressed, but is it that bad, Margie?* Black hair blowing in the wind. *Do you really want to be with a guy who would hurt you like that?* Emptiness. *But what am I going to do now?* General store. *I have no options. I'm stuck in Dad's general store for the rest of my life without David.* Blackness. *Oh God! What's the point…?* I tried to shake off anything close to suicidal thoughts. My brain war continued to rage, while the rest of me was numb to the point of barely functioning. *Breathe…Just one breath.*

Next, I found myself thinking about God. I wasn't especially religious, having had plenty of reasons to question my Catholic upbringing. Regardless, I believed in some sort of Divine someone or something. I wondered if God had forgotten about me, or maybe He was punishing me for being such an idiot and ruining my life. *No,* I argued with myself, *God doesn't randomly punish people, does He? Of course, He does, Margie. The Bible is full of examples of His punishing ways. On the other hand, the scripture is full of examples of His mercy, too. So, I don't understand why He's left me in this fog of darkness. Couldn't He help lift me out of this funk?* The next thing I knew, I did something I rarely did before. I began to pray:

God, I need help. I'm in a bad place and I'm sinking fast. I need some kind of miracle to lift me out of this. I need You to show me how to open up to the world instead of letting it close in on me. I need help to feel something again, to start to heal this gash in my heart. I don't know what to do next. Please, God. Help me.

What happened next counts as, well…a miracle, at least to my way of thinking. I opened *The Banner* and on page two, it appeared: An audition notice for "King Vido's Swing Band." A ridiculously tiny notice on the bottom of the page, easy to over-look, but it glared at me as if encircled by neon lights. I read it over several times, my heart beating faster each time.

```
Looking for singers who move well for
permanent tour of the U.S.. Must be
proficient in several genres, includ-
ing pop, Broadway style, country,
and gospel. Call the number below to
schedule an audition appointment by
April 12, 1978. Bring sheet music in
the correct key and wear comfortable
clothes to move in. Studio located
in Little Italy, Baltimore, Maryland
on Albemarle Street. Directions pro-
vided when appointment is scheduled.
```

This is it. My ticket. The numbness began to disappear. In its place, scary, excited feelings surged. But at least I felt something! While it may sound crazy in hindsight, in that moment I knew for certain that I would audition and be selected for that tour.

Later, as I carefully glued the audition notice into my writing journal, I felt a new confidence that going on the road with a swing band was exactly the change of perspective I needed at that point in my life. I hoped it would revive my passion for music and writing too. I printed the words "Excited" and "Scary" and "Amazing" on that journal page, as I wasn't feeling inspired to write much more. *Hey, it's a start!* As Ram Dass says, "Everything in life is there as a vehicle for your transformation. Use it!"

I planned to do just that!

2

Audition Nerves

Cambridge, Maryland – April, 1978

Despite protests from Dad, who declared I was beyond crazy, and Mom's concern for my safety, I grabbed my sheet music and pointed my car toward Baltimore. *You'd think they'd at least be glad I'm not still moping around, but I guess my mood swing caught them off guard.* Frankly, even I surprised myself with this sudden surge of courage. But convinced I'd chosen the right path, and ignoring the occasional wave of nerves, I trudged on.

With a map of Baltimore laid out on the front seat and Jackson Browne's "Running on Empty" playing on my 8-track tape player, I headed North on Route 50 over the Choptank River, watching Cambridge disappear in my rearview mirror. I sang along with the chorus as I scanned the flat, Eastern Shore scenery. *My life may be running on empty, but I'm hopeful this audition will be what I need to turn it around.*

Easton, the next town of any size, was sixteen miles ahead with plenty of nothing in between. I watched for hawks and vultures over open fields, while praying my old junker of a car would complete the trip. Dad had bought me the used AMC Gremlin before I graduated from high school.

"Happy graduation, Margaret. I've been thinkin' about this. You'll be needin' an auto to get around now that you're older."

"Nifty." I said as I examined the white exterior with the red stripe running along the side panel, curving up to meet the roof in the back.

"Now it's seven years old but runs good. Ya gotta keep it up, though. I'm goin' teach ya some of the basics. Ya know, like how to check the oil, add water to the radiator, change the air filter, and whatnot. Every car owner needs to know how to do these things."

"Wow, I dig the red interior and oh look…there's a hatch-back here in the rear."

Dad yelled to get my attention. "Jesus, Mary, and Joseph! Margaret, are you listenin' to me?"

"Yes, yes."

My initial suspicion about the whole car thing was eventually confirmed. The real reason Dad bought me a car was because he didn't want to take the time away from his general store to have to transport me to college. I was fine with that. But for anyone who knows anything about AMCs, the 1970 Gremlin was the pits! Oh, I loved the look of it but overall, for a seven-year-old car, the thing ran like crap!

That's what confused me about Dad, though. Did he really think it was his fatherly duty to buy me a car, or was he trying to pass off his responsibility to transport me to college because it might take him away from his precious general store? And then, when he did decide to buy me a car, he went for the cheapest used vehicle he could find. I understood that we didn't have a ton of money sitting around. Obviously a general store in Church Creek, Maryland didn't rake in the dough. But the gesture left me puzzled. His values usually clashed with mine and left me in the dark. I guess that's why we didn't communicate very well.

Mom, on the other hand, was totally the opposite. With her,

I knew where she held her values: Education, first and foremost. From my first memories I can hear Mom telling me how important it was.

"Remember, sweet Margaret, you must learn all you can in Kindergarten. Listen to your teacher and don't fool around."

"Will I like school, Mommy?" I remember asking.

She took me on her lap and gave me a squeeze. "You will love, love, love school. You'll have picture books to read and colorful puzzles to work and fun art projects to do. And there will be new boys and girls to meet, not just Mommy to see every day."

Mom had attended college in Virginia, majoring in elementary education, and she was determined I would attend college too, even though Dad was lukewarm on the idea. The only way she won him over was to dangle the Catholic College idea and to make sure I was eligible for grants, scholarships, and work-study opportunities at St. Angela's. She valued academics, even though she gave up teaching first grade to follow Dad to Church Creek – a move I never understood. She must have really loved the guy. *Either that or there's way more to their relationship than I can figure out.*

I supposed Dad may have been a looker in his younger days, but twenty-five years of single-handedly stocking and running a general store had taken its toll. A graying, receding hairline framed his ruddy, lined complexion. While still muscular in the upper body, Dad's sagging belly and stooped posture told the story of a worn-out, fifty-eight-year-old. Mom, on the other hand, still looked radiant to me. Petite, active, and lovely, although she kept any gray hair concealed with monthly applications of Clairol's Loving Care #77 Medium Ash Brown. It might be snide to say, but I always thought Dad got a much better deal in marrying Mom.

Despite her outward composure, a bit of sadness lurked behind Mom's pretty eyes. She tried to hide it, but her melancholy had a way of trickling out, especially during my high school and college years. Did she miss her old teaching life, or did she feel stuck? Or was she re-living her life through me by encouraging me to pursue a college education and look beyond the limits I had been setting for myself? *Could she be living vicariously through me or does she know I need pushing, since I tend to shy away from taking initiatives? On the other hand, here I am driving to Baltimore to audition for a traveling swing band! Totally out of character, Margie!*

After reaching Easton, I continued to drive another thirty-six miles to the Bay Bridge, crossing the Chesapeake Bay. Due to construction on the second span of the bridge, traffic was diverted to a single extension of two-way traffic, causing delays and a potential late arrival for the audition. *Thank goodness the wind isn't raging. The Bay Bridge can be freakin' scary when the wind is blustering.* Despite the narrow bridge and two-way traffic, I stole a few glimpses over the guardrails at the choppy bay below. The sun peeked out between dark puffy clouds. White caps lapped in the distance. Beautiful gulls of all sizes soared overhead. I spotted a few boats on the water, despite the unseasonably cool April weather. The combination of gulls and brave seafarers gave me hope that summer would be here soon, my future brighter as well.

Once over the Bay Bridge, I needed to pay attention to the unfolded map spread out on the passenger's seat. I still had another forty-five miles or so until I hit Baltimore, but after getting off Route 50, the directions became a bit complicated with several turns onto different roads.

I had been to Baltimore a few times with Mom and Dad

to pick up merchandise for the general store in the Lexington Market when deliveries were backed up, but that's different from driving there yourself. On this trip, I was heading to a different section of Baltimore. Once I reached the Little Italy neighborhood, I kept my eyes peeled for the King Studio & Creative Talent Agency, located at 324 Albemarle Street. Spotting a huge "Little Italy" sign hanging over a main thoroughfare, I knew I arrived in the right neighborhood. *So far, so good,* I encouraged myself as I maneuvered through the narrow streets.

324 Albemarle Street. I searched for the address, driving like a ninety-year-old geezer through charming streets lined with bakeries, delis, restaurants, and brick rowhouses set off by wide sidewalks, I acclimated myself as I scanned street numbers. Many streets were one-way, which the map only indicated for main thoroughfares. Humming to warm up my voice, I ultimately circled through the neighborhood four times before I found the right block and building.

324 Albemarle Street! Found it. Huh! The building didn't look like a commercial studio, but more like a residential, red brick rowhouse. A sign over the door read: King Studio & Creative Talent Agency. Another plaque on the right side of the door read: Conti Cabinet Making, LLC. *Hm, a bizarre mix of business interests, but what do I know?*

God, I hope I don't have the wrong address. That would be disastrous. I started to feel that crushing weight in my chest again. A few deep breaths brought relief until a quick look at my watch created another wave of panic. *It's already two o'clock, my scheduled audition time!* Pleased with my decision to wear my "comfortable clothes to move in" for the nearly three-hour drive, I wouldn't have to waste time changing at the studio. Throwing together an Indian print, wrap-around skirt over a brown, short-sleeved leotard with matching brown tights meant all I needed to do was slip off my clogs and change into jazz shoes for the dance audition. I found a parking spot on the street nearby and rushed to the front door of the studio.

"Please be the right address, please be the right address," I repeated to myself, as I knocked on the heavy oak door.

A "bottle blond" woman in her early twenties, reeking of Jean Naté cologne, opened the door a crack, and sized me up. "You're late," she snapped, opening the door wider. I took this as an invitation to enter.

I stepped into a small foyer, taking in the view of a long, narrow hallway ending with a door. To the right, a staircase with an ornate wooden banister led to the second story. To the left, an archway opened into what would have been the living room of a regular house. Instead, I found an office with a desk outfitted with a typewriter, desk accessories, and a phone, engulfed in a cloud of cigarette smoke. Behind the desk, a row of gray metal file drawers stood guard, heaped with piles of folders, binders, and loose papers. In an adjoining room, perhaps the original dining room, sat a grandiose, shiny, mahogany desk, surrounded by two oak file cabinets, a mimeograph machine, and a steel safe. Two large, framed posters of saxophone players hung on the side walls.

Blondie pointed impatiently to a few mismatched plastic chairs arranged along the wall facing the desk in the smoky room. An older woman, cigarette dangling from her lips, firmly anchored behind the desk, simultaneously typed and answered ringing phones. I sat like an obedient third grader. *Blondie could have introduced herself*, I thought to myself, as she disappeared around the corner and down the long hall.

"Don't let Princess shake youse, hon. She's threatened by

newcomers," said a gravelly voice from behind the typewriter, before answering another call. "King Studio & Creative Talent Agency. How can I help youse? Oh hey, George. Yep, confirmed for Saturday at the Masonic Hall in Philly. Eight o'clock show-time for the hour and a half magic act. Seven o'clock call. Okay, bye hon." The woman hung up, puffing another cloud of smoke into the atmosphere. "I'm Ruby, by the way, and youse must be Margie."

Her voice startled me, as I had begun to lean around the corner to sneak a peek at Blondie's exit route. Straightening up, I bumbled a nod. Ruby's distinct dialect placed her as a Dundalk resident, a blue-collar suburb east of Baltimore. Her silver-blond hair was piled up on top of her head in a beehive hairdo, secured with a headband that matched the zig zag print in her tight-fit-ting, brightly colored dress that looked like something Twiggy would have worn on the runway in the 1960s.

"Here's a trick. Try to suck up to her, hon. Compliment her. It's the best way to win her over," Ruby said. "But it's damn hard, I'll tell you!" With that, Ruby brayed a husky, uncontrollable laugh, as if she'd just told a dirty joke.

Blondie suddenly appeared around the corner, shooting Ruby a dirty look. "Did you bring sheet music?" she barked. I nodded, holding up my two musical theatre selections. "Are these in the right key?" I nodded again. She grabbed my music and disappeared.

The crusty manner of Blondie, or Princess, or whoever, started to unnerve me. I really hadn't felt anxious about this audition. In fact, the practice I received from auditioning for theatre productions in college and community theatre musicals had taken the edge off the whole process. Although, since David came into my life, it had been a long time since I'd done any auditioning. Still, I felt confident. That was until Blondie started messing with my brain cells. She had a superior way of rattling off orders with her pointy nose in the air. Kinda shook me to the core. It did not give me a warm or welcoming feeling, nor did it help build my confidence in any way. I needed to snap out of the bummer trip of self-doubt that I felt myself slipping into – and fast! "'Be here now,'" I reminded myself and took a few deep cleansing breaths I'd learned from yoga.

A few minutes later, Blondie appeared again. "Okay, follow me." As I rose to follow her, I said, "That's an off the hook top you're wearing. Where'd you get it?" Rounding the corner, I caught Ruby's eye and saw her wink in approval. I smiled to myself. *I'm on my way.*

Blondie led me down the long, narrow hallway and through the door I observed when I first entered the foyer, to a basement stairway. *Would it be rude to cover my mouth and nose from the wafting cologne odor? Probably. Why would a girl my age need to wear so much fragrance to an audition! It seems more of a date night thing. Very funky.* Once downstairs I discovered the "studio" of sorts. More like a regular basement filled with music stands and chairs, a drum set and a Hammond B-3 organ. Behind the drum kit sat a young man, about 17 or 18, and at the organ, a guy in his mid-20s with a dark moustache. Blondie pointed to a spot in the center of the room to which I quickly moved.

"Costanza, how about some intros," said the guy at the organ. *Finally, some real names.*

Blondie said, "That's Antonio Conti on organ and Enzo Conti on drums. Oh, and I'm Connie Conti." *Hmm. Quite the family affair! Okay, so Blondie-Princess-Costanza is also Connie. Crap! Not only brusque and bossy, but the whole name thing makes this chick stranger-than-strange.*

I smiled. "Hi, I'm Margie Stevens. I'm incredibly happy to be auditioning for you today." Neither organ guy nor the drummer kid looked up. *So much for a cordial welcome.*

Antonio proceeded to describe the audition process. "First, Costanza will teach you a short dance routine to 'Everything's Coming Up Roses.' You know it?"

"Sure," I said. "Peppy showtune from the musical *Gypsy*, right?"

He half nodded and continued. "I'll listen to the two selections you brought along, and then we'll work on a couple songs from the band's playlist. Once we're done with that, we'll get King in here for you to perform the dance routine as well as a couple pieces for him." *Of course, King, the band leader of King Vido's Swing Band!*

"I'm ready," I said with feigned confidence, despite my stomach doing flip-flops at the suggestion that Connie would teach me the dance routine. Between the "oh-so lovely" welcome and the fact that dance was not my forte, I began to have doubts about my chances at getting into this band for the first time. *Did I make a mistake thinking I should try to spread my wings and fly away from my Church Creek roots? Do I have more of Dad in me than Mom and I'm simply a small-town girl at heart? Oh God, I'm doomed to spend the rest of my life working in Dad's general store waiting for a local guy to marry me! Maybe a college education was wasted on me. Studying music, performance, writing, liberal arts — what on earth will I ever do with that?* The negative chatterbox in my head was unrelenting. *How can I imagine I have the voice, dance, and performance skills to make it through a professional audition?*

As it turned out, I wasted my energy worrying about the dancing. Connie not only served as dance captain, teaching the steps, but she also functioned as the choreographer and, well, let's just say I grasped the "routine" to "Everything's Coming Up Roses" almost immediately:

> Make an "okay" sign with right hand and hold
> through 1st and 2nd lines of lyrics.
>
> Extend right hand with palm up in front of body
> through 3rd line.
>
> Point down with both hands to represent
> "Starting here."
>
> Extend both arms up overhead in a "V" shape for
> the big finish!

Oh brother. Gotta love the "classic" arms in a "V" ending! Hardly mind-blowing. If this was going to be the extent of the choreography for the entire tour, I had nothing to worry about.

Next, I ran through my two selections: a ballad and an up-tempo song from two Broadway musicals I had performed during college. I sang "Much More" from *The Fantasticks* as my ballad selection and "I Cain't Say No" from *Oklahoma!* for my peppy piece. Maybe it was adrenaline but I felt psyched about my performance of both pieces. *Whew, Margie, you overcame the nerves, stayed on pitch, added some dynamics, and sang from the heart. And it was even fun!* With crazy intervals and high notes, "Much More" was vocally more challenging than the *Oklahoma!* piece, the personality number. *Thank God, I wasn't as rusty as I thought I might be. And I'm especially grateful that my musical muse hasn't been completely destroyed by the whole David fiasco after all.*

"Okay," Antonio said. "Let's try a few bars from the band's

repetoire. I've pulled out *Ain't She Sweet*, *Proud Mary*, and the country song *Two Doors Down.*"

"That's cool. I know the first two tunes but I've never heard of the country song before," I said. "Don't worry, though. I'm pretty good at sight-singing. If you don't mind me looking over your shoulder, I can follow along with the score."

Antonio agreed to the sight-singing arrangement. Based on her impatient sigh, Connie seemed annoyed that I didn't know the country song. She plopped in a chair across the room, oozing exasperation. The drummer, Enzo, played very lightly to these snippets of songs, which became more distracting than helpful. Antonio's accompaniment consisted of chords and occasional notes from the melody. Except for that damned country song, I knew these tunes well enough to keep belting out the melody, despite the strangest accompaniment I'd ever experienced at an audition.

Upon completing the band pieces, a booming voice from the doorway startled all of us in the room. "She's good, yes?" asked a short man with dark, deep-set eyes, set off by thick framed glasses and jet-black hair, receding above the temples. *Ah, the infamous King Vido, I presume! Kinda a letdown.* I was expecting a man of elegance. What I got was an elfin-like male in black polyester pants and a white dress shirt with buttons straining across his overly large stomach! *Certainly not regal in any sense of the word!* I guessed he'd been watching the audition for most of the vocal portion.

"A bit too much vibrato, but we can work that out of her," Antonio said. It felt weird being talked about as if I weren't in the room. *Why hadn't Antonio mentioned anything about my "vibrato" while we were working together. It's true, I did train under a classical voice teacher in college,, where vibrato was encouraged, but I take direction very well.*

"Welcome to King Vido's Swing Band, Margie." King's voice bellowed as he turned and swaggered out of the room.

So that's King Vido, or, as I later learned, Angelo Conti. Stage names. Italian variations versus American names. Pet names. It was hard to keep track of this family. One thing for sure, despite his small stature, dark rumpled hair, and beady eyes, King had a way of making his presence felt. He exuded a cocky confidence, making him appear commanding and taller than his actual height. While it seemed silly to refer to him as King when we weren't at a gig, Ruby later instructed, "It's expected."

Back upstairs in her office, Ruby outlined the details of working with King Vido's Swing Band with extreme efficiency. "After a week of rehearsals here in the studio, startin' Monday bright and early, the band'll break in new material at local performances with its two new singers, youse and another gal, Evelyn, who just signed on. The followin' week, the schedule expands to a coupla regional bookings. By the end of May, the official U.S. tour begins."

My heart pounded with excitement. "Unreal," was all I could squeak out.

"Youse'll get a schedule for tour dates a few weeks ahead, but beware, hon: it's all fluid. Pay attention, be flexible, and mosta all, be on time! That's a biggie."

"Flexible, right. And be on time…I'm so psyched!"

"I'm sure youse are, hon. Now, durin' rehearsal week, youse girls'll be fitted for two costumes. Also required: two pairs of shoes for the first day of rehearsal – a pair of white and a pair of black heels."

"I feel like I should be writing this down." I started to freak out over all the information she was spewing, and I guess it showed.

"Don't worry, hon. I gotta whole packet for ya. Now, pack one suitcase for travel. Be sure to include several dresses as youse girls'll be required to wear a dress whenever youse arrive at a venue. It's part of King Vido's image that his girls always appear feminine and pretty." *That's kinda weird, but I guess that's how it is with these road shows.*

"How does the band get from place to place, Ruby?" I pictured a Greyhound Bus with a bunch of musicians and instruments.

"Of course, transportation." Ruby flipped ahead to the next page in the packet. "The band members travel in trucks and a Volkswagen van at this point, but there's a plan in the works for convertin' a second truck for the girls before the official summer tour begins." *I'm seeing a VW van full of suitcases and band equipment, with girls in hot rollers climbing all over themselves trying to put on makeup as we ramble down the road. I hope it's not like that but I'll find out.*

Referring to her checklist, Ruby muttered, "Now what else? Oh, right. Housin' arrangements. When the band's on the road, King Vido'll provide housin' in the form of a hotel or motel room for the girl band members. Until the tour begins and even for those rare occasions when the band's home between gigs durin' the tour, Angelo's not gonna to leave youse girls out on the pavement."

"Angelo?" I was confused by the introduction of an unfamiliar name.

"Ah, Angelo's King. King Vido's his stage name. Angelo Conti's his real name. But you'll call him King. Everybody calls him King. Even his own kids call him King. Make sense?" I nodded, thoroughly intrigued.

Ruby continued her spiel. "So, on the third floor of this building are a couple of dorm-style rooms with a bathroom and a small area with a hot plate and a teeny frig."

"Where do the guys in the band stay when we're in town?"

"The guys either go to their parents' homes if they live in the area or rent a room somewhere in the Fells Point neighborhood."

Not entirely trusting this arrangement, I probed for details. "If I stay here at the studio, would they take rent out of my paycheck?"

"Nah, hon. King wants to make sure his band girls are safe. And youse should know that the rest of the Conti family lives on the second floor, so they appreciate privacy."

Flipping to the final pages of the packet, even Ruby seemed fatigued. "Now, you'll be paid one hundred and fifty dollars a week startin' next week, payable on Fridays. In addition, you'll receive eight dollars and fifty cents per diem for each day the band's on the road to cover meal expenses. It's not a huge daily food allowance, but if you're careful youse can even cover the occasional Natty Boh!"

"I do like the occasional beer," I said, chuckling at Ruby's reference to Baltimore's local brew, National Bohemian Beer. I tried to act cool taking in all this information, especially the salary, but a hundred and fifty dollars a week was like striking it rich for me. The most tips I could ever expect at the diner was sixty-five bucks on a phenomenal week, while Dad paid me next to nothing to work part time at his store. *And all this for singing and dancing!*

Ruby handed me a packet of papers to look over and asked me to call her by Friday to confirm my acceptance of the band's offer. If I did accept, I'd be expected to show up for rehearsal at ten o'clock on Monday morning.

Feeling thrilled, scared, yet oddly confident, I began processing this mess of emotions as the skyline of Baltimore faded and I headed to the Bay Bridge toward home. I reviewed the events of the past several months and considered what the future may hold. A Ram Dass passage came to mind, one that later I neatly printed on the first page of my journal to review frequently: "It is important to expect nothing, to take every experience, including the negative ones, as merely steps on the path, and to proceed." Despite my jumbled feelings, one clear thought cut through: I had to do this tour, "to proceed." Between finding a way to get over David breaking my heart, picking up the pieces of some sort of career path, and getting away from Church Creek and Dad's persistent messages of "work here until you get married, little missy," I needed this badly!

All I had to do was convince my parents to let me travel in a Volkswagen van or converted truck all over the country with a group of musicians, living in either motels or some sort of dormitory in the middle of Little Italy in Baltimore.

Convincing my parents? *That should be easy! Oh, crap... breathe, Margie.*

3

Rehearsal Red Flags

Little Italy, Baltimore, Maryland – April, 1978

I arrived at 324 Albemarle Street early on Monday morning with my paisley print suitcase crammed with the recommended dresses, rollers, makeup, and black and white dress shoes for stage wear along with my personal books and writing journal. Ruby escorted me to my room on the third floor "dormitory." *Looks more like an attic with walls slapped up, dry walled, and painted "prison beige." But hey, what did I expect for zero dollars?* The room was furnished solely with a twin bed and a sage green dresser with an attached tiny mirror. A polyester spread with huge pink, white, and green roses adorned the bed. At the head, a pillow covered with a blue pillowcase had been casually thrown. I wondered if Connie was "Chief Room Decorator" as well as Head Choreographer. A brass pin-up lamp hung on a bare nail over the bed, the single light source in the room. No art on the walls, no closet, no chair, no desk. I overlooked the fact that the short beige curtains barely covered the window opening and sadly blended into the drab wall paint, focusing instead on feeling grateful that at least my assigned room *had* a window! We'd be on tour most weeks out of the month anyway so I only had to endure this miserable space for a brief time. *Good thing I didn't know what this dorm room looked like when Mom and Dad decided to let me embark on this adventure.*

Mom had appeared more supportive than Dad when I returned home after the audition and broached the subject of joining the band. I'm sure Dad hoped I'd fall on my face, see the error of my thinking, and realize that my only future existed in what he thought was best. His plan for me consisted of staying in Church Creek to help him with the general store until some local guy swept me up and proposed. Dad's philosophy for women was old-school and dusty. "Margaret," he'd often say. "Girls should keep their mouths shut, do as they're told, and be happy about it!" He liked having me around as an "employee" at the store, since he paid me less than half what the male part-timers received! I had only been able to push against Dad's ancient philosophy in the smallest of ways: I went to college and I talked about graduate school. In all other ways, I silently complied, rarely talking back or even speaking up when I disagreed with him.

Unfortunately, Mom was my biggest role model in the voiceless department, so what did I expect! Although at times Mom came to *my* defense, she seldom spoke up to voice her own concerns, despite her obvious sadness. This touring opportunity was the first time I took a major action all on my own, using valid reasoning to make Dad hear me. Of course, it didn't hurt that Mom had my back.

"I'm against it. For cryin' out loud, no daughter of mine's goin' to go galivantin' across the country and that's it!" Dad fumed, taking a nip from his flask to punctuate his proclamations. Despite feeling intimidated and terrified to confront him, I didn't let it deter me this time.

"Well, Dad," I began, taking a deep breath to calm myself and giving me time to review my memorized speech. "I believe this opportunity will be good for me, because a) it pays more than the diner, and b) it's an opportunity to use some of the skills I learned getting my college degree, and c) it's a chance for me to start a career, and d) I'll be traveling with a group of people, which *is* safer than if I decided to set off on a cross-country trip all by myself."

"Oh, Lord, that's very true," Mom said, freaking out at the thought of me traveling cross-country by myself. I really had no desire or courage to travel cross-country by myself. I threw that in for leverage. It worked, because it got Mom talking to Dad about how it would be good for me to have some experiences outside of Church Creek and Cambridge.

After much discussion between them, he relented…dubiously, offering the most encouragement I could ever expect from him: "Watch the deer and watch the cops." *Typical!* But the point was he relented. Less because of discussing the issue with me, more because of Mom's persuasive arguments. At least, it had been the first time I mustered up the tiniest bit of backbone to speak up to him and made some headway…well, with Mom's help to seal the deal. *I wonder why Mom never confronts Dad that way for things she feels are important for her.* I never understood that. Even though my heart pounded and I had to stop to catch my breath at times, it felt good. I hoped someday I wouldn't feel so intimidated about expressing myself to Dad.

• • •

Having made my first major decision on my "next steps," I settled into my room at 324 Albemarle Street. I had a few minutes before I needed to report to rehearsal at ten o'clock. Since the band would be in town for a couple of weeks rehearsing and performing local performances, I decided to unpack whatever fit into the dresser and hang my few dresses on a hook I discovered on the back of the door. As I began placing peasant skirts and sundresses on the few clothes hangers Mom *insisted* I bring along, a friendly voice came from the direction of the doorway.

"Hey, neighbor."

I looked up to see a tall girl about my age, magazine-model gorgeous with wavy auburn hair, emerald eyes, and long legs like a Radio City Rockette dancer.

"I'm Evelyn, new girl number two. You must be Margie." I must have looked like a Sika deer caught in the headlights off a marsh road. She continued, "Ruby told me you'd be moving in early this morning."

"That's me." We chatted a bit about our hometowns and our auditions. Evelyn grew up in Harrisburg, Pennsylvania and went to college at Penn State as a voice performance major.

"Have you ever sung in a big band before?" she asked.

"No, it's my first time doing anything like this, outside of musical theatre. I've done a lot of choral and solo work in college, but this is all new to me. What about you?"

"I've done a bit." She didn't go into any details. "I'm sure you'll be fine. We'd better get downstairs and vocalize before rehearsal begins."

I followed her down three flights of stairs and entered the studio, where a couple of band members were warming up, creating a cacophony of noise. According to Ruby's schedule, the singers would be working with the Conti family band members without the rest of the band during the first part of the week. The full band would layer in later in the week. *It might have to do with not wanting to pay the full band while we were in training, or something like that.*

No sign of Connie, but I did recognize Enzo on the drums. He gave us a nonchalant chin nod as he pounded on the drums in his own personal warm up. The others were practicing individual scales and rifts on their trumpet, trombone, and organ. Since I had so little experience with bands, I didn't want to pass judgment, but to me it sounded kind of....well, like they were trying to be as loud as possible. Or drown each other out? *Hmm. Some ego clashing or sibling rivalry going on here?* I didn't know for sure. But what I did know: It was incredibly loud!

No way Evelyn and I will be able to vocalize in all this noise. In the future, I'll either come down to the studio early or do my vocal warm up upstairs in my room. The other players, presumably Conti brothers, never stopped to introduce themselves, so Evelyn and I stood around humming until King and Connie entered the studio. Immediately, the room became silent.

Antonio repositioned himself at the organ and began organizing music without a word, while the other brothers spread out to various metal music stands and prepped their music. Meanwhile, Connie clung to King's arm. It was a little embarrassing to see this obvious display of possessiveness, a demonstration for the benefit of Evelyn and me. It screamed, "Look how much my Daddy loves me!"

"Boys, this is Evelyn and Margie, our new singers." King began to introduce the others as he pointed to each player, "Giorgio on trumpet. Enzo and Antonio of course you've met. And this is my eldest, my Simone on Trombone."

"It's Simon," he corrected, glaring at King.

Unfazed, King said, "Okay, Costanza. Let's get to work!" Like a bratty child, Connie stomped over to Evelyn and me. King took control of the rehearsal with his deep commanding voice by outlining the three numbers we would work on that morning.

"We'll break for lunch at one o'clock then review and add

three more pieces. King finalized his instructions as he was about to exit the studio. "I'll be back at the end of the day to see where we are, yes?"

As King turned to leave, Connie caught his attention. "Uh, King?"

"Oh, yes." King faced the band but rested his gaze on Evelyn and me before continuing. "And Costanza oversees the girls. All questions go through her, *capisce?*"

Evelyn and I nodded. I noticed Simon raised his eyebrows at this announcement, while Connie maintained the smuggest of expressions. Evelyn shot me a quick look, more like a grimace, then looked away. Ruby warned me about Connie, and she hadn't exaggerated one bit. Fortunately, my musical theatre experience prepared me for working with egos like hers. I knew better than to cross her and planned to treat her with a combination of kid gloves and avoidance!

Connie began to explain how the band booked two types of gigs: dinner-dances and show performances. "When we do shows, King puts together specific set lists, like the Gospel, Country, and Patriotic mini shows, and then fills in with big band numbers. When we do a dinner-dance, it's almost all big band and swing music with a few pop pieces thrown in." She lectured us as if we were middle school students.

"So, we've got to learn movement routines for all the mini show music. Got it!" Evelyn said. "What about the music? Will we be learning harmonies?" Connie stared at her disapprovingly. Frankly, I thought it was a little too early in the morning for Evelyn to be poking that cranky bear. *Let Connie be the teacher if it feeds her ego. At least that's my game plan!*

"Dance steps first. We'll worry about harmonies later. *GOT IT?*" Connie said it in a way that let everyone in the room know that she didn't appreciate being challenged, but Evelyn didn't seem bothered. I admired her confidence and guts: two qualities I generally lack.

The first piece we worked on was the song "Oklahoma" from the Broadway musical of the same title. The so-called dance steps were a cinch to pick up because they consisted primarily of marching around, moving our right arm across our body on a certain phrase, marching around some more, and moving our left arm across our body on a different phrase. Oh, and at the very end of the song, bringing both arms up in a "V" shape overhead. *An apparent signature move for Connie's choreography!*

We always learned the song first with Antonio on the organ. He was all business, all the time. Nice enough, but rarely a smile or a laugh. Never any conversation outside of teaching us a number or reviewing a segue. When it came to anything beyond the song, Connie oversaw the girls and that was that!

Once Antonio taught us the numbers, then Connie introduced the movement. The final step in the process consisted of layering in the other band members. To tell the truth, the accompanying music was a bit disorienting with the Conti players. The horns may have overwhelmed the small space, but it became difficult to hear the melody when the Conti ensemble played. I couldn't put my finger on the problem.

Despite the accompaniment challenges and the dorky choreography, it felt wonderful to sing and dance with Evelyn and even Connie. The rest of the choreography followed the same way, although some songs added clapping, or props like small flags and straw hats, or rhythm instruments like a tambourine. *Nothing like marching around with a teeny American flag to excite the audience, I suppose.* Not surprisingly, Connie made sure Evelyn and I knew she would be performing all solos as well as duets with a certain band member who would be showing up the next day.

"And *that's* show biz," I whispered to Evelyn, as we walked out of the studio at the end of rehearsal.

• • •

The following day Evelyn and I arrived at the studio a full half hour early to vocalize before any of the other band members arrived. As we ran scales and arpeggios, a handsome, six-foot tall young man walked through the doorway carrying a knapsack slung over his left shoulder and a guitar case in his right hand.

He approached us and introduced himself. "Ted, guitar and occasional vocals."

"Hi there, 'Ted-Guitar-and-Occasional-Vocals'," Evelyn said. Ted laughed, tossing back his sandy brown surfer-tousled hair while casually dumping his knapsack on the floor.

"What'cha girls working on?"

"We're doing some vocalizing before the band guys come down and start warming up," I said.

"The Conti brothers warming up? Hm, that's generous of you." Ted let out a snarky laugh. "You sure it's not more like a contest to see who can overblow their instrument the loudest?"

"Well, I don't know. I'm a vocalist–" I began, but Evelyn cut me off.

"–I think we get the picture, Ted." We all chuckled nervously, although I still wasn't sure what Ted was driving at. With my limited experience around full bands, except pit orchestras for musical theatre, I didn't have a discerning ear about the instrumentals. *Even though he is joking around, can Ted have hit on the problem at rehearsal yesterday?*

A moment later, Connie entered the room and stopped short. She observed the three of us talking. A hateful scowl appeared on her face. God knows what ran through her little blond head. We found out soon enough. She threw her shoulders back, stuck out her large breasts, and marched right over to Ted, grabbing his arm, and declaring in a loud voice, "I'm so glad you're back, honey!"

Giorgio and Simon arrived with instruments in hand, pulling Ted away with banter about a piece of music that King added to the band's set list. *Did I notice an expression of relief on Ted's face? Interesting?* As I pondered that thought, I felt a sharp tug on my arm and realized that Connie had yanked both Evelyn and me to the corner of the studio.

"Teddy and I are dating. *Got it?*" she said with a threatening tone that was quite pitiful.

"Yeah, okay," Evelyn and I said in tandem, although I knew I had no interest in pursuing him, or anyone for that matter. This tour was my chance to focus on healing my ruptured heart, forgetting David, and figuring out what the hell I wanted to do with the rest of my life. I wasn't here to get hurt again by becoming involved with anyone of the male persuasion.

• • •

Despite the ominous start with Connie, the second day of rehearsal went quite well, except for the same strangeness with the sound of the band. We reviewed the numbers we worked on yesterday, adding Ted into the choreography, and struggled a bit to keep our dance steps in synch. It wasn't that the routines were difficult. When we learned the dance routines and songs with Antonio on the organ, it was easy to follow the melody and hear the downbeat. But as soon as we added Enzo on the drums and the Conti boys on the horns, it seemed like the beat and melody got garbled up.

The rhythm problems continued until we began working on

the Pop mini show, which included "Joy to the World," "Bad, Bad, Leroy Brown," and "Proud Mary," among other pop and disco hits. Then a bizarre thing happened. Surprisingly, these tunes were much tighter, the sound less disjointed, and the downbeat became easier to hear. I zeroed in on the major difference: Ted played guitar for these numbers. He set up right next to Enzo's drum kit and used his entire body to "conduct" the rhythm of the songs for Enzo. *Was it possible that Enzo needed this additional support to play the drums properly?* While I didn't know enough about how musicians work, or how it all fits together to make sense of it, I began to see that Enzo needing Ted's guidance could be a real possibility – that good musicians can enhance the playing of mediocre ones.

I asked Evelyn what she thought later that evening upstairs in the dorm. She smiled like she possessed some secret knowledge and I wasn't part of the club. I pressed harder.

"I want to know what you think, Evelyn."

"You might wanna take a chill pill about this." She sensed my disappointment. "Why does it matter so much what I think?"

"Well, for one thing, I don't have a lot of experience working with bands and I'm trying to learn something about it. You seem to know a lot about singing with a band. At least you said you had experience, so–"

Evelyn cut me off. "Look, something I've learned is to not criticize the musicians you're singing with! That got me in trouble before and I'm not going to get bitten twice."

"What do you mean? What happened?" Super curious, I hoped she'd open up to me.

She hesitated before she spoke. "This goes no further than you, okay?" I nodded as she continued. "I was hired by Mr. Waring to be a part of The Pennsylvanians', a member of his elite choral group that performs all over Pennsylvania and the surrounding states."

"Wait, I've heard of Fred Waring. Didn't he have a TV show, do a lot of big band music stuff?

"Right, that's how most people know him, from "The Fred Waring Show" in the 1950s, but vocalists know him as a master in choral technique. 'Fred Waring and The Pennsylvanians' was the name of the touring choral group. Mr. Waring's method is all about precision and tone syllables, where the song is equal parts words and music. I was lucky enough to be in Mr. Waring's summer choral workshops after my Freshman, Sophomore, and Junior years at Penn State. As a vocal performance major, I learned tons that I was able to apply to music theory and to improve my voice training.

"After those three summers, Mr. Waring invited me to join the band during my Senior year, which was a huge honor because only the best, the most professional vocal performers are asked. He was even more demanding with the performance group, asking all of us to work at our top level of commitment and abilities. And I rose to the challenge. Eventually, he rewarded my efforts with a solo."

"That sounds off the hook to the max. So why aren't you still with them?" My curiosity was stoked.

"Problem was I let the honor of getting that solo go to my head. At one rehearsal, while trying to work out the tempo of a particularly tricky riff with the combo that accompanied our group, I snapped at the musicians. Instead of collaborating and working out the issue, or taking responsibility myself, I blamed them. When Mr. Waring stepped in to call me out for acting like that, I made matters even worse: I criticized the skills of the musicians. For Mr. Waring I had stepped over a line. I was fired.

"That was about a year and half ago and I gotta tell you, I ate a lot of humble pie over that incident. Since that time, I've been singing with a few local pop bands, but nothing matches the experience and love I had for working with them and the big band sound. I regret taking those musicians for granted and for getting such a swelled head over the whole thing. But I'm still trying to move forward."

"Gee. That's…." I wasn't sure what to say.

"But this is only between you and me, right?"

"You got it."

"Big day tomorrow." Evelyn changed the subject, already walking toward her room. "We get to meet the rest of the band *and* get fitted for our costumes. See you in the morning!"

As I slipped into bed, I couldn't shake Evelyn's story from my mind. *Here is someone with a ton of musical knowledge and experience, who had an opportunity to excel with a well-known group, and her ego got in the way.* I thought of Gandhi: "When the ego dies, the soul awakes." Never an easy lesson to learn. I knew Evelyn's story was her own but hearing it made me feel it held some significance for me as well. As I drifted off to sleep, I envisioned beginning my own journey and wondered what experiences I might encounter along the way.

I knew two things for sure: I felt the spirit of music slowly seeping back into my heart and I was psyched to see what tomorrow's rehearsals would bring!

4

Meet the Band

Little Italy, Baltimore, MD – May, 1978

By the time Evelyn and I arrived at the rehearsal studio the next morning, the room was already hopping with activity. The entire band was either unpacking instruments, warming up or gabbing with each other. Enzo randomly beat on his drums, creating an eruption of noise. Horn players ran scales or licks from the tunes. Most of the new instrumentalists looked up as we walked through the doorway, but then continued with their preparations for rehearsal. Eventually, one fellow carrying a huge saxophone approached us and introduced himself.

"Hiya sweet things. I'm Ricky. You must be the new gals." This guy totally came on too strong in his delivery. *Does he think we're impressed?* "What do we have here? A former runway model or basketball pro?" referencing Evelyn's height and the fact she wore white shorts and a striped polo shirt.

"Hilarious," Evelyn said with utter coldness.

Undeterred Ricky turned to me. "And a little flower child?" *I get that a lot due to my long, straight hair parted in the middle and my go-to attire – bohemian-style maxi skirts and peasant tops, Dad always calls me "a hippy chick." What can I say? I'm more comfortable in skirts than Levi bell bottoms jeans.*

Evelyn jumped in again. "You're wrong on both counts. I'm

Evelyn and this is Margie."

While I tried to give people a chance when I first met them, my radar went up immediately with this guy. In addition to trying too hard to impress, he ogled us in a creepy way. I had customers at the diner who did that, and it made my skin crawl. For another thing, the way he dressed seemed like, well…like he was on the prowl. His slicked back, dirty blond hair, shorter in front and longer in the back, mullet-style, was styled too perfectly with gobs of hairspray. He wore a polyester shirt that fit closely to his torso with wide pointy collars. The abstract print of the shirt in browns, tans, and greys matched the brown in his tight-fitting flared pants. The outfit was more like something a guy would wear to the disco on a Saturday night. The rest of the players dressed in Levi jeans and pullover jerseys or tee shirts. Oh, and the cologne. He was wearing cologne – to a band rehearsal! *What is it with these people wearing cologne to rehearsal!*

"How's King's mood been lately?" Ricky asked.

"Mood?" I wasn't sure what he was trying to get at.

"Has he been in an okay mood or cranky or, you know, worse?"

Evelyn tried to diffuse the conversation. "We haven't seen too much of him."

"Well, don't you fret, ladies," Ricky said. "I'll fill you in when we get a break." Evelyn rolled her eyes in disgust. *My sentiments exactly! Was he trying to impress us with his hero act or something?*

Saving us from Ricky's hot-air, King and Connie walked in and, as usual, everyone stopped what they were doing and gave King their undivided attention. It amazed me how King took control of the chaos in an instant, simply by entering the room. *Is everyone so intimated by this gnome-like band leader? Does he possess some magical powers over all the musicians that make them snap to attention like that? It is true, his booming voice can be a bit frightening. Frankly, I hope I never tangle with him.*

King dove right in by announcing that we had a gig Saturday night. *Yikes, three rehearsal days away!* He described it as an "abbreviated" big band concert for a local street festival.

"You girls don't have to worry about any of the new show pieces. It's all big band music, *capisce?*" *I still didn't "capisce" what the girls do during a concert or dance show, though I'll find out soon enough. But cool, our first official performance! It's all crazy exciting!*

We spent the morning reviewing the show numbers we had learned on Monday and Tuesday, but this time incorporating the entire band. *Wow, what a difference in the sound!* Suddenly, I felt and heard the downbeat easily, musical nuances appeared that didn't exist before, and tempos were consistent. While the band took a break, Connie taught Evelyn and me the choreography for the final three show numbers, which required very little movement. Before the one o'clock lunch break, King arrived to deliver the afternoon's schedule.

"At two o'clock sharp, the band will meet in the studio to review for Friday night's event. It's only an hour show. I'll go over the set list, but as most of you know by now, be prepared for anything," King announced. "And girls, right after lunch report to Connie in the storage room for costume fittings." He pointed to a door adjacent to the studio. "Two o'clock, *capisce?*" Everyone in the band mumbled something in the affirmative and put down their instruments to prepare for break.

Evelyn and I had decided to splurge for lunch by walking over to Vaccaro's Italian Pastry Shop for something yummy. We were already tired of eating tuna fish out of a can in the dorm kitchenette. Even though cannoli and cappuccino were at least three times the cost of our usual fifty-nine cent can of tuna, we agreed we deserved a treat. Exiting the front door of the building, we bumped into three of the band members standing by the front stoop.

"Where you girls headed?" asked a skinny guy around five-foot-eight with a curly red afro, dragging on a cigarette.

"We're grabbing a decadent lunch at Vaccaro's," said Evelyn, then she introduced us to the guys.

"I'm Jimmy." Between puffs on his cigarette, he motioned first toward the short guy with Coke-bottle glasses, the sax player, "This is Bernard and that big guy is Chaz."

Bernard and Chaz could not have been more different in stature. Bernard was nearly a foot shorter than Chaz, and, with his cropped brunette hair, thick glasses, and neatly trimmed moustache, he had the appearance of the class nerd. Chaz, the trumpet player, towered over his friends with his six-foot plus frame and athletic, muscular build. A clean-shaven, freckled face gave him a preteen look, although my guess was he was in his mid-twenties. He sported a camouflage print ball cap over straggly medium-length straw-colored hair. *These two remind me of The Odd Couple! And the three of them together? Jimmy, Chaz, and Bernard make a curious-looking trio, a friendly but peculiar ensemble.*

"You can come with, if you want," Evelyn said, without consulting me, but I was getting used to her taking charge like that.

"Thanks, but we're gonna grab some chips and a soda from the market around the corner. Check ya later." *Jimmy seems like the ringleader of that little gang.*

Making our way up the street, I said to Evelyn, "At least those guys made an effort to start a conversation, unlike the Conti boys." We chuckled as we continued toward Vaccaro's.

I had my eye on Vaccaro's Italian Pastry Shop from the first time I drove into Little Italy for my audition. The corner brick building with large black awnings protecting the outdoor seating areas looked so inviting. Once inside, you had to love the place – a huge board with painted menu items and prices hung over glass cases of gorgeous mouth-watering pastries, a few tables and chairs scattered about the intimate indoor dining area, and the aroma of oven fresh delicacies to die for. I ordered one of Vaccaro's famous cannoli and washed it down with a cup of cappuccino. Evelyn wanted an expresso and a piece of rum cake, another Vaccaro specialty. Between these yummy treats and the cozy atmosphere, we were in heaven. While we ate, I pounced on the opportunity to ask Evelyn about the difference in the quality of the music at this morning's rehearsal.

"I know you won't criticize the musicians but I'm trying to learn about this whole band thing. Did you notice how different the band sounded this morning?"

"Yes," was all Evelyn offered.

"There was so much energy and they seemed more together. Don't you think?"

"Yes."

"Well?"

"Look, Margie. I told you my story and I'm not falling into the same pattern again. But if you really want to learn about bands and how they work or don't work, then focus on observing. Listen. Watch. It sounds like you're already doing that, so good for you."

It didn't sound like she was going to give me any specific musical feedback and I didn't want to make the conversation awkward, so I dropped it. We finished up our coffees in silence until I noticed the time. "Yikes, it's almost two o'clock. We'd better head back."

"Okay, but I think I'll grab a gelato for the walk back to the studio."

"I kinda think we should start back, Evelyn. You know what a big deal Ruby made about being on time." I looked at my watch for what felt like the twentieth time.

"Oh, it'll only be a minute." Evelyn was already ordering the gelato at the counter as I waited not-so-patiently by the door.

By the time we got outside it was one fifty-eight and we still had two long city blocks to hike back to the studio. "Come on, Evelyn. Double time!" I urged, picking up the pace, although Evelyn seemed distracted by her gelato. We'd be late no matter how we cut it. We were greeted at the door by a very smug Connie. "You're late! King wants to see you in his office!" *Man, I want to slap that self-righteous sneer right off her face.*

Evelyn and I reported to the office next to Ruby's, where King sat like royalty at the shiny mahogany desk. Ruby was nowhere in sight. *At least she'd be a friendly face to help diffuse the tension in the air.* Like an emperor summoning lowly commoners, King gestured for us to approach. Standing in front of that massive desk, waiting for him to speak, we knew we had broken a cardinal rule of the band. The whole episode caused my heart to beat rapidly and my breath to become labored.

After what seemed an eternity, King suddenly blasted, "You were late," causing us both to jump.

While I was about to agree, ready to add a huge apology, Evelyn jumped in first. "It was only a couple minutes, King."

Boy was that the wrong thing to say. King freaked out. "I don't care if it's one minute, five minutes, or thirty minutes. You're in a professional organization now. This is first and last warning. Next time you're late, you're out." Then he looked right at Evelyn and added, "And you, don't ever talk back to me, *capisce*? That's all. Now go!"

We left the office like wounded puppies. I understood that professionals needed artistic discipline and all, but King's reaction seemed a bit aggressive. I hadn't seen this side of him. *Was that what Ricky meant when he asked us about King's mood earlier this morning? I'm kinda surprised with Evelyn's defensive, knee-jerk response, given her history with the Fred Waring Band and her desire to make this job work. Or was that the compliant side of me coming out again? I don't know...*

As we walked downstairs and into the small room next to the studio to meet Connie and the costumer for fittings, I had an epiphany. I had been letting Evelyn do a lot of the talking and thinking for me in the brief time we had been together. She jumped in to introduce me to people when I should have introduced myself, she invited the guys to our lunch outing without asking me, and she decided to cut it too close to make it back to rehearsal on time. I don't think she meant anything malicious by it. It was more letting myself be pulled in. *I kinda let David do that too, didn't I? And Mom...I always rely on Mom to plead my cases with Dad, never standing up for myself. Why do I keep doing that, letting other people speak for me, dictate my actions, overpower my feelings? When am I gonna be my own person and be responsible for my own actions? I guess I can start with getting myself to rehearsals on time!* I remembered a quote by Aristotle from Philosophy class: "Happiness belongs to the self-sufficient." *I'm sure Aristotle won't mind if I adapt his quote to "Survival belongs to the self-sufficient!" Seems appropriate for the time being.*

Connie met us with her typical, holier-than-thou glare, and began assuming command of the costume fittings. "We're already behind schedule!" Verna, the costumer a.k.a. tailor, seemed numb to Connie's behavior and went about her work with efficiency. *I don't blame her. I'd want to get my work done and vamoose as soon as possible, too.*

"Don't worry, Connie. Margie and I already brought our show shoes down to the studio that morning," Evelyn said as we slipped on the first outfit and let Verna do her thing. The first costume was a white sleeveless jumpsuit with wide bell bottom leg openings. The bodice had a deep V-neck, embellished with three-inch wide red fringe.

I twirled and danced around as Verna pinned the bodice of Evelyn's jumpsuit for a better fit. "This nifty fringe does pop against the white fabric." Connie frowned at me, clearly disapproving of my antics.

The second costume was part of what Connie labelled, "The Rainbow Series." Each girl wore a distinct color jumpsuit with a bodice that fit tightly clear down to the knees, where it flared out dramatically, enhanced by twelve inches of fringe. Sewn on the yoke of the sleeveless jumpsuit were three rows of twelve-inch-long fringe. My costume was canary yellow, Evelyn's kelly green, and Connie's a pretty pink, of course. Both my white and yellow costumes fit fine, except for the length. At five 5'3", hemming was the norm for me.

The need for hemming led to Evelyn and me learning about Cheryl, Simon's wife, who had been in the band previously. Verna let the cat out of the bag when she muttered, "Cheryl was at least two inches taller than you, Margie," causing us to pounce on Connie with questions.

"Who's Cheryl?" Evelyn and I asked at the same time, forcing Connie to fill in the background story.

"Cheryl's married to Simone," Connie said, using the Italian pronunciation of Simon's name, which apparently everyone in the Conti family did. "She performed with King Vido's Swing

Band for about four years."

"Okay," I said. "So why isn't she still with the band?" *She probably had enough of bossy Connie!*

"Well, since she's pregnant now, she's not traveling anymore.

"Doesn't Simon want to be at home with Cheryl? asked Evelyn.

"I guess part of him does, but Simone knows how important family is. It's a matter of family pride that King has his sons play in the band with him."

"The truth is King insists that Simon stay on the road," Verna clarified. "Simon would rather be a carpenter working with his hands and make a living on his own to support his growing family." Connie turned up her nose and snorted.

Ahh! Conti Cabinet Making, LLC. The sign on the side of the front door. Does Simon do a bit of carpentry on the side when the band is in town?

"But I agree with Daddy…I mean King, of course. Your main family comes first. Besides, when Cheryl married Simone, she became part of the Conti family, even though she's not Italian." Connie added the last part under her breath.

Hmm. More family drama with the Conti gang. Does this explain why Simon is so insistent that King calls him Simon rather than Simone, and why King refuses? The family power struggle is on full display. I wondered on which side of the family divide Giorgio, Antonio, and Enzo fell, or did they feel as intimidated to bend to the will of King as Connie clearly did? I was sure I'd have an opportunity to get to know them better as time went on, but during that pre-tour rehearsal period, the routine consisted of studio rehearsal time, grabbing a bite to eat, and sleeping. That left little time for much else. Though exhausting, I felt exhilarated at times. The rehearsal pace became the perfect salve for my personal ailment. No time to think about David or the aching wound in my heart!

• • •

Rehearsals continued much in the same vein on Thursday and Friday that first week. We reviewed the show numbers in the morning, broke for lunch, and the band reviewed the big band numbers in the afternoon. Sometimes they needed Connie for the afternoon rehearsals. A few tunes required either a violin part (although an entirely odd instrumental contribution for the big band sound) or a vocal solo for which she was the appointed vocalist (as she so "delicately" pointed out every chance she got!) Evelyn and I had to stick around in case Connie had a break and required us to go over the numbers we had learned, so I chose to sit in on the big band rehearsals to absorb whatever I could. I marveled at the sound difference once the entire band was assembled! Of course, the band was louder and fuller. But there was something more. A pulse or drive or…I couldn't describe it. Those Glenn Miller pieces really did swing. Like "Pennsylvania 6-5000," a Miller tune recorded in 1940. This number starts out with simple trombones in the opening and then requires precision playing by both the trumpets and trombones throughout with lots of syncopated rhythms. I heard the Conti boys playing part of this earlier in the week, especially the section that leads up to King's solo on alto sax, and it sounded, well…kind of sloppy. But with the full band in place, the number was hot, swinging, and sharp. *Can excellent players help mediocre players raise the bar? Or were the Conti boys having an off day when I heard them earlier in the week? I must admit, King's sax solos are freakin' good. He's quite talented, but did the rest of the family inherit his talent?*

• • •

On Friday afternoon we all gathered in the studio to receive our final instructions for Saturday evening's show. The event was part of the Mother's Day Crowning of the Blessed Mother festival at Saint Leo's Church, a big deal in Little Italy's Catholic community. The church made this event more unique with a traditional procession of the statue of the Blessed Mother through the neighborhood streets. The procession and Mass took place on Sunday and the outdoor festival near St. Leo's Church on Saturday.

King began to outline the schedule. "Saturday's festival is a fundraiser for St. Leo's Church and our band is scheduled to play at seven o'clock to close out the festivities. You are to report to the Studio at five–"

"–in costume," Connie interrupted with that annoying air of superiority.

"–and we'll be walking to the festival site at St. Leo's Church at Stiles and South Exeter Streets," King finished.

"Girls will be wearing the white jumpsuits and guys will be in the white tuxes with red shirts," Connie added with her arrogant flare. At one point I glanced over at Simon, who refused to look at his sister. *Definitely some sibling friction going on there.*

King added, "Simone and Giorgio will drive the equipment truck over to the stage at eleven tomorrow morning to set up. We'll only need the men for set up this time around. Guys, be there at eleven o'clock sharp, *capisce?*"

"You're not needed to set up this time, ladies," Connie said with slightest of smiles. *Did I dare to believe that the she-wolf was being nice?* "Don't get used to it," she threw out, as I began to let my guard down. *Figures!*

I wasn't going to let Connie deflate my excitement over our first performance. At the same time, questions filled my head. *Is a week of rehearsals enough to pull this concert together or will we fall on our faces? Which of the numbers will King have the band play? Will there be a large crowd? Do people dance at these outdoor events? How will the audience receive King Vido's Swing Band? And what the heck do we girls do when we're not performing the mini show?* I started to visualize the band on an outdoor stage with the girls in our fringed jumpsuits and two-inch platform sandals. The next thing I knew I heard my name being called, snapping me out of my dream state.

"Margie," Ruby called out. She had slipped into the studio and was distributing envelopes, while I was in a trancelike stupor. *Pay attention, Margie!*

"Right here!" I said as I made my way to Ruby near the studio doorway.

Ruby leaned in and whispered as she handed me the envelope. "Congrats on gettin' your first King Vido's Swing Band paycheck, hon."

Sitting at a cozy corner table at a pizzeria later that evening, I took stock and recorded my thoughts in my journal. I made it through my first week, met some new people, learned a bit about how bands work, and even had a performance to look forward to tomorrow. *What could possibly make this week any better? My first paycheck!* Half-tempted to glue the check into my journal, I settled for a napkin with Vaccaro's logo on it to represent my temporary new home and my love of cannoli. I closed my eyes and relaxed into a breathing meditation for a few moments. When I opened my eyes, I felt energized, inspired to write again. Waiting for my salad, I wrote about beginning to feel settled, about loving the big band swing music, about my excitement to perform. Even though he popped up into my mind and danced around in there ever so briefly, something I didn't write about was David.

Hmm That's interesting. I was truly "in the moment" and, well...
simply feeling.

Psyched to be *feeling anything again*, I wallowed in anticipation of my first official gig tomorrow.

5

First Baltimore Gig

Little Italy, Baltimore, Maryland – May 1978

Saturday arrived at last. Our first show was at the outdoor festival at Saint Leo's Church, right in Little Italy! A huge deal according to Connie and the Conti family – the festival preceded Sunday's procession and Mass for the Crowning of the Blessed Mother. Even as a "fallen" Catholic, I got wrapped up in the excitement and energy of these festival events. In fact, I missed the Catholic rituals since I stopped attending Mass. But I never was really down with the religious doctrines and politics. Disillusionment with the lack of spiritual connection at church led me to search for answers to a slew of questions (none of which Dad allowed me to bring up at home). What unites all faiths – Christians, Hindus, Buddhists, Muslims, Jews? Is God only connected to the church, or does He exist outside of the church? Or is God inside each of us?

In many ways, I was ripe for David's eye-opening introduction to new ways of thinking about spirituality. But I still had moments of conflict where I craved my comfortable Catholic foundation. Witnessing a festival and procession honoring a special saint, like the Crowning of the Blessed Mother, was one of those moments.

Since the singers didn't have to report until five o'clock,

I took the morning to run a few errands, like opening a bank account and making sure my car would start, before devoting time to exploring the neighborhood. It was a gorgeous May weekend, perfect sunny weather for the outdoor festival. The small trees lining the side streets in Little Italy announced the arrival of Spring with their sprouting buds. I purposely made my way over to South Exeter and Stiles Streets, home of St. Leo's Roman Catholic Church, to check out the festival grounds before the activities began at noon.

Approaching the large red brick church, I noticed red, white, and green bunting draped across the Stiles and South Exeter intersections at six equidistant intervals in both directions, creating a festive atmosphere. I stood across the street to take in the full view of St. Leo's façade. A double staircase led to a second-story entrance under a porch canopy, where a large round window hovered under a golden statue peering down from the peak of the pointed roof. A turret-like appendage flanked to the left with another building annexed to the right. Toward the back of the main building, a bell tower rose to the skyline, while along the Stiles Street side of this building, a row of four colorful stained-glass windows indicated the placement of the sanctuary.

I crossed the street and continued up Stiles, walking past the roadblock set up to reroute traffic. Many small, tented booths and tables already lined the sidewalk with volunteers scurrying around organizing food, games, and craft items for sale. At this point, the vendors had little under an hour to finish decorating the booths with red, white, and green bunting or paper flowers, or to secure colorful signs to draw in customers.

A freakishly immense number of games of chance filled the festival activity area, including roulette wheels, gift basket lotteries, 50/50 raffles, many sponsored by the Knights of Columbus or other St. Leo's organizations. *Ah yes, we Catholics love our raffles and roulette!* And despite the closed booths, early-bird crowds began to mull around, sizing up the prizes and greeting the workers. Everyone knew each other, but I could tell they also meant business. I read one of the signs announcing that all proceeds benefited St. Leo's School, which first opened in 1882. *That's impressive!*

Dozens of food and drink booths, woven throughout the games of chances, provided a wide selection of offerings. The tantalizing aromas of calzone, chicken and eggplant parmigiana, lasagna, pizza, fried mozzarella were enticing. *Why did I skip breakfast this morning? I'll go broke at this festival!* Gelato and flavored ices and cold drinks and, of course, vino were all available as well. My favorite booth, the cannoli and other pastries provided by Vaccaro's, looked like a miniature Italian café. A professionally printed sign indicated that Vaccaro's supported St. Leo's events through donations of pastries. In addition to food and game booths, individuals sold their homemade preserves or baked goods as well as craft items, including garlands and whistles for the kids. Indisputably, the spirit of community and support for the church pulsed through the growing crowd.

A sad thought popped into my mind followed by a twinge of pain in my heart. This festival was exactly the kind of event that David and I would have enjoyed together. While I hadn't had much time to think about David this week, an occasional feeling or memory had wiggled its way into my psyche. *It's odd how just when I think I'm over the hump, moving forward, full steam ahead, the slightest thought or image releases the stopper and allows David to spill out. Will I ever get over that?* It did help to keep busy. Fresh music, choreography, people. Each day became easier to focus on the present and let go of negative thoughts about the past. The hurts, mistakes I'd made, or feeling like a fool. Most importantly, I enjoyed rehearsing and rediscovering what I loved about having music in my life again. *One day at a time, Margie.*

I wandered through the vendors' booths until I spied the platform stage where the band would be performing later that evening. I watched Jimmy, Chaz, and Ricky hauling Antonio's huge organ onto the stage, while Giorgio and Ted set up the bandstands and microphones. Simon, Bernard, and Antonio stretched cables across the stage. Enzo seemed absorbed with his drum set, of course. I know Connie said that the girls weren't required to help this time, but I felt a bit guilty watching the guys laboring while I was able to have the day to myself. I decided not to make my presence known. *Why rub it in, right?*

At four o'clock I wandered back to the dorm to plug in my hot rollers, curl my hair, and start my makeup. I wanted to have plenty of time to report to the studio in full costume by five o'clock on the dot. Evelyn quizzed me about my day as she slipped into her costume.

"You saw the stage? What did it look like? Does it look professional or amateurish? Will we be cramped or is there plenty of room for everyone?" She drilled me with question after question, leaving me little time to answer.

Without coming right out and saying, "Take a chill pill," I blurted, "Whoa. Slow down. It's all new to me, Evelyn. I'm sorry but I don't know how to answer." After Evelyn composed herself, I said, "You'll have to wait and see when we get there." She calmed down enough to let me get back to putting on my makeup.

From the studio we walked as a group the couple of blocks to the venue, which felt a bit like a circus parade. Three girls in white jumpsuits with bright red fringe accompanied by nine fellows in white suits with red ruffled shirts prompted quite a few gawks from shop keepers and pedestrians. The Conti boys led the march, greeting neighbors, friends, and fans along the way. Ted and Connie followed behind, arm in arm, and the rest of us formed pairs or trios. Despite the fact that my shoes were new and not broken in yet, I enjoyed the stroll a lot.

King met the group as we arrived at the stage area, having driven the VW over separately. As soon as we gathered on the stage platform, King asked the singers to stand in front of our microphones for sound check. He cued us to speak a few words individually, as Giorgio made a few minor adjustments on the sound board set up on stage between his chair and the organ. Then the entire band played the one song we would all be singing together later, "My Country Tis of Thee," while King listened from the audience area. The entire sound check took about ten minutes.

"Not the most sophisticated sound system," Evelyn whispered to me. I shrugged, not having a frame of reference.

We had some time to kill before the performance started at seven o'clock so the band members scattered. Bernard, Ricky, and Chaz wanted to check out the booths and grab a calzone. Connie and Ted walked off to who knows where, hand in hand, and Evelyn decided to try her luck at one of the raffle booths. My feet hurt from walking in new shoes, so I hung out behind the stage until showtime with Jimmy, while he smoked a cigarette.

"What brought you to King Vido's Swing Band, Jimmy?" I asked.

"Aw, hell. Kinda a long story." He took a long drag, exhaling a puff of smoke. "I saw Angelo Conti, uh, King, play when I was first learnin' trumpet, 14 or 15 years old. My teacher took a group of music students to a show at the Civic Center in Baltimore to see the Temptations."

"The Temptations? How cool was that?"

"Yep! So, a local group called the Admirals was the openin' act, and Angelo was sittin' in on alto sax that night. Maybe 'cuz it was his big chance, or he was bein' a hothead, but he played his ass off that night. Man, he stood out. I don't know if the rest of the Admirals appreciated it, but the dude was rad. Anyway, it impressed the hell of this snot-nosed kid."

I laughed at this story but was still confused. "Okay, but that was a long time ago. I'm missing the connection to this band."

"Right. Later, when I was playin' local spots, I'd bump into Angelo now and again, and mention that Admirals' gig, and we'd laugh. But I kept my eye on different bands King formed – I'd go out to hear him. He's a damn good sax player."

"So, what happened? He formed bands in the past. Didn't they stay together?"

"He told me once, he always wanted to front a big band doin' this Glenn Miller, Duke Ellington shit but he knew there wasn't a big enough demand for it in Baltimore alone. He'd have to tour. With six kids and a wife, he couldn't pick up and leave so he had to wait it out."

"Wait a minute, six kids? I thought there were only five: Simon, Giorgio, Antonio, Connie, and Enzo." I counted on my fingers. "Who am I missing?" I asked, totally intrigued.

"Yeah, *he who shall not be named… .*"

"Come on, Jimmy!" He loved teasing me.

Skirting the mysterious sixth Conti sibling, Jimmy continued. "So once the kids are old enough, Angelo begins to groom them, teachin' them to play the right instruments, whether the hell they want to or not. He gets everyone to call him 'King' and he starts to act like he is one! And there you have it… King Vido's

Swing Band. He got the big band he always wanted. He plays local gigs to start, but when his wife passes away he's finally free to tour. He takes Enzo out of high school and home schools him on the road, for God sakes! Poor kid. Anything to make King's dream work. And even though the family members are mediocre players, King's smart enough to hire halfway decent musicians to fill in the gaps and sorta, I don't know, lift them up."

"Wow, this sounds almost oppressive. How do the family members feel about it, Jimmy?"

"That's the damnedest part. King inflated their egos to the point that they really believe they *are* talented musicians."

"Do you think any of them ever wanted to do anything else?"

"They've all been brainwashed by the damn family loyalty thing, and King's convinced them that this swing band's gonna be the greatest musical offering the country's ever seen. I mean, man, we all know he's an egotist, but I didn't realize how much he's livin' in the past. Swing bands are washed up. But he's convinced this clan of his that they're makin' a comeback and that King Vido's Swing Band's gonna 'make it to the top.' He can be very persuasive and intimidatin'." *I can't disagree based on the little bit I saw of King's aggressive side already.*

"So, all the Conti siblings have bought into King's dream? Like to the max?"

"Pretty much. Except for Simon. I think that's Simon's problem. He's startin' to think for himself for the first time. Now that he's got a kid comin' along, he's pushin' back – lookin' for a way out. And King Daddy don't like that one damn bit. Simon's torn on how to deal with it. But look, it ain't our problem. I try to keep my nose out of Conti family business. Just look the other way. That's my motto."

At that moment I saw Simon and a woman I'd never seen

before walking toward the stage area. Wearing a pink maternity top to cover a slightly swollen belly, I assumed the woman was his wife, Cheryl. They stopped at the foot of the stage, where Jimmy and I overheard most of their conversation.

"Tonight, Simon. You said you were going to tell him that this ends tonight. I need you home with me. You promised." Cheryl held back tears.

"I know, babe, but you know how difficult King can be," Simon said.

"What about you wanting to get off the road? What about your plans to start your own business?"

"I know, I know. This isn't the best time with the tour starting."

"It's never a good time, Simon, and you know it." Cheryl started to get angry. "He always finds some excuse. The band's working in fresh players. The band's prepping new materials. The band's starting a tour. The band's got an important gig for VIP clients. The band, the band, the band. What about *your* family?"

"This is my family, too, Cheryl," Simon said, and she broke down in tears.

I whispered to Jimmy, "I see what you mean. King does have a hold on him."

"Like I said, man. It ain't our problem. Just look the other way." And with that, Jimmy flicked his cigarette and moved to his position on stage. The Conti boys and other band members began making their way to the stage, so I did the same.

The stage sported black glossy bandstands painted with fancy, overlapping "K" and "V" in red with gold highlights, positioned in front of the trumpet, trombone, and sax sections. The back of the organ branded the band with a large sign reading, "King Vido's Swing Band." Next to the organ sat Giorgio and Jimmy on trumpets with Simon and Chaz on trombones, making up the back row. Enzo anchored stage right with the drum set and Ted stood next to him with his guitar. In the center section, a chair and bandstand were placed for King when he joined the sax section with his alto sax. Otherwise, he stood in front of the sax section for his featured solos. Next to King's chair, Bernard on tenor sax and Ricky on baritone sax completed the sax section with bandstands in front of each chair. The three girls' chairs were arranged diagonally at stage left.

By the time we were seated, a crowd had already gathered around the platform stage. When King entered from the steps at the rear of the platform, the audience members began shouting greetings to King. "Ciao, Angelo! Ciao! Salve, Angelo!" King knew most of them personally. Saint Leo's was the Conti family's church and this was their neighborhood. But the way King ate up the attention, he did act a bit like royalty. Jimmy was right about that.

We began the show with "My Country Tis of Thee," which got the crowd singing along immediately. That was fun. Next King had the band launch into several Glenn Miller tunes including "In the Mood," "Chattanooga Choo Choo," and "Tuxedo Junction." He featured himself on sax, which set him up as the "star" of the show, naturally. *If you're going to have a band called King Vido's Swing Band, you might as well be the star.* He was a good sax player, exactly as Jimmy described. Other band members had short, featured solos, especially Jimmy on trumpet and Chaz on trombone. Connie sang Rodgers and Hart's "Blue Moon" as a solo and Gershwin's "Embraceable You" as a duet with Ted.

Evelyn and I finally got the answer to our question: What do we girls do while the band plays these big band numbers?

Following Connie's lead, we swayed. That was it. We swayed to the big band tunes…a lot! During the swaying, I had plenty of time to observe the audience, taking in the way they experienced King Vido's Swing Band. How cool to see the excitement mounting. People stood right up against the raised platform, keeping time with the music, cheering between numbers. A few brave couples danced, some cheek to cheek, others swing dancing, but all enjoying the music in their own way. Even though I did *a lot* of swaying, I loved sharing this energy with the audience. *Can you even believe it, Margie? You're sitting on a stage, part of a swing band, and even getting paid!* But looking back, that night represented much more than those initial, adrenaline drenched outpourings. I took a significant step toward reigniting the flame I felt certain had been extinguished forever. The joy and electricity and connection that music can bring between performer and audience reminded me of the very reason I loved to sing and have music in my life in the first place!

● ● ●

On Sunday, Saint Leo's Church offered the traditional Mother's Day Mass, including the crowning of the Blessed Mother statue. I considered going to the Mass, if only to watch the pageantry. I stopped attending Mass during college once I started questioning the whole "Catholic doctrine," specifically the lack of support for the birth control. *Hmm. And yet, here I am working with a band, the result of a prayer and a miracle. Ironic, isn't it?* I hadn't told Dad I'd given up on Catholicism. I was too afraid of the confrontation. He was so unreasonable, especially when he'd been drinking. It was useless to try to have a rational discussion. And Catholicism was a hot-button topic for him.

Instead of going to Mass, I took Ruby up on her suggestion to go directly to the procession following the service, where the congregants paraded the statue of the Blessed Mother through the streets around Saint Leo's Church. I made sure to position myself along Exeter Street to get a clear view. The statue of the Blessed Mother sat on a float decorated with large vases of beautiful white flowers, followed by a line of children making their First Communion, clergy, and parishioners, escorted by members of the Knights of Columbus. The adorable little girls in their white dresses with matching veils and little boys with slicked back hair in white shirts and dress pants all took their roles in the procession quite seriously. I loved the sense of community and pride from both the parishioners and the spectators as the statue of the Blessed Mother passed through the streets of Little Italy that morning.

Later in the afternoon I found a corner phone booth, searched for two dimes to insert, and asked the operator to reverse the charges on a call to my parents. I figured it was about time to check in. Dad was busy working at the general store, of course, but Mom was off the hook happy to hear from me.

"Happy Mother's Day, Mom."

"Margaret, I've been thinking about you so much. How are you? Have you been eating right? It's important to eat breakfast every day. Are you getting enough sleep? You're not staying up too late? You need your rest."

"Mom!" I protested even though it surprised me how her voice and concern felt like a long-distance hug.

"Okay, okay. Tell me all about your adventures."

I gushed about everything: the rehearsals, the Conti family, the band's first show at Saint Leo's festival, the beautiful procession of the Blessed Mother that morning, and the people I'd met so far. I left out a description of the dormitory to save her from worry, or at least that was my rationalization. Hearing Mom's voice made me the tiniest bit homesick for Church Creek, which I could not EVEN believe I admitted to myself.

"You sound happy and excited and healthy, Margaret. I love you. Oh, and remember, 'All experience is education for the soul'," Mom said, before hanging up the phone.

I hung up, chuckling to myself. "Look at Mom doling out the 'Quotes to Live By'. Nifty."

6

Connie's True Colors

Little Italy, Baltimore, Maryland – May, 1978

Our first regional booking took place on Friday of my second week with King Vido's Swing Band. We headed to York, Pennsylvania for a dinner-dance, traveling in what would become our typical mode of transportation, at least for the next few weeks. At the appointed time, three vehicles pulled up in front of 324 Albemarle blocking traffic and creating a scene – two huge commercial delivery trucks and a bright orange and white Volkswagen van. The guys threw their instruments into the equipment truck and then piled into the back of the larger truck, where a normal door had been retrofitted into the rear roll-up cargo door.

"That's 'The Kennel'," Connie's authoritative voice announced. "We girls travel in the VW van." Evelyn and I turned to see Connie with a head full of curlers. I almost laughed out loud but stifled myself.

The guys traveled to gigs in the back of The Kennel, a 22-foot cargo truck, converted into 12 bunks, six on each side of a narrow central aisle, equipped with privacy curtains and small windows. Not sure if the nickname implied that the guys were a bunch of animals, I chose not to ask. At the far end of the bunks, two closets faced each other, providing space for tour costumes.

A second 16-foot truck carried the band equipment. Both vehicles were obnoxiously branded with "King Vido's Swing Band" on every available outer surface: sides, front, back, and doors.

Connie said, "When the band started out and was smaller, the guys used to travel in a separate camper. You know, like a lot of bands do. But then King got the idea of converting a large delivery truck and adding bunks. Isn't he brilliant?" I simply nodded my head, taking it all in.

As Ruby described, and Connie reminded us in her snippy manner, the girls traveled in the Volkswagen van with King at the wheel and Connie in the passenger seat, of course. I couldn't help thinking that we girls had the better deal and wondering if packing a horde of guys in the back of a moving truck was safe or even legal. *But wasn't King ordering a similar Kennel-type vehicle for the girls, including his own daughter? Surely he wouldn't do anything illegal to put his Princess or family members in danger, would he?*

Evelyn and I settled into the back of the van, pushing aside the orange and brown paisley-print privacy curtains on the side windows to watch the cityscape as we made our way to the Elks Club venue.

About ten minutes into the journey, King shouted to us, "Girls, the band will be expected to perform "God Bless America" to kick off the evening. Review it, si?"

Reluctantly, Connie climbed from the front seat to join us. Evelyn had a pitch pipe to get us started, much to Connie's chagrin, and we breezed through the number.

Then Evelyn pushed Connie's buttons even further. "What if we added a bit of harmony to this song?" pointing to the finale where we could break into three-part harmony.

Connie was about to protest when King jumped in. "That

would be *perfetto*. Work that out, girls."

It became clear why Connie had been so resistant about working on any complexities with the music. She couldn't hear anything but the melody line. As Evelyn and I effortlessly added harmonic intervals in thirds, Connie continued to lose her way in the music. She attempted to keep her frustration in check, since "Daddy" was within earshot. Otherwise, I felt sure she'd either blast us or we'd receive the cold shoulder treatment. Evelyn and I weren't purposely trying to frustrate her, though. The song sounded much richer when adding three-part harmony.

Evelyn discovered a way to placate her. "Here's an idea, Connie. You sing melody throughout and Margie and I will adapt to you." Connie was thrilled, boasting that she had the star status of being "lead voice." In the end, King seemed pleased and that was what mattered.

I thought it strange that Connie kept asking King about arrival time. *Why does she keep bothering him?* I finally figured it out when we were about ten minutes to our destination. At that point, Connie took those freakin' rollers out of her hair, brushed out the curls, and sprayed her hair within an inch of its life, choking me and Evelyn with aerosol fumes in the meantime. I'd never seen anyone use so much hairspray in one sitting! Her hair looked nifty though, I had to admit. She wore a ton of cosmetics, too. I hadn't thought about the makeup thing that much. Slowly I put the pieces together. *Our first gig was outside under natural light. But tonight, we'll be under stage lights, which will wash out our features.* I had to give Connie credit for knowing her end of the business!

When the band arrived at the Elks Lodge, our first task was to set up the sound equipment, microphones, cables, monitors, bandstands, and lights on the platform stage at the end of the large hall. The caterers and volunteers darted around prepping buffet tables and arranging linens and dinnerware on circular tables. An elaborate impromptu ballet evolved between musicians and staff as we scurried around the hall, attempting to stay out of each other's way. New to the stage set up process, Evelyn and I received the full force of Connie's oversight. She seemed to relish in shouting out orders at us.

"Drum cases go there, lay out microphone bases in a straight line out front, place one mic cord near each base," on and on she ordered. Evelyn and I did our best to keep up but relied on Bernard, Ted, or Chaz for help every now and then when Connie looked the other way.

"Is she always so bossy?" I asked Chaz in a hushed voice, as he demonstrated how to assemble the microphone cables to the mics.

"Yep," was all I got out of him. *Chaz is a man of few words.*

The guys lugged most of the heavy items from the equipment truck, including wrestling the Hammond B-3 organ into place, thank goodness. But the girls needed to pull drum cases to stage right, unroll microphone cords, lift heavy microphone bases, and place them across the stage, screw the mic stands into the bases, and assemble seven wooden bandstands, and set up twelve chairs for the musicians and singers – all while wearing dresses with strappy sandals! I felt envious of the guys' blue worker coveralls.

Once the stage was set, microphones were connected, and the vocalists completed a quick sound check, everyone prepared to retreat to either the van or The Kennel to change into costumes for the evening. But before they left the stage, Connie blasted the evening's costume instructions.

"Rainbow jumpsuits for the girls with black shoes, black suits with yellow ruffled shirt for the guys," she shouted, her grating voice set to "extra arrogant."

I made sure to apply additional makeup after slipping on my costume, although my long brunette hair sat flat against my head after all that physical work. *Hm. There is a method to Connie's curler and excessive hairspray madness after all!*

The Elks Club audience responded with enthusiasm to our "God Bless America" opener. *Seems like the little American flags really do add a big punch!* At least that's what I kept telling Connie so she'd feel like her "choreography" made an impact. I felt confident the three-part harmony played a bigger part in the crowd's response. Some of the folks sang along, others stood with their hands on their hearts. They were moved. At the end they clapped, cheered, and made their way to the buffet. *Ah, the all-American response – "let's eat!"* King segued immediately into an instrumental version of Les Brown's "Sentimental Journey" and gentler dinner music. This meant that the girls did a lot sitting and swaying in our chairs. At first it felt awkward to be swaying for such a long time, but after a while I realized that no one paid attention to the girls anyway. The audience either ate and talked or occasionally glanced at the sax or trumpet player belting out a riff, especially when King soloed on alto sax.

The first half of the evening included two featured vocal solos: Connie sang "Blue Moon" and Ted crooned Bobby Darin's "Mack the Knife." Not surprisingly, the crowd went wild for Ted's smooth, sexy voice. My parents listened to Darin's albums all the time and I swear Ted sounded identical to the pop star! On the other hand, the audience responded blandly to Connie. Oh, they applauded politely for her performance but they generally seemed disconnected. The thing is, Connie had a fair voice but she "over sang" too much as if always trying to prove something. Vocally, when a singer pushes, it often results in going sharp, which is as bad as singing flat! It made me cringe and I wondered if she knew the crowd was less engaged, or if her ego didn't allow their response to register.

The second half of the evening focused on dance music, including a variety of Glenn Miller swing tunes as well as pop and disco numbers like The Commodore's "Brick House," Creedence Clearwater Revival's "Proud Mary," and Three Dog Night's "Joy to the World." The crowd filled the dance floor, swing and disco dancing with equal abandon. As I sat swaying in my chair on stage left, I shared the energy of the music filling folks with joy and fun – smiles, laughs, and movement.

Since the Elks Club's dinner-dance was a longer gig than Saint Leo's festival, the band took several breaks throughout the evening. King planned the song list in advanced so that the band always ended the set with a peppy, swinging tune like Glenn Miller's "Pennsylvania 6-5000" or "Take the A Train," leaving the audience with a feeling of "Aw, we want more!" It worked. They were super enthusiastic when we returned for the next set. King knew how to work a crowd! Most of the guys took their break behind the band platform, smoking and trading jabs on where they might have missed a note – or "hit a clam" as they called it, jokingly.

"Man, I hit a damn clam on my trumpet solo in 'Tuxedo Junction,'" Jimmy admitted, as Bernard, Ricky, and Chaz laughed.

"Sure did," Chaz teased.

"But you covered it very well," Bernard said. "And you know what they say: If you miss a note the first time, make sure you miss the same note the second and even third time, so the audience thinks you did it on purpose." They all cracked up, including me.

I looked around to see where Evelyn had gone and noticed her chatting with Ted at the other end of the stage. The Conti's were having a family conference outside, so Ted had a moment to breathe without Connie suffocating him. But Evelyn still put herself in a precarious position by chatting with Ted. Connie's possessiveness had been made crystal clear.

I was about to invite them both to join our little group, when the outside door opened and Connie bounded in. Her ability to size up a situation and turn it into something nefarious was beyond paranoia. Her eyes bulged, her body tensed, and, in this case, she reacted like she had found Ted and Evelyn in bed together or something.

"Teddy! Really!" she shrieked, reminding me of a screeching osprey when fighting for territory along the Chesapeake Bay. Her abrupt interruption caused both Evelyn and Ted to jump, which in turn made them look guilty when all they were doing were talking.

"Oh shit!" I heard Jimmy say under his breath.

"Ted's in deep, deep trouble, man. We know that voice," Ricky said.

She looked like a banshee, her eyes wild and bulging. Ruby warned me that Connie was challenged by newcomers, but she never indicated her ego was this flimsy. I sensed a boiling core of hot lava simmering below the surface with Connie. I felt it in the way she barked orders, attempted to cover her musical deficiencies, and how she overreacted when another female got within two feet of her boyfriend! Hating confrontations, I tried to defuse the situation.

"Evelyn and I were just now telling Ted what a fantastic job he did on "Mack the Knife." Uh, what a wonderful job you *both* did on your solos, that is. Right, Evelyn?

"Right. Both solos were super. I, er, we were just talking about that, Connie."

Ted picked up the cover story. "Yeah, Connie. You did great with "Blue Moon" and the crowd seemed to respond. And what about opening with "God Bless America"? Didn't they go crazy, guys?" By this point the rest of the guys had gathered around to aid Ted and further defuse any potential fallout. I wasn't convinced that Connie was a hundred percent appeased, but she displayed that smug smile I'd already come to know, so maybe.

Driving back to the studio late that night, I thought about Connie and her controlling personality. After that evening's discovery about her musical ability, or lack of, I felt a bit sorry for her. *She probably feels like she has to show that she can cut it musically, but she doesn't have a great ear. Jimmy said that King pushed all his kids into music, whether they had talent or not. Maybe she's trying to prove herself. And then losing her mom…Does she feel she needs to fill the female void for the family? That must be a lot of pressure.* Even though my efforts to pay her a compliment about the choreography and her solo were half-hearted, the situation reminded me of a passage I read in *Autobiography of a Yogi* that I should apply more often: It was about spreading kindness and making other people happy – that is truly a sign of greatness. *Maybe Connie needs some confidence boosting from time to time. But boy, she sure makes it hard.* I smiled to myself as I remembered my introduction to Ruby and how she said nearly the same thing to me that first day.

What about Ted? He seemed nice enough and his bandmates certainly supported him. *What's the deal with him and Connie? If she's that uptight and distrustful to the point that Ted can't even talk to another girl without having a freak attack, what does that say about their relationship? Why does he put up with it? Either he really likes her or there's something else going on there. I don't see the attraction, but then I'm not a guy.*

Who knew about other people's romantic liaisons? What I knew was that I was searching for something different right now. A boost, a spark, a reconnection, clarity? I wasn't even sure how to define it. *Is being on this tour about running away from the pain of a broken romance or genuinely wanting to be a singer? Is being a singer for rest of my life the career I'm looking for? If not, then what do I want to be? Or who do I want to be?*

Despite my haze, I was confident that this tour was the right place to start looking for some answers.

7

King's True Colors

Roland Park, Baltimore, Maryland – May, 1978

Our second local performance took place at the Wyndhurst Country Club near Roland Park, Maryland on Thursday the following week. King made a big deal about this club being "very high end" and how we needed to be on our best behavior. *What did he expect us to do, go bananas and act all dorky?* From his stern instructions, it was clear this gig had some significance that I wasn't aware of.

A short drive northwest from our Little Italy studio, Roland Park was known as an elite Baltimore suburb. We drove through tree-lined avenues in the ritzy neighborhood, viewing neatly landscaped yards and gorgeous gardens attached to massive houses – some with Tudor-style architecture, others more Georgian with large stone columns, and others Victorian with turrets or wrap around porches. Each home was more impressive than the next. Finally, our parade of vehicles turned into a long private driveway onto the grounds of the Wyndhurst Country Club where a sign caught my attention: "No Dogs, No Coloreds, No Jews." I couldn't believe my eyes.

"Did you see that sign, Connie?" She half shrugged, indicating she had, but otherwise she offered no reaction. "You don't find that disturbing?

"At least they don't mind Italians." *That's all Connie cares about! She lives her whole life in an Italian Catholic mirage. I wonder if she has any Jewish or Black friends. Heck, or any dog friends, for that matter!*

In Church Creek, I attended Cambridge High School, which was integrated by 1969, my freshman year. There were five or six Black students in each of my classes, mostly from Cambridge. I remember the local news reporting about parents ranting and raving against desegregation when I was in middle school. Our high school principal did his best to encourage the students to embrace it, but it didn't seem that hard to me. All the students, White and Black, were finding our way through our mutual interests, whether it was sports, chorus, or the school newspaper. Although thinking back, the "embracing" did seem focused on a panicked message of "Let's all just get along, people!" coming from teachers, who were all White with few exceptions, and the PTA. As long as the Black students quietly participated in the sports and student activities already established, and didn't cause a fuss, the administrators were happy. I don't remember receiving much encouragement for the White students to mingle socially with the Black kids. No one ever suggested we learn about their lives beyond school, what their neighborhoods were like, or where they went to church. *Yeah, it's weird that we never really talked together. Did the teachers not know how to guide us in conversations, or did they not want to? Were they secretly as prejudiced as those parents in the newspaper articles? Gosh, I don't know.* But we students *seemed* to get along fine. *At least, that's how I viewed it back then but I wonder....*

But one warm Saturday morning in late April, when I was still in high school, something happened at Dad's general store that had a major effect on me. I was sweeping the steps outside his store when a Black kid I knew from school walked by. I knew where Kevin lived, or at least I assumed he lived where most of the Blacks from school lived, several miles in the opposite direction from our general store. I said hi and asked him where he was going. He told me he had a job for the day helping a farmer clean out his barn on the other side of Church Creek. Kevin looked hot and sweaty from his trek. I offered him a glass of water, which he welcomed, and he went on his way. As soon as Kevin was out of sight, Dad stormed out of the store and reamed me out.

"I don't ever want to see you spending time with a colored boy again, do you understand me, Margaret?"

"But that's someone I know from school, and I only gave him a glass of water."

"I don't care if the school system forces our kids to mix it up in the classroom. Damn bussing. But there'll be no fraternizing with coloreds outside of school. Do you understand me?"

I was speechless. I could not believe what I was hearing. This was a man who went to Mass every single Sunday, who said grace over every meal he ate, and who had no problem selling his overpriced merchandise to anyone who walked into his general store, including Blacks, Whites, or whatever. The idea of true tolerance for all people didn't fit into any of those Catholic principles for Dad.

But I didn't speak up or defend Kevin or my Black acquaintances from school or say "No, you're wrong." I didn't know how to talk about it, especially to someone like Dad. I knew in my heart something didn't feel right. I didn't know the words to say or have the courage to say them. While our principal at Cambridge High School may have encouraged White and Black students to get along, we were never taught *how to talk to each other* about things that mattered, like differences, hardships, or what to do if we encountered intolerance. Or was I simply a weak girl, who lacked courage to stand up for what felt confusing and wrong in my heart? Regardless, after that incident with Dad, I never looked at him the same way again.

And there I was again. As the band trucks continued to wind through the long, shaded country club driveway and well-groomed lawns, I faced someone with the same ignorance as Dad. I couldn't help but feel the same way about Connie, yet again, I didn't push the issue. I became silent, a slow anger simmering inside. *Was this Connie's ignorance or did her whole family feel the same way? And why don't I say something to her?*

We approached the clubhouse, although "clubhouse" was a bit of an understatement for the palatial mansion that rose before us – a gorgeous brick, stone, and frame building surrounded by lush, landscaped gardens, an adjoining patio, and tennis courts with the golf course greens looming in the distance. The vehicles pulled around to the back of the clubhouse, where a large platform stage had been erected facing elegant outdoor porches furnished with wrought iron tables and chairs surrounded by large potted palm trees and exotic grasses. A stone patio extended beyond the porch area, perfect for dancing under the stars.

Simon and Giorgio took charge of the set up and mic check, while King disappeared. Once all the equipment was in place, Connie instructed us to change and remain either in the van or The Kennel until summoned for sound check. This entire event clearly had a different feel. Not only was the venue classier than the Elks Club or Saint Leo's, but the whole Conti family mood felt strange and tense. Connie's uptight order snapping, the instruction to stay out of sight until sound check, an uneasiness between Simon and his brothers – all created a sense of apprehension. Being so new, I couldn't put my finger on the source, but I heard Ruby's words echoing in the back of my mind, "Pay attention, be flexible, and mosta all, be on time!"

Before leaving the stage to head to the van to change, I caught a glimpse of King at the porch bar sitting with a very distinguished looking gentleman in a gray pinstriped, three-piece suit with wide lapels. A maroon ascot tucked around his neck gave him a classy vibe. "Ascot man" handed King a thick envelope, which King shoved into the inside pocket of his show tux. *Payment for this evening's performance?* I hurried to catch up with the others.

In the tiny van space, Connie, Evelyn, and I worked like contortionists as we slipped into our white jumpsuits and applied some last-minute makeup and hair fixes. I observed Connie for any clues about what could be causing the tension with this gig, but she appeared calm and cool. In fact, she was downright chatty. I'd almost say too friendly!

"Evelyn, I really like your hair tonight. Did you do something different?" Connie never mentioned our hair or makeup, let alone complimented us.

Evelyn seemed suspicious at first, proceeding with caution. "Uh, no. The usual hot rollers and hair spray."

"I'm thinking the harmonies work well on that 'God Bless America' piece now that I'm good with the melody line." Connie's interest in musical harmonies was completely out to lunch, but Evelyn lost her head and dove in.

"Yeah, I think so too, Connie. And there are a couple other songs we can work harmonies into. If you'd like to, that is." Connie gave a casual nod, as she applied more mascara to her already made-up lashes.

Simon called us to report to the stage for sound check. As we reached the platform steps, Connie turned to us. "Oh no, I left my violin in the van. Evelyn, could you run back and grab it for me? I have to remind King about a change in the set list." Not thinking twice, Evelyn did what she was told.

Meanwhile, Connie and I took our places on the stage in front our mics, as did Ted. King began the sound check immediately...without Evelyn in place. Connie never talked to King about any set list change. At that moment, I suspected Connie had set up Evelyn to get in trouble.

"Where's Evelyn?" King bellowed with a sudden anger that was downright terrifying. Even Connie jumped, then kept her eyes down, avoiding any contact with King. I'm sure I looked panicked, intimidated by his anger. *Why don't I say anything? Think of some way to cover for Evelyn. But no words are coming out of my mouth.*

"I said, where's Evelyn?" King yelled, his face turning bright red.

"Here. I'm here." Breathless, Evelyn ran up the steps and took her place in front of her mic. "Sorry."

King walked up to Evelyn and got right in her face. "You're late for sound check," he blasted. "You embarrass me at this fine establishment. We are a professional band." *Boy, he's fuming. Why's he so uptight?*

I noticed Evelyn didn't have Connie's violin when she returned. I glanced over to Connie's chair, where her violin rested against the leg, right where it was supposed to be. Connie *had* set her up! *What a witch! I should have known something was up when she was being so nice to Evelyn.*

Evelyn became desperate. "Look, King. I was sent to get an instrument–"

King put his hand up to silence her. He wasn't buying it. "I don't want to hear it. You made an excuse the last time you were late, and what did I tell you? I said, I didn't care if you were five minutes or an hour late, didn't I?

Evelyn tried again. "Yes, sir. But you see, I was sent–"

"Are you challenging me? I've had about enough of you. I told you once and that's it! You're done. Now get the hell out of here."

"What? Now? Are you serious?" Evelyn looked at Connie in disbelief but got no help. Connie's gaze was glued to the floor. "Leave now?…uh…I at least need to get back to the studio and get my things."

"That's not my problem. Find your own way back! Get the hell off my stage and out of my face! The band has an important show now and you're in my way." Holding back tears, she staggered off the stage, shoulders hunched, deflated.

And I never saw Evelyn again.

I looked over at Connie, her eyes still cast to the floor attempting to conceal that damned smug look of self-righteousness. *That little bitch. That dangerous, little bitch!* I glanced back at Chaz and Jimmy, both shaking their heads in dismay. Ted, Bernard, and Ricky were in my direct sightline. Ted's face became red with embarrassment. Bernard appeared horrified. Ricky looked pissed. *This is what Ricky was alluding to when he asked about King's mood that first day when Evelyn and I met him. I bet Ricky and the guys have seen this explosive temper from King before.*

We finished sound check as the guests entered the porch area, requiring the band to quickly take our places and begin the first number. I wondered if Connie's brain could feel the laser-like glares coming from Jimmy and Chaz, who were positioned behind the girls' chairs. Somehow Evelyn's chair had been magically removed. It was all too contrived.

To top the evening off in even more bizarre fashion, about halfway through the first set, I noticed a note passing through the sax section, from Bernard to Ricky to Connie, who of course read it. I paid little attention, thinking King had some important message for her, until she handed it to me. It read:

Margie: Sing harmony on the next song

Panic set in. *Harmony? What's the next song?* I whispered to Connie asking if she knew, but she only shrugged. She wanted me to fail. *Yikes. I'm going to fail.* I began to hyperventilate and felt a panic attack coming on. My heart pounded out of my chest, my throat tightened, and I began to sweat. *Breathe, Margie. Slow, deep breaths. You got this. In and slowly out. Again. In and slowly out.* Somehow I calmed myself, regaining control.

The band finished "Chattanooga Choo Choo" and Connie moved to the microphone. I followed her, glancing back at Chaz, who mouthed "Blue Moon." My mind raced through the lyrics of "Blue Moon." *Crap! I only know the words to the first verse, and not the chorus of "Blue Moon."* The band finished the intro and plowed ahead into the first verse. *Too late now, gotta wing it!*

I improvised a harmony on the fly to the first verse, keeping my ear tight to Connie's melody line. For the second verse, I echoed the word "Moon" and threw in "oo" at the end of the next two phrases to cover for the fact that I didn't have a clue what the lyrics were. Since that worked well, I decided to "oo" and "ah" and "oh" my way throughout the entire chorus while Connie sang the melody. At the very end of the song, I bravely joined Connie on the last lick, a line repeated in all verses. She seemed shocked, which delighted me to no end.

At break, King called Connie and me over to the side of the

platform stage. Connie's face oozed pompous judgment and I braced myself to be confronted by King's wrath for not knowing the lyrics. *Well, that's it. I'm out on my ear, like Evelyn!*

"Did you two rehearse 'Blue Moon' together. I mean, back at the studio?" he asked.

"No, King. I got your note and—" I said.

"So, you made up all that harmony on the spot?"

I felt worried, terrified of experiencing King's temper first-hand. "Well, yes. And I'm sorry I didn't know all the lyrics." My heartbeat began to ramp up again. "I can learn them for next time."

"No, no, no. I thought you'd sing it in unison and throw in some harmony on the last phrase, no. Keep it exactly as you performed it tonight, cara." Connie's pompous expression melted into indignation as she stomped away toward Ted on the opposite end of the stage.

Jimmy and Chaz approached me backstage before the next set. Between giggles and half hugs, Jimmy told me they'd overheard the exchange with King.

"Man, Connie's gonna need to take a chill pill after that performance. Whew! She looked like she was ready to blow!"

"Thanks for the heads up on the song, Chaz," I said, giving him a little hug. "You are a life saver." He blushed a bit, laughing it off. *I've got to admit it feels good to know the guys had my back. I was able to calm myself enough to get through that duet, AND to feel connected to the audience.*

What a strange, sad day. Returning to the dorm that night, all evidence of Evelyn had vanished, her room packed up and empty. Sitting on my bed with my open journal in hand, I recorded the day's events. An abrupt, cruel ending to Evelyn's involvement with King Vido's Swing Band, both in the way

Connie framed her and in King's firing her. I replayed the whole scene in my mind like watching a grainy home movie, hoping for clarity. I could see Evelyn had been set up. I knew the truth. Where the plot went wrong was with me? *Why did I remain silent? Why didn't I defend for her? Was I weak? Intimidated?*

I glued the tiny scrap of paper with King's scribbled order on a blank page in my journal. Continuing to pour out my emotions, I wrote about my other discoveries. I felt fantastic belting out "Blue Moon" despite my improvisation of both harmonies and lyrics. The energized connection with the audience reaffirmed my passion for singing and music. The good news was I seemed to have won a bit of King's confidence. The bad news was that it freaked Connie out even more. *Not quite sure what to think about that.* I learned that King could flip on a dime: one minute he's firing someone and the next minute he's offering up a compliment. *Not sure what to think about that either.* Regardless, "Sing harmony on the next song" became a secret personal motto, reminding me to be ready for anything and go with the flow.

I pulled up the bed covers and turned off the light for the night, still concerned about my non-response to Evelyn's firing but excited to see where this tour may lead me.

8

Enter Amy

Little Italy, Baltimore — May, 1978

When I woke up the following morning to get ready for our ten o'clock rehearsal, I heard Ruby talking to someone in Evelyn's old room. "Here's your room, hon. Bathroom's over there, and here's the kitchenette with hot plate and frig that youse can share with Margie." *They didn't waste any time bringing in Evelyn's replacement. Were they already planning to add a fourth girl for the tour?* I had quickly learned to avoid second guessing how this band worked. Throwing on a sweater over my pajamas, I stuck my head into the new girl's room.

"Oh, here's Margie, Amy. I'll let you two gals get acquainted," Ruby said as she exited down the staircase.

Amy was not only as cute as a Cabbage Patch Doll but she also exuded energy and giddiness. With bobbed auburn hair and a freckled complexion, it struck me that Amy could not have been more different than Evelyn in both looks and personality. Amy was short and bubbly, where Evelyn was tall, reserved, and sophisticated. *Was that an intentional replacement choice and did Connie have any say in the matter?*

"Welcome to the dorm and King Vido's Swing Band, Amy."

"Thanks." Amy said through an irrepressible giggle.

"What's so funny?"

"It's just…whoever decorated this place must have been out to lunch!" she squealed. I liked Amy immediately. Her sense of humor, her perky energy, her unrestrained giggle. I felt sure we'd get along great. As she unpacked a few personal items, I asked about her audition and last-minute hiring.

"I know, it's bananas. I'm still kinda buggin' out! I got a call from Ruby late last night asking if I could report this morning. I mean, cool beans! It wasn't like I was doing anything else, so I said, 'Far out!' and here I am. It's all a dream. I mean, I auditioned a few weeks ago and heard zilch. Then out of the blue… Wham!"

I debated whether to tell Amy what happened to Evelyn, deciding to warn her about the "Conti Rules of the Game."

"Look, this whole band thing is new to me, but here's my take so far: it's very cool to perform in front of the audiences and see them enjoy the swing music–"

"But?"

"But King and company have some strict and even peculiar rules about being in this band. So…it's best to follow along and not make waves. At least that's been my plan so far."

"Right on," Amy agreed, although I wasn't convinced I made my point.

"Oh, and one more thing," I said. "The family can be weird about their names. Some of them go by their Italian names and some hate going by their Italian names. It can be confusing, but you'll figure it out."

"Cool beans," she said, giggling as we walked downstairs.

At rehearsal in the studio, King introduced Amy to the band and then stressed that we had three short days to work Amy into the full show, including costume fittings. Our next booking was quite unique – we were opening for Vic Damone at a venue called Painters Mill Music Fair in Owings Mills, not far from Little Italy. Amy turned out to be a quick study, picking up the movements to the show numbers super fast. Without Evelyn to push the issue, Connie did not have us work on any harmonies for the show songs. At one o'clock, King announced, much to everyone's surprise, that we would reconvene at three-thirty rather than our usual two o'clock. Ricky whispered to Amy and me that the longer lunch break was to accommodate Connie so she could go downtown Baltimore to shop for tour clothes!

Already skeptical about Connie, Amy quietly cracked, "Do you really think she's going shopping, or straight to the nearest salon to get her dark roots dyed?" Even though it was mean, I thought I'd wet my pants trying to suppress my laughter! *Yep, this gal is already proving to be a fun addition to the band!*

As Amy and I exited the studio, Jimmy and Chaz invited us to join them for lunch at a place called Bertha's Mussels in the Fells Point neighborhood. *Sounds rad to me.* On the sidewalk outside of 324 Albemarle our merry little troupe gathered: Bernard, Ted, Ricky, Jimmy, Chaz, Amy, and me. Acting as tour guide, Bernard reported that Fells Point was a historic neighborhood on the Patapsco River, known for its shipyards, busy port, and markets during the 1700s. I chuckled as his glasses kept sliding down his nose, distracting him from making key points in his historical lecture. The warm breeze and sunshine made it a perfect day to hike the several blocks to Bertha's and even more lovely to sit along the waterfront to indulge on delicious, steamed shrimp and buttery mussels.

Heading down Broadway toward the water, I noticed the most amazing aroma of fresh baked bread coming from a bakery nearby. Despite some derelict buildings and warehouses here and there, Fells Point supported small shops, row houses, industrial buildings, and a smattering of restaurants, giving the area an interesting, almost quirky feel. After grabbing our food at Bertha's, we continued down South Broadway to Thames Street, which led us to the Patapsco River. Chaz, Jimmy, Bernard, and I hunkered down on benches near the pier overlooking the river. Ted, Ricky, and Amy perched a short distance away on some pylons. I wanted to get to know more about my bandmates and this seemed like the perfect opportunity, but before I could open my mouth, Bernard beat me to it.

"I'm curious about your interest in singing with the band, Margie."

"Ah, kind of a long story." *I'm cool with quizzing others about why they wanted to join the band, but less eager to share my tale of woe.*

"We all have a story. Whether it's for music or something personal, we're all here for some reason," Bernard said with a slight shove of his glasses.

"Then let's hear yours, Bernard? What brought you to the band?" I used my pivot strategy to steer the conversation to anyone but myself.

"I'm here because of Jimmy, thankfully. I met Jimmy when I subbed as a sax player in Two Worlds, an R&B band. Jimmy was a regular. Since we're both from Essex, we hit it off, kept in touch. I studied jazz at Towson State University, but after graduation I was struggling with subbing here and there. Horn bands are hard to book in clubs, and when they do get a gig it's usually for a single night – a one off. So anyway, Jimmy got hired by King and the first time they had an opening for a tenor sax, he recommended me."

"Why did you leave that Two Worlds band, Jimmy, if you were a regular?" I asked.

"It's what Bernard said. At the time, gigs were drying up for Two Worlds. Hardly ever got extended club dates. Shit, I wanted to play. The players in Two Worlds were dynamite – some of the greatest horn players in Baltimore. Man, those cats could play the shit outta Chicago, Tower of Power, Earth Wind and Fire."

"Some great guys," Bernard mused.

"But like I said, I wanted to play more, and the steady money of this gig didn't hurt," Jimmy said.

"And Chaz, what about you?" I redirected the conversation. Chaz was usually quiet to the point of shy. Although athletically built, he had a sweet face with chubby, pinchable cheeks, and as I later learned, always dressed in well-worn bell bottom jeans and an oversized navy blue or brown tee shirt. A Chaz uniform of sorts.

"Did you go to college for music too?" I asked.

"Yep,"

Bernard said, "Yeah, I knew Chaz from the jazz program at Towson. He transferred in after two years at Catonsville Community College."

"Are you from Baltimore, Chaz?" I asked.

"Hell no!" Jimmy said, laughing. "Chaz is a farmer boy from the corn fields of Westminster, Maryland. He broke his Daddy's heart when he loved music more than plowing and planting."

"Is that right, Chaz?" I pressed.

"Pretty much." *Well, we're graduating to multiple word answers at least. A sign he's warming up to me?*

Jimmy continued to fill in the background. "The point is it's nearly impossible for horn players to get steady work and steady money right now. Chaz, Bernard, and I jumped at a secure $250 a week."

"Don't forget that *generous* $10 per diem on tour!" Bernard interjected.

Jimmy laughed. "Dude, how could I forget! We went for $250 a week and more playin' time."

My brain took in this latest information and began to process. *The guys are getting $250 a week? But the girl singers are only making $150 a week. Okay, the guys are trained musicians, so maybe that's fair. But wait, I'm a trained vocalist. Although, they do have to set up equipment. But wait, I've got to set up equipment, too – and in heels and a dress! Am I doing $100 a week less work than the fellows? Does my training for my position in this band equal $100 a week less than their contribution? There must be some reason the women get less. Yeah, that's gotta be it.* I needed to talk myself out of being angry or feeling like there was any injustice done solely because we were women. *"Don't make a big deal out of this, Margie."* I could hear the programmed messages of my parents and teachers of my youth playing over and over in my head. *"Don't make waves. Keep it to yourself, Margie. No need for confrontation. People will label you."*

Chaz continued his story. "Least I'm earnin' some money playin' music, so my Dad's off my back." *He speaks!*

"Damn good horn player, too. Even if he *is* a hick farmer from Westminster," Jimmy threw a wadded-up paper napkin at Chaz, all in good fun. Chaz took it in stride, laughing and nodding in agreement.

"Yep," he said, chuckling.

Once the laughter and kidding died down, Bernard turned to me. "Okay, Margie, your turn." *Crap, I can't escape this time.*

I told them my life story, the whole girl-from-tiny-town-goes-to-college thing. "And that's about it…until I got distracted by a guy who ended up breaking my heart. The end."

"No, no," Bernard said. "That's not all there is. I can tell."

By this point, the rest of the gang had gathered around, awaiting my response. *This is a position I hate: Standing center stage reciting the monologue of my life. I much prefer to reflect in the privacy of my journal or shove hurtful feelings deep inside.*

Bernard persisted. "What did you mean 'got distracted'? What happened with this guy?"

Once I began, the saga gushed out of me. I described how David taught me about love and how I thought he had all the answers but in the end that relationship cost me my passion for music and writing, how my whirlwind romance with him ended in deception, how I fell into a deep depression.

"Depression can be a total bummer," Amy said, while the others nodded in agreement.

"Yeah, I felt myself sinking into a dark, bottomless crater. I felt so stuck in our small town, thinking there were no paths out, with Dad's voice in my ear saying, 'get married, have babies, live here for the rest of your life.' It sounds stupid now, but I felt hopeless."

Jimmy piped up right away. "Listen, Margie. You ain't alone."

"So, how'd you find your way to 'ah-King ah-Vido's ah-Swing ah-Band,' of all places." Bernard lightened the mood with a piss-poor Italian accent, attempting to imitate King's voice stating the band's name, not that King's accent was that heavy at all.

After getting a few chuckles out, I continued. "As amazing as this sounds, I was so depressed that I found myself praying for a miracle to lift me out of my...I don't know...darkness, despair...or at least to show me a new path. The next thing I know, I see the notice for the band's auditions and here I am."

"Cool beans," Amy said. "So, a freakin' miracle is what led you to this band?"

"I guess so. I needed to get away from Church Creek, do

something just for me, and stop thinking about this guy. But more than that, I needed a fresh start, to meet new people, and... well, rediscover myself and my passions, maybe...I don't know."

"We get it," Bernard said. "It might sound corny, but there's a lot of world out there to help you find yourself."

"Yeah, and a lot of county fairs and rodeos and dinner-dances. You'll see," Jimmy added, while the rest of the guys laughed. Amy and I weren't sure what the laughter was all about. *I guess we'll find out soon enough.*

As we walked back to the studio, I reflected on Jimmy's salary conversation. Like a green-headed fly in the dog days of summer, a thought kept nipping at my brain: Equal pay and equal rights for woman was exactly the point of the ERA legislation that women had been working so hard to get ratified in Congress. *I haven't been following these efforts very closely but now, look...this affects me. Here I am in a band that treats the guys differently than the girls. I need to pay more attention.*

• • •

Sunday night we prepped for our first full show performance. "Rainbow jumpsuits/black suits with yellow shirts!" Connie's shrill instructions rang in our ears! King Vido's Swing Band opened for singer Vic Damone, who had started touring again after a season in Las Vegas and a few movie roles. The Painter's Mill Music Theatre attracted quality performers and audiences wanted to get up close to their idols. The large theatre-in-the-round configuration didn't work for a band set up like ours. However, for this venue Vic Damone's band used a standard proscenium set up too, so we didn't make any adjustments for the "in-the-round" stage arrangement. And since the event wasn't a sell-out, most of the audience sat directly in front or slightly to the side of the stage. The seating spread out like a huge fan, helping with acoustics and keeping the audience close to the stage. A patron never sat more than seventy feet from the stage, creating a feeling of intimacy, even though the auditorium appeared cavernous with stage lights hanging on an overhead grid in plain sight.

Aware that Vic drew an older audience, King planned for our performance to include the Broadway, Patriotic, and Country mini shows, filling with swing tunes in between. The crowd's excitement revved up after each section, even the country numbers, which didn't seem to fit with the whole evening to my way of thinking. The audience jived to the swing music, swaying and snapping their fingers in time with the rhythm. A few brave couples even danced in the aisles! I got a kick out of seeing these gray-haired seniors enjoying the music so much.

Of course, Vic Damone was the real draw. Seated behind the stage for his performance, Jimmy, Chaz, Amy, and I clustered together to watch the audience's reactions from our vantage point. Demonstrating their appreciation after every song he sang, the audience went crazy when he sang "What Kind of Fool Am I?" and "The Glory of Love," two of the more popular tunes from his albums. His polished style, smoothly segueing from song to song and bantering with the fans, engaged the audience beautifully.

When the house lights came up after his encore, Mr. Damone retreated to his dressing room, but not before pausing in front of our huddled quartet to say hello. Super nice guy. Amy and I asked for his autograph on our programs and he signed them with a smile before being escorted backstage. Amy kept repeating, "Far out!"

At the end of the performance, we waited for Mr. Damone's roadies to break down their equipment before we could pack up and load out. This made for a long, late night. We stood around, trying to stay out of the way to let Mr. Damone's team do their thing.

"I guess that's the difference with being a star," I said to some of the guys. Ted approached our group, a rare occurrence since he was usually always with Connie. He talked fast, his eyes darting around nervously.

"Hey, just heard. Trouble brewing with the Conti clan. King wants the show to have a bigger, flashier look. He's thinking of adding Enzo to the show as singer, but that would mean bringing in another drummer and you know who that would be?"

"Do you *really* think they'd bring Stefano back on the road?" Jimmy looked worried.

"Who's Stefano?" Amy asked.

"He who shall not be named," Jimmy said with a quick wink in my direction.

"Ah, the other Conti son," I whispered to Amy, bringing her onboard.

"What's the story with Stefano?" Amy asked innocently, but the whole group shot her a look letting her know not to ask any more questions for the moment. I was glad she did the asking because I was curious, too. Ted wandered away, leaving us to wonder what it all meant.

"Hell, King's been desperate to get this band to 'the next level' ever since I joined," Jimmy said. "It's a freakin' pipe dream he returns to every now and then. He's livin' in the past, man. Don't get me wrong. I love playin' swing. Shit, I love playin' anything, but the gigs and the audiences are dryin' up for swing music. Throwin' a bunch of money into this band? What's that gonna get him? A couple more state fair gigs. He's delusional." Jimmy seemed disgusted about this news from Ted.

"Yep, you're right," Chaz said. "Industry's changing."

"Damn right. Disco's puttin' the hurt on venues hirin' live musicians. I'm tellin' ya, King ain't keepin' up with the times!"

Ricky and Bernard nodded and looked concerned. *I understand if King wants to make improvements in his band, but I don't know enough about running a band or the music industry to contribute to the conversation. I don't understand why Jimmy is so angry or upset about this news. There must be something about this Stefano sibling. But what?*

When we finally returned to the studio it was nearly two o'clock in the morning, but Amy and I felt wired. Adrenaline pulsed through our bodies! Amy munched on cookies in the dorm kitchenette and I worked on my journal as we reflected on our first actual show.

"Can you believe we met Vic Damone? How cool was that?" Amy said. "And what about that radical theatre! Not to mention the audience's reaction to our singing."

"My parents aren't going to believe we opened for Vic Damone tonight," I said as I looked over Vic's signature on my program. "I think I'll stick this in the back of my journal instead of gluing it. It'll be easier to show Mom next time I go home for a visit."

"I'm so stoked! This is so groovy! I can't wait to start the tour." Amy bounced around and giggled like a toddler at preschool.

"Shh! Next thing you know, we'll get a visit from The Princess herself with orders to shut up," I warned, but had to agree with Amy. "It is super cool, isn't it? I didn't even know I liked swing and big band music as much as I do. I remember my parents had a few albums back home, but I listened to Broadway musicals and stuff on the radio."

"Me too. The radio stuff. Not the Broadway stuff. I mean,

I know show tunes, but I don't listen to them for fun." Amy became serious. "Why do you think Connie is such a grump-wad all the time?"

"That's a tough question. I feel sorry for her."

"Really! That's out to lunch!"

"I'm serious. Look at it this way. She's the only girl in a family of five boys with a domineering father. She doesn't have a mother figure to look up to when she could really use one. Connie doesn't seem very secure with herself so she overdoes it – acts bossy and possessive when she can. You see what I mean?"

Amy thought about it for a moment. "You mean like hanging all over Ted, or making sure we know she's in charge of us?"

"Right. Sort of sad, isn't it?" We looked at each other for moment, nodding.

"Hey, we better hit the sack," I said. "Big day tomorrow!"

We headed to our rooms, but before I closed my door I heard Amy yell at the top of her Cabbage Patch Doll-size lungs, "But she can still be a pain in the tush sometimes!"

What a long, exhilarating, fun day! And it's only the beginning.

9

Tour Takes Off

Morehead City, North Carolina – May, 1978

The first leg of the official tour took us from North Carolina to Chicago to Missouri and several points in between during a three-week stretch. For a girl who'd never been beyond Ocean City or Baltimore, my heart raced when we received a mimeographed tour schedule.

```
King Vido's Swing Band 1978 Tour Schedule -
First Leg

Wed 5/24 - Morehead City, North Carolina -
Morehead Marina Festival

Fri/Sat 5/26 & 27 - Little Rock, Arkansas - Fair

Tues 5/30 - Clay County, West Virginia -
Community Fair

Fri/Sat 6/2 & 3 - Chicago, Illinois - O'Hare
Airport Hotel - Convention

Sun 6/4 - Chicago, Illinois - Cicero Racetrack

Mon/Tues/Wed 6/5, 6 & 7 - Omaha, Nebraska - No
performance

Thurs 6/8 - Sioux Falls, South Dakota - Fair
```

The retrofit of the new truck for the girls arrived in the nick of time for the tour, thank goodness. Traveling to tour appearances in that VW van proved to be way too cozy! Our girls' vehicle was a smaller version of the boys' Kennel and much nicer and cleaner with more storage and privacy. Its eighteen feet housed two sets of bunks with room for suitcase storage underneath and two, 2-foot-wide closets for costumes. Nice full-length mirrors graced the closet doors, essential for the makeup and hair process. I still wondered how it was legal to be transporting people in the back of moving vans, even if these trucks were retrofitted with small windows for air flow, but I assumed that King knew what he was doing.

Our first tour performance in Morehead City, North Carolina took place near the Town Marina as part of an outdoor festival. A slight ocean breeze off the water provided a respite from the southern heat. As the sun set behind us, reflecting beautiful fuchsias and corals on the water, the band played swing music into the evening to an appreciative audience. A memorable way to begin our journey.

That evening I learned how the overnight accommodations worked when the band traveled. After loading up at the end of the gig around eleven-thirty, the trucks traveled about five miles or so out of the city limits. The drivers turned into a Motel 6 near a shopping center, and pulled towards the back of the parking lot, a bit out of sight. Amy and I followed Connie and King to the Motel 6 entrance and waited outside while King went into the lobby to register. When he returned, King told us that Connie, Amy, and I would share one room, while King took a second room. At least that was the set up for that particular night. But the kicker was that the guys slept in The Kennel! I couldn't believe it. I was shocked. *The girls get a room, but the guys don't. If this is one of the perks of being a female in the band, I'm still not sure it warrants the sizable difference between the guys' and girls' paychecks.* While I was glad I got to sleep in a room, at the same time I felt guilty. I had no idea what to do or say to make it right.

A few days later the motel situation got worse. We arrived in Little Rock, Arkansas on Thursday, the day before we were scheduled to play. King and Connie each had their own rooms at the motel this time while Amy and I shared a third room.

"Cool beans," Amy said in response to our room assignment.

"Seems odd," I whispered.

Early Friday morning, we learned the new drill.

Connie popped her head into our room. "I need you to go out into the hall and grab extra towels off the maid's cart. But make sure the maid doesn't see you, got it?"

We weren't sure why, but we did as we were told. The next thing we knew, several of the guys sneaked into our room so they could take showers! The Conti brothers were doing the same over in Connie's room. *Of course, it makes sense. How else would the guys get a chance to take a freakin' shower, since they never get a motel room of their own!* This was how it worked throughout the tour: every few days the girls had two rooms booked at a motel, which meant that the guys would be sneaking in for showers the following morning. On the off-shower days, Connie, Amy, and I bunked together, as a cost-saving measure, I supposed. *I'm sure running a band is an expensive proposition but it seems like King is kind of promoting cheating and, well...stealing! And Connie is acting like it's a normal thing! It feels wrong but if I question it, I'm afraid King will tell me to hit the road. Look what he did to Evelyn for being a minute late to sound check! Crap, everyone else seems to go along with this arrangement. Maybe I'm being too naïve but stealing from the motels like it's a normal function of band business bugs me.*

Traveling between shows meant long hours on the road in the back of the girls' truck. Connie rarely wanted to talk to Amy and me, often closing her bunk's privacy curtains as soon as she got into the truck at the start of a trip. Sometimes Amy would sit in my lower bunk, looking over my stack of spiritual books, munching on Fritos or other snacks.

"How can you read these funky books?" she blurted out after opening the Ram Dass book *Remember: Be Here Now* and flipping through the pages. "I can't follow any of it."

"Yeah, I get that. It's not for everyone. I think it's interesting to read about different philosophies, religions, and spiritual paths. I like to see how they are similar. And sometimes I find quotes or sayings that are helpful reminders of how I want my life to be."

She looked relieved. "Oh, cool beans. I was a little afraid you were one of those religious freaks. You know, like those dudes who wear the robes and follow you around at the airport and make you buy little flowers, singing Hari Krishna?"

I started laughing. "Nope, nothing like that, Amy. You're safe."

After Amy and I got tired of giggling about something goofy Connie did or looking at a fashion magazine together, we'd retreat to our separate bunks. This created lots of personal time to take naps, read books, watch the world go by through my small window or reflect in my journal. I wrote about things like the exchange of performer-audience energy and the rush of adrenaline that occurred when performing. I slowly began to express myself more in my writing, using my journal to hash out my thoughts about coming on the road. I wondered if this tour was truly the miracle I had thought at first or simply an excuse to run away from David and repair that hole in my heart. *Or is it a matter of how we perceive these events in our lives? If I believe what I read, there are no wrong choices, only different paths to getting to my own personal truth, whatever that is! David did introduce me to so much. Eastern philosophy, mediation, yoga. Even though he hurt me, I keep thinking and writing about this idea that I needed him in my life. Do I need these touring experiences to help me grow into the phase of "the next me," too?* Regardless, the more I wrote, the more my passion for writing reignited. Daily journaling was not only a terrific way to fill the time and the miles between gigs, but also became an essential mode of self-expression.

We often stopped for meals at Cracker Barrel or Big Boy-type restaurants, unless we were falling behind schedule. In those cases, we'd more likely get fast food. Eating healthy on the road could be difficult. I liked eating at a sit-down restaurant because it gave me a chance to talk to the guys, breaking up the long hours of travel. On our drive to Chicago during this first leg of the tour, we stopped for lunch at a Cracker Barrel. The Conti clan called a special "family only" meeting at a separate table, giving Ted the rare opportunity to sit with the rest of the "lowly players," resulting in gentle ribbing from Jimmy, Chaz, Ricky, and Bernard. He took the teasing in stride. *He's probably relieved to be spending time with the "non-Conti" part of the band for a little while.*

"Got away from the ole' ball and chain and decided to eat with the peons?" Jimmy teased, while Ricky gave Ted a slight shove.

"Something like that." Ted smiled while glancing over to the

Conti table to make sure they couldn't hear us.

"Well, come grab a seat and join us. Happy to have you," Bernard said. Always the positive voice in the crowd, Bernard was super down-to-earth, even though he sometimes had a bit of an inferiority complex. Maybe being short and kinda nerdy, with those thick glasses that tended to slide down his nose, contributed to his low self-esteem.

"Give us the scoop, Ted. What's up with the Conti clan? Cough up the intel. You're an insider," Ricky pressured, half joking.

"Come on! Tell us what you know! What's up?" The others jumped in, hounding him.

"Seriously, guys. I think they're going over set lists and scheduling for the next leg of the tour, so take a chill pill."

When the waitress arrived with our food, I changed the subject. I wanted to get to know Ted, since we didn't often have a chance to talk. I asked him about his background in music and how long he'd been in the band. I learned that Ted grew up in Ocean City, so I commented on how we were both from the Eastern Shore. At 26 years old, he and Jimmy were the oldest members of the band, besides a couple of the Conti boys, and they both had been in the band the longest, a little over four years.

Ted was well liked by the rest of the band. His humor, charisma, and good sense set him apart. *Good sense in most cases. Except perhaps when it comes to Connie!*

"Teddy!" That grating voice from across the restaurant cut through our conversation and just like that, Ted turned into a simpering sap, threw some money on the table, and shuffled over to where Connie eyed some ridiculous stuffed animals displayed near the cashier.

I wanted to respect Ted but found it difficult in moments like those. *What did Connie have on him that could make him pivot like that? Okay, I get that she's blond with big boobs, but there's got to be more to a relationship than that.*

"Who wants to bet that vixen will get him to buy her one of those silly animals?" Ricky challenged the group but everyone was already nodding in agreement.

"I ain't bettin' against that. I'd lose my money," Jimmy said with a chuckle.

Amy sighed as she watched Connie and Ted interact. "I don't get that. He seems beaten to the max when he's with her, and so relaxed with us."

"Uh oh, kid," Jimmy said. "Don't be gettin' any ideas about Teddy-Boy, if you know what's good for you."

"It's best to leave it alone," Bernard said. "Who can understand what people see in each other and what holds them together?"

"How did you get so wise, Bernard?" I teased. He smiled back at me.

Getting settled back on the truck, Amy and I lounged on my lower bunk, complaining about eating too much, when the door flew open. Connie strutted in with a stuffed Snoopy dog. I caught Amy's glance and we burst into laughter.

"Isn't it the cutest?" Connie said in a silly baby voice. "My widdle Teddy got it for me."

As I searched my brain for a non-sarcastic response, Amy jumped on the situation. "You mean, you asked Ted to get it for you!" *Yikes, that was direct. I might need to have another talk with Amy about keeping the peace with Connie.* But for some reason, Amy's comment went right over Connie's head.

"I tink I'll name him 'Teddy Weddy'." Connie squeezed the

stuffed toy within an inch of its pretend life!

Amy couldn't let it go. "You do know it has a name, right? 'Snoopy' ring a bell?"

"No matter," Connie said, drawing her privacy curtains. *I guess Amy doesn't threaten Connie, at least for the time being.*

• • •

The next part of the tour included three full days in Chicago. The first two performances at the exquisite Hilton Chicago O'Hare Airport Hotel included dinner-dance music on the first night and a full show on the second night for a convention of medical professionals. There were 400 guests in attendance for the performance in the hotel auditorium with full lights and a professional house sound system. This crowd was revved up for the Pop mini show with songs like "Y.M.C.A.," "Proud Mary," and "Brick House." The audience sang from their seats, danced in the aisles, and hooted and hollered throughout the entire show. I suspected that alcohol may have had something to do with their enthusiasm, but we still soared on their energy.

I learned to expect highs and lows while on tour. One of the lows occurred the following afternoon in Cicero, a suburb on the south side of Chicago, our third performance in the Chicago area. We assembled on a rickety flat-bed trailer. A pickup truck literally pulled the band onto the Cicero horse racing track to entertain all of twenty-five or so gamblers and spectators in the stands, who only wanted to see the ponies run. I laughed when Connie pretended to be insulted because she thought some of the men in the audience were checking her out "with their binoculars!" In reality, they were watching the racehorses make warm up runs around the track behind our stage. The smell of manure, the shoddy stage platform, the disinterested viewers – a strange comparison to the previous night's Hilton Hotel event.

Man, we couldn't wait to get that performance over with! One high point of the day: Our skimpy audience did take their eyes off the horses for a moment when we sang Jim Croce's "Bad Bad Leroy Brown." *I mean, how can they not at least look up when we mention the south side of Chicago being the baddest part of town?*

Since we didn't have any scheduled performances immediately after Chicago, we traveled to the Conti's condo in Omaha, where we lolled around for several days of nothingness. At the condo, King's son Stefano greeted the band as the trucks rolled into a nearby parking lot. *At last, "he who shall not be named" in the flesh.* With his slick dark hair, full sideburns, and menacing moustache, the guy reeked of trouble, but I may have let my imagination be influenced by Jimmy's comments. It didn't help that Stefano wore a tan leather jacket, despite the unseasonably warm May day, and very dark sunglasses that screamed, "I'm hiding behind here!" His overall look – the facial hair, clothing, glasses – created a cross between a used car salesman and Michael Corleone.

Giorgio and Antonio hugged Stefano, exchanging claps on the back. Stefano messed up Enzo's hair, then pulled him in for a close hug. Connie received a giant squeeze, lifting her right off the ground and making her squeal. But when Stefano came around to Simon, he pulled him in tight, head-to-head, and said something very quietly. It looked intense, causing Simon to pull away. *Hm, what's that all about? An intense sibling conflict?* King jumped in to intervene with more hugs and greetings in Italian, whisking the family to the condo entrance. On her way in, Connie told Amy and me she'd be back later with instructions.

Since the sunny, cloudless day was gorgeous and the condo had a radical pool, Amy and I took advantage of it. After nine hours on the road, it felt great to chill out in the fresh air.

"So that's the infamous Stefano," I said to Amy as we settled onto a couple of lounge chairs. "I'm guessing he lives here in the condo, but what's his story?"

"I was able to get the skinny from Bernard. At least some of it. Stefano runs some kind of Conti business from Omaha but Bernard doesn't think it has anything to do with band."

"Intriguing. Does he have any idea what the business is?"

"No clue. He said I should mind my own Ps and Qs. He's such a dork." Amy's infectious giggle got me laughing, too.

"What did Bernard tell you about this condo in the middle of cow country?"

"Oh, right on. He said King leases it as a mid-way rest stop for the band between tour gigs. A total tax credit or something like that. Plus, Stefano gets a groovy place to live for free! Sounds like a far out deal for 'He who shall not be named'."

We were interrupted by her royal highness, who told us to follow her into the condo. Once inside, Connie described the sleeping arrangements. The girls would share the spare room in the three-bedroom condo. King had the master bedroom, and Stefano took the remaining room. The condo had a kitchen area, painted blood red, and a large living/dining space, covered in embossed red and black paisley print wallpaper with flecks of gold. The crimson sofa, armchairs, and dining set attempted to pull the two rooms together but... *Whoa! Decorating is not a Conti strength!* There were two bathrooms, one in the master bedroom and one in the hallway. Of course, the guys would be showering in the condo during our three-day stay, which went without saying. Once Amy and I got our suitcases up to the room, it was late afternoon with plenty of sunshine left in the day.

"Hey, Connie, is it okay if Margie and I go for a swim in that groovy pool?" Amy asked.

"Look, for the next three days, your time is your own." Connie handed us each a key ring. "Here's a key to the condo and the downstairs door for each of you. But don't come in super late and be all stupid drunk. And don't lose the keys."

"Cool beans!" Amy said. Connie acted like a Mother Hen, a grouchy hen at that, but at least we didn't have to ask permission for every little thing for the next few days. I felt liberated.

While Amy and I changed into our bathing suits, we overheard bits and pieces of King talking with the rest of the Conti clan in the living room. Something about needing Stefano to come on the road and play drums so that Enzo could do more singing in the mini shows. King wanted the show's production to look bigger and grander. Enzo was whining because he wanted to play drums. His "life's calling," he proclaimed! Stefano pushed back, too. He thought the "other" business would suffer.

"It needs constant attention, or you'll lose important connections, King, and you can't afford to lose a single one. It could be dangerous," Stefano said. *What does he mean? Of course, any business needs attention, but how can losing a business contact be dangerous? Is Stefano being dramatic or is the band in financial trouble or something else?*

Ricky, Bernard, and Chaz were already in the water splashing around like goofballs by the time Amy and I arrived poolside. Even though we'd only been on the road for two weeks, it felt amazing to chill out and have some fun doing nothing for a couple of hours. I began to realize that life on the road took a lot out of a person and I needed to learn ways to strike a balance. I recalled an apt saying about balance from my days with David: "Life is a balance between rest and movement." I decided to make it my mantra for surviving this tour.

"What a dork!" My thoughts were interrupted by Amy's

squealing laughter as Ted cannonballed into the pool, creating a huge splash. "I'm soaked. Thanks a lot, Ted."

"I'm so, so sorry." Ted continued to splash Amy until she got into the pool. Meanwhile, Jimmy walked over to join me on the lounge chairs.

"Well, here we are in Condoville for a borin' three days." He seemed unhappy about this downtime.

"Is this a regular thing?"

"Hell yeah! We have a few weeks of gigs, then land here for a couple days. Frustrates the shit outta me. I wanna play, man."

"What do you love about playing, Jimmy? Is it solos? Being in front of the crowd?

He thought for a moment before he spoke. "Nay, man. It's not only the audience, even though they're a part of it. It's the energy, the buzz I feel when all the horns are in synch and crisp, and I feel the audience groovin' and...I don't know...it's hard to explain. Great music connects people, whether you're listenin' or playin'. I love bein' part of it." He seemed self-conscious. "That's why I wanna play, man!"

I was a bit surprised by his heartfelt answer since Jimmy didn't seem super deep. *A good reminder not to be so quick to judge people, Margie!*

"What's this 'other business' I overheard Stefano talking about with King in the condo? Do you know what that's all about, Jimmy?"

"You ask a lot of questions, don't you, Margie?" Jimmy smiled so I could tell he wasn't annoyed. "Look, a word of advice. You don't wanna go stickin' your nose into the Conti family affairs. Just go along to get along! That's my motto." I could tell Jimmy was trying to protect me, though I wasn't convinced he knew any more than I did. He changed the subject. "Hey, a couple of us are goin' out to a local bar tonight. You in?"

"Sounds like fun." I could use a night out. I was sure Amy would be up for it, too.

• • •

Rosie's Bar and Grille turned out to be a hopping place. Tasty food, arcade games, pool tables, a disco floor, and cheap draft beer. What more could a touring band ask for? Amy and I tagged along with Bernard, Ricky, Jimmy, and Chaz. Connie and Ted said they might show up after their "movie date," as Connie stated loud and clear. I gorged on stuffed potato skins with cheddar cheese and chunks of real bacon, while Amy gobbled down a greasy cheeseburger and plate of fried onion rings. While we ate, Bernard and Ricky strategized on a plan to pick up girls.

"Check out those two foxy mamas over there, Bernard. What do you think?"

"Do they look tall? It's hard to tell while they're sitting. But what do you think? I can't ask a girl to dance if she's towering over me." Bernard adjusted his glasses as he tried to nonchalantly size up the girls.

"We're gonna talk first. We might not have to dance...if they're easy."

"What?" Amy interjected. "That's sleazy, Ricky." *Gosh, I admire how easily Amy spoke her mind. Confrontation is not my thing.*

"Shut it, Amy. Mind your own business." Ricky could be rude when he wasn't turning on the fake charm.

But Amy ignored Ricky. "Bernard, both those girls look like space cadets. Are those the kind of girls you want to be with? Girls you won't even be able to have a conversation with?"

Bernard hesitated. "Um...Well... I just want to dance."

"Far out, then go over and ask one of them to dance," Amy

said.

"Butt out, Amy. I know what Bernard wants better than you," Ricky snapped, as he grabbed poor Bernard off the bar stool and headed across the bar. *My initial feelings about Ricky are panning out. He is a sleaze. The perfectly coifed hair and fancy cologne is his method for scoring a pickup.*

Amy and I watched as Ricky dragged Bernard over to the unsuspecting girls' table and struck out cold. I wanted to laugh but thought better of it. I wasn't sure how frail Ricky's ego might be. *No sense whacking that hornet's nest.* Plus, I really liked Bernard and didn't want to hurt his feelings.

The rest of the night was a blast. I had a couple of drafts, shot some pool, danced with Amy, Chaz, and Bernard. But Jimmy refused to get on dance floor, saying he was "standin' or rather sittin' in protest against disco music." I didn't understand what he was talking about until I heard the guys talking back at our table about how disco music was hurting the livelihood of live musicians because so many venues were switching to DJs and recorded music.

"Damn *Saturday Night Fever* movie and that John Travolta. Makes the disco world look so sexy and glamourous." Jimmy was all worked up.

"Lots of musician friends are struggling cuz their gigs are drying up," Bernard said.

"It's not only the movie that's the cause, though, right, Bernard?" I asked, thinking I'd get a less biased answer from him.

"No, that's true."

"You're right," Jimmy conceded. "It's cheaper for clubs to spin discs than to pay for full bands. I get it. But I hate that damn movie!" *One thing about Jimmy: he doesn't mince words!*

I wondered what could be done to help musicians, especially

since disco was such a hot trend. *It feels odd to be concerned about this music industry issue, and at the same time, to enjoy dancing to disco music. Should I be standing with Jimmy and refusing to dance, too? I don't usually take a stand on…well, much of anything.*

After his early rejection with the girls, Ricky pouted at the bar for most of the evening. Despite his forced self-confidence, I sensed Ricky was a glum guy inside. Toward the end of the night, I went over to try to cheer him up.

"Hey, Ricky. Why don't you give it a rest and come join us?"

"Look who's here. Little Miss Cheerful." He seemed super down and kinda drunk.

"Aw, come on. We're all just chillin', having a few beers, dancing. Thought I'd ask, is all." I turned to leave when Ricky stopped me. "Wait. You'd really dance with me?"

"Sure, Ricky. I hate to see you missing out on all the fun." We headed to the dance floor to join the others, who clapped and welcomed him into the space, impressed that I was able to break through Ricky's funk.

At the end of the evening, we all walked back to the condo as a group, laughing and singing the chorus of "Brick House" over and over, slightly off-key and way too loud. Once we got to the condo parking lot, the guys split off to return to The Kennel, while Amy and I stopped at the entrance of the condo to moon gaze a bit. I was thinking about how I never realized how rude those "Brick House" lyrics were. I wonder why King included that song in the Pop show.

"You know, Ted and Connie never showed up," Amy said.

"Hm? Oh yeah, I doubted they would. Connie has him on a short leash. Hey, while we're on the topic, I don't want to tell you what to do but –"

"But?"

"I like you, Amy, and I'd like you to stay around. I didn't tell you all the details about what happened to Evelyn, the girl before you, but maybe you'd want to know."

"Sure. Give me the skinny."

"Connie thought something was going on between Evelyn and Ted, which wasn't true. And I'm pretty sure Connie set her up, purposely making Evelyn late for mic check at a show to get her fired. You don't want to mess with Connie and what she views as her property."

"Connie really is bitchy, isn't she?"

I nodded in agreement and continued, "And remember, Ted and Connie have been together for a long time."

"That may be true, but I know for a fact that he's totally bummed out about it. He told me today in the pool. He wants to break it off with her, but he doesn't know how. Connie and the family have their hooks into him too deep. He's too freaked out to even bring up the subject, afraid she'll run to King and get him fired, afraid that the Conti brothers will go bananas.

"Wow," was all I could say. *I may have misjudged Ted. Maybe he just doesn't know how to speak up.*

I understood that *all* too well.

10

The Incident

Omaha, Nebraska – May, 1978

During our second night in Omaha, the whole group planned to go to Rosie's Bar and Grille, including the Conti brothers AND Connie and Ted. Even King showed up for a bite to eat before excusing himself, making it an early evening. The Conti brothers stuck to themselves most of the evening, taking turns at some stupid *Space Invaders* arcade game. It gave me a good opportunity to observe Enzo display some major acting out around his older brothers. What a baby! Temper tantrums and whining when he bombed out and the aliens overwhelmed him on the screen. Even Antonio and Giorgio acted immaturely. *Is it the dumb arcade game causing them to regress or are these guys emotionally stunted? Outside of Simon, they never mingle with the other band members, don't know how to converse, and can barely function without instructions from King. Pitiful.*

At one point in the evening, Connie and Ted began arguing at the far end of the bar. Something about Ted wanting to hang out with the rest of the guys more and feeling that Connie acted too possessive. *Whoa! Pretty bold for 'Teddy' boy! Is he learning to speak up after all?* I tried not to stare, but I couldn't help myself. "Like moth to flame," as Mom would say! In an attempt to stop staring and eavesdropping, I joined Jimmy, Chaz, Ricky, and

Amy at a high top near the pool tables. Ricky had struck out again with a young woman on the dance floor and Jimmy was teasing him relentlessly.

"Stop trying so hard, Ricky. They can smell the 'prowl' on you. Or is that your cologne?"

"What happened to your sidekick?" I asked Ricky, referring to Bernard. Chuckling, Jimmy, Chaz, and Amy pointed to the dance floor where Bernard and a cute blond danced and laughed together. My question and the attempts to suppress giggles seemed to tick off Ricky, who retreated to the end of the bar and ordered a shot.

I turned to the group. "Touchy."

"He tries way too hard. Shit, I don't know what the hell he thinks he's gotta prove." Disgusted, Jimmy flagged down a waitress to order another beer. "Ignore him. He's in one of his *moods* tonight."

The evening progressed much the same as the night before. Lots of dancing, laughing, talking, yummy food, and a few beers. I updated Amy on the Ted and Connie argument, which interested her immensely. I even talked with Simon a bit at the bar, after he was tired of playing *Space Invaders* with his whiny brothers.

"We never get a chance to talk outside of setting up for a gig, Simon. How are things going with Cheryl and getting ready for the baby? It must be exciting," I said.

"Yeah, she's doing all that pre-baby stuff. You know, decorating the nursery and picking out a crib, all that stuff."

"It'll be hard to be away so much once the baby is born, won't it?" *I may be wading into dangerous waters.*

"Yeah, but I'm working on a way that I might be able to be home more."

"Cool. I'm sure Cheryl and the baby will like that, too."

Just as I started to ask about his plans, Ricky interrupted from his perch at the end of the bar. "Ya know S-Simon's married, Margie," he said, slurring his words. "You should stop trying to pick up everything that wears pants in this joint." I felt uncomfortable at the implication that my conversation with Simon was something more than friendly banter but laughed it off.

"Sit on it, Ricky!" Simon shot back as he got up to mingle with his brothers at the pool table. I moved to the dance floor to join Chaz and Amy, avoiding further fallout from Ricky.

Walking back to the condo at the end of the night, a small group gathered out by the pool before calling it a night, talking and staring at the star-filled sky. As some of us began to disperse, I said my goodnights to Jimmy, Chaz, and Amy and headed inside.

"Catch you on the flip side," Amy called out, before I rounded the corner of the building and headed to the condo door.

Before I reached the door, I heard Ricky's voice. "Hey, Margie. Wait up." He and Bernard hadn't walked back with the rest of the group, but I figured he wanted to apologize for being such an ass at the bar. When he caught up, I gave him a quick once-over: greasy hair falling into his eyes, shirt untucked, one cuff unbuttoned and flopping. *The impeccable Ricky is a mess!*

"You...you're a g-good dancer, ya know that?" Ricky said. Between his appearance and the slur of his words, I realized he was still drunk.

"Thanks, Ricky. See you in the morning. It's late." I fumbled through my purse looking for my keys.

"Wh...why didn't cha dance with me tonight, Mar-gee?"

"Well, for one thing, you were moping at the bar most of the night, Ricky. Why don't you go to bed now, okay?"

I looked down to find my keys in my purse again, getting my left arm tangled up in the long strap. The next thing I knew I felt the pressure of Ricky's body against mine, pushing me against the door, the handle of the condo door digging uncomfortably into the small of my back. He was trying to kiss me, his hands all over my body, tugging at my blouse, groping my breasts, and grabbing my butt. I was completely caught off guard. The moment was surreal, moving both extremely fast and in slowing motion, if that was even possible.

At first, I couldn't think straight or breathe for that matter. My mind tried to process: *What's happening here? This doesn't make sense!* While I tried to think, Ricky continued to grab at me, tearing my blouse with a snicker. My thoughts raced, attempting to simultaneously untangle multiple problems at hand: disengage arm from purse...fix torn blouse...relieve pressure on body... stop groping...stop pain in back...run from danger!

While pinning my right arm, he clumsily grabbed at my breasts and began thrusting his pelvis against me, each time banging my back against the damned door handle. His attempts to kiss me were met with my head flailing from side to side so he settled for my neck. He began to fumble with the zipper of my jeans, trying to slip his hand between my panties and belly. I squirmed making his maneuver difficult. He smelled of whiskey and Old Spice. My stomach turned. Ricky acted like a caged animal set free, wild and detached, as if he'd found his target and was determined not to strike out again.

I tried to scream. Nothing came out. *Where's my voice?* No sound. It was like those dreams where you try to yell over and over, but nothing comes out. Voiceless. Then I realized I wasn't breathing. *Of course, I can't speak. I need to breathe. Breathe,*

Margie.

I started to hyperventilate and could feel my heart pounding, pounding, pounding. *I can't breathe. I...can't...breathe!* Nothing. I felt lightheaded. *I...must...breathe. One time. Do it! One breath...slowly. Good. One more. Again.*

As my breathing started to normalize, my thoughts came into focus and the danger became even more real. Pressure, pain, unwanted hands, tearing, pushing. *Run away, Margie. Run away, Margie. No, you can't run away this time, Margie.*

Do something, Margie! Breathe, Margie! Make this stop! Make this stop, Margie! You've got to do something! Suddenly, a voice exploded from deep inside of me and I formed a word. I screamed "No!" An unexpected strength surged in me. I pushed with all the energy I could summon from deep inside me. This explosion of strength must have shocked Ricky because with an untangled left arm I was able to shove him hard. He fell back a few feet, staggering in his drunken state.

Ricky looked at me with a shocked expression of utter disbelief. "Gawd, Margie. What'sa big deal?" He tried to straighten up but staggered. "I mean ya asked for it. You...you some kinda prude?" was Ricky's response as he stumbled away and rounded the corner of the building.

Finally grasping my keys, I unlocked the outside door to the condo vestibule and crumbled to the floor, gasping for breath between sobs, as the door closed and locked. A second panic attack rose inside me. *Pounding in my chest. Tightness. Difficult... to...breathe.* I talked myself through it, taking slow, deep breaths and releasing, coaching myself. *You can do it, Margie. Breathe in slowly for four counts, breathe out gently through your nose. You're safe now. Close your eyes and focus on the breath going in and out. Again. Now again. There now, breathing is better.*

With breathing and sobbing barely under control, I climbed the stairs to the condo and headed to the shower. I scrubbed my face and neck and breasts and stomach, trying to wash off the cologne stink, as if I could make the incident disappear with soap and steaming water. My thoughts returned Ricky's words, "You asked for it." *Why would he say that? Did I? I did ask him to dance last night, but that was being friendly, right? Did he misunderstand? Did I send him the wrong message? Maybe this is my fault?* That phrase, "You asked for it" haunted me. *How do you wash away words that have been imprinted in your brain?*

• • •

The next day I cocooned in the safety of the condo bedroom even though Amy asked me to hang out with her at the pool. I pretended I had cramps. At lunchtime, I lied and told her I wasn't hungry. Truth was I needed time to regroup, to think what to do next, to figure out how to face Ricky. That night, everyone planned to hit Rosie's one last time before heading out the following day for tour dates at Sioux Falls, South Dakota and St. Louis, Missouri. I begged off despite Amy's pleading.

"Aw, come on, Margie. It's our last night here. It'll be far out!"

"I don't feel up to it. I'm gonna do some reading and hit the sack early. You go. Have fun."

"You seem kinda down in the dumps. Is everything okay?"

"Yeah, sure. Wiped out, that's all. I'm cool. I'll catch ya tomorrow." I wanted her to stop prying. I didn't want to dredge it up again. I needed to bury the whole incident as deeply as possible. Whenever an image or sensation or Ricky's words bubbled up, I pushed it down. It was all I could think to do. *Otherwise, I might hear the "You asked for it" again and again and again.*

As I laid in bed looking for peace or inspiration in my

books, I found only mental and physical exhaustion. I dozed off, depleted. About an hour later I awoke to loud voices in the condo living room. At first I recognized King and Simon, but then it became clear that Stefano made up the trio. They must not have realized that I was in the condo, or they would never have let their voices get to that level. At first the argument centered on Simon's desire to leave the band and return to Cheryl when the baby arrived as well as his desire to open his own carpentry business. He kept saying, "I kept my end of the bargain, now keep yours, King. You promised."

Stefano interrupted. "Be reasonable, Simone."

But Simon jumped down his throat. "Quit calling me Simone and butt out, Stefano. Get your nose out of my business."

"The band is family business," Stefano said. "You must be loyal to the family, Simone." Then everyone started yelling strange accusations I didn't completely understand.

"I never agreed to the stuff you're doing, Stefano. You're going to take the band down and the family with it," Simon shouted.

"*Testa di cazzo*! Asshole!" Stefano countered.

"*Basta, basta*! Enough! Both of you!" King said, trying to stop the argument. "Stefano is only trying to help the band grow."

"No, Papa. He's working with bad people, doing illegal shit. And he's got you so turned around that you're convinced it's okay if it's in the name of the Almighty King Vido's Swing Band. It's not right! Before this whole thing goes south, I want you to honor your promise to me. I'm off the road when the baby comes and I get my seed money to put into Conti Cabinet Making."

The next thing I heard was the door slam. King and Stefano continued to discuss Simon's request, but I only overheard bits and pieces since they were talking at a normal level. King asked

Stefano something about how much longer he'd have to work with "them." Stefano said, "You want money for new costumes and a promotional album, don't you?" Then King started pressuring Stefano about coming back on the tour to play drums again, going on and on about his grand vision for expanding the look for the band and how "that's the better way, that will increase the quality of bookings."

Stephano pushed back. "Better bookings require *molto denaro*. Come on, King. You've been doing this long enough to know that. The performers, the costs of gas, hotels, per diem, the transportation, costumes. The fee for a gig barely covers those costs. Ask Ruby yourself."

"That's why we have to take this band to the next level, Stefano." King's volume escalated as he spoke. "If we don't, then we fade away. I will not have everything I worked for fade away. I will not have King Vido's Swing Band become obsolete. I won't have it! That's it! I'm King Vido!" King was yelling at an obscene volume by the end of this tirade.

"Okay, okay, King. That's why you've got me here, keeping track of this side of the family operation, and why I can't go on the road right now. Trust me. You keep doing your part and I'll do the rest. And ignore Simone about it being illegal. He doesn't know what he's talking about. We got our people covering our backs. We're good." That must have calmed King down because the next thing I heard was the front door open and close, and the living room was quiet.

• • •

The following day, as we loaded up to head to Sioux Falls for the next appearance, Ricky approached me. My body tensed up immediately, throat closed, shoulders tightened, stomach ached. I was in no mood to talk to him, but what could I do? I didn't want to make a scene in front of the whole band. I did what I usually do in these situations, I shut up and complied with his request to talk.

"Margie, I wanna talk for a minute." Ricky placed his body between me and my path to the girls' truck. Amy glanced back, but kept walking, having no reason to think anything would be amiss. Why would she? I gave no indication. In fact, I acted downright stoic.

"Look, about the other night. I had a little too much to drink and was kinda lonely." Okay, sort of an apology and a feeble excuse, but I still felt…well, I didn't know how I felt. I stood there, silent.

"And I mean, come on, you were kind of flirting with me, so…" *What the hell!* Thoughts exploded in my head. *Was I flirting? I felt sorry for Ricky and was nice to him. We were all dancing together that night. What makes him think that dancing together gave him an invitation to… Holy crap!* I had a bad feeling about Ricky the minute I met him. The smooth talking, overdressing, cologne overdosing…ew. I should have listened, trusted my instinct, stayed away from the creep. But I didn't.

"So, still friends, right?" Ricky asked, as King shouted last call to load up for departure.

I mumbled an incoherent response, although beneath the surface thoughts raged like gale winds on the Chesapeake. *Why don't I blast him? Tell him what I think of him and his stupid apology right there in the parking lot.* But the anger and stormy thoughts swirled in my brain, never close to becoming articulated words. All my energy went to stifling tears.

"I…I guess so," I said, failing once again to find the courage I needed to get what was in my head and heart out into words. *Shove it down and keep on going.* I kept repeating these words to myself, echoing my mom's advice after the David break up.

Why do I do that? I let men manipulate me, even when I figure out they're bad news. First David, now Ricky with his "You asked for it." David had little phrases he created to manipulate me to his point of view, mostly bastardizations from Ram Dass. Like if I made a decision that he didn't like, he'd pull out his own little ditty: "Flow with my flow." It was his way of guiding me toward his point of view. *I can see it clearly now, of course! I'm sure that was not what Ram Dass had in mind with his spiritual philosophy.* But it was my own freakin' fault. I let David distract me from my passions and dreams with the promise of a one-sided version of a loving relationship. It suited him well as long as I stuck around to support him. I didn't listen to my soul, and I rarely spoke up for myself, never ended it properly with David. *And here I am with Ricky, facing similar intimidation, similar manipulation, and not speaking up to express how I really feel. Worst of all, I'm overwhelmed with the sensation that running away from this "Ricky situation" is my only option…again.*

• • •

After the show in Sioux Falls, King rounded up the band for a meeting. The following day, we planned to travel nine hours to St. Louis, Missouri to open for country singer Waylon Jennings at a large, outdoor, riverfront venue. King stressed that this was the type of A-list event he wanted to continue to book, and therefore he wanted a top-notch performance. With set up not until three-thirty, King mentioned that we would have some time to explore the city, while he met with a business associate earlier in the day.

I dreaded nine hours in the back of the girls' truck as we traveled to St. Louis the next day, staring at the corn fields of Iowa and Missouri. After our first rest stop, Jimmy and Chaz asked me if I wanted to ride with them in the cab of the truck, while Jimmy took the wheel of the equipment truck. Jimmy often spelled either Giorgio, Antonio, King, or Simon as one of the designated drivers.

Thrilled at the chance to get out from the back of the truck, I situated myself between Chaz and Jimmy in the cab as we followed The Kennel and the girls' truck, last in line in the King Vido's Swing Band caravan. I soon learned why these guys volunteered to drive as often as possible, when Chaz lit up a joint as soon as we entered the highway. He offered me a toke, but I passed, handing it over to Jimmy.

"Don't you get high, Margie? I mean, it's cool if you don't, but..." Jimmy asked.

"I have. It's super harsh on my throat and, well, as a singer, that's kind of a problem."

Chaz stared at me in disbelief. "Dang. Bummer."

I laughed. "I think I'll live, Chaz."

The other reason the guys loved to be in the cab was because of the 8-track tape player. Between the two of them, Chaz and Jimmy had an extensive collection of tapes and the cab of the truck was one of the few places they could listen to their music. For me, getting out from the back of the girls' truck provided a respite from thinking about Ricky and the assault, even if it meant listening to Jimmy and Chaz dissect musical genres nonstop.

"What kind of music do you listen to, Margie? Like when you're by yourself, hangin' out at home?"

"Well, a lot of musical theatre." Chaz and Jimmy both looked at me like I was a scaley one-eyed alien. "You know, Broadway show tunes...and stuff on the radio, I guess."

"Well, shit! We need to musically educate this woman, Chaz, my man!" Jimmy laughed as he pushed a tape into the tape player. "Let's start with somethin' easy to grasp. The amazing horn band, Chicago."

"Oh, I remember 'Color My World' by Chicago," I said.

"Of course, you do." Jimmy had a sarcastic edge to his voice. "I'm sure you danced your little heart out to it at your first junior high dance."

The usually quiet Chaz said, "Did ya know 'Color My World' was only one part of a thirteen-minute mini-rock opera by Chicago called 'Ballet for a Girl in Buchannon'?" *Quite the burst of conversational input from Chaz!* I shook my head as this was all news to me.

"Thank you, Dr. Chaz," Jimmy said. "But let's introduce Margie to some real funky Chicago tunes. We gotta teach her some rad musical elements, okay? Chicago's known as a 'rock and roll with horns' band, combinin' rock, jazz, R & B, pop, and even high-brow techniques that you classically trained folks might recognize." Then we listened to a tune off the Chicago IX's greatest hits album that Chaz had cued up for me to hear.

"Okay, this tune, 'Does Anybody Really Know What Time It Is?' is one of their earliest, before they changed their name from Chicago Transit Authority to Chicago. I think it was from 1969 or 1970." I couldn't believe Chaz was talking this much. He clearly enjoyed the topic. "Listen to how the horns, the voices blend together, and how the drummer drives the whole thing forward." Listening to music this way sucked me in.

Jimmy introduced the next tune by asking me to listen to the way "Saturday in the Park" began with a keyboard introduction, then layered in horns before the singer began. He challenged me to listen for the section where there was a complete tonal modulation in the middle of the song. I kinda dug that he tested me with a listening quiz. I remembered hearing "Saturday in the Park" on the radio during my senior year of high school, but I hadn't *really* heard its nuances, as Jimmy and Chaz were asking me to do. As I listened from this fresh perspective, I heard the moment in the song where it diverges, changes style and tone. I passed Jimmy's quiz!

"This is super nifty, guys. As a voice major in college, we were only allowed to learn classical songs."

"Hey, that ain't a shitty thing," Jimmy said. "Music, dance, theater, all the arts have a foundation. The trick is not gettin' stuck there."

"Yep, very wise!" Chaz teased.

"Shut the hell up, Chaz," he said, laughing. "It's true though."

I considered this idea about getting stuck from a broader context. "I think you're both right, guys. We can get stuck in our thinking about a lot of things, can't we?" Jimmy and Chaz glanced at each other, not sure what I meant.

As we rolled down the highway, groovin' on more great Chicago tunes, I allowed my mind to wander to other questions. How do people get stuck in unhealthy thinking patterns? How on earth do we break free of them? The truth was I started to think about wanting to run away again, to leave the band because of Ricky. It would have been the easiest thing to do after the attack and it was my typical pattern. *Why can't I speak up, use my voice, state my objections, stand up for myself and other people when I feel these injustices burning inside me? Why is my first impulse to run away from my hurts, instead of facing them?*

It wasn't only the Ricky thing, though that hadn't helped matters. Everything seemed all jumbled up in my brain. *Where will I run away to next? What answers am I hoping to find in the next place that I can't answer here? When will it become clear to me where to go next in my career?* I didn't come to any conclusions as we bounced down the highway.

One thing I knew for sure: As hard as it was to do, it felt important to be asking these questions, to be pushing myself toward some sort of understanding and clarification.

11

Voiceless, Again

St. Louis, Missouri – June, 1978

We arrived in St. Louis with an entire five hours to kick around before reporting for stage set up. Amy, Bernard, Jimmy, Chaz, and I decided to focus on seeing the famous Arch, checking out old-fashioned riverboats on the Mississippi River, and then walking a few blocks for a closer look at the Old Courthouse. If we had time, I wanted to check out the Museum of Westward Expansion, located near the Arch.

Bernard grabbed a pamphlet about the Gateway Arch, assuming his tour guide persona.

"At 630 feet high, the Gateway Arch is designed to sway as much as eighteen inches and can even withstand earthquakes." We all chuckled at Bernard's travelogue description of the engineering feat as he attempted a British accent, his glasses resting on the tip of his nose.

"That is the worst English accent I've ever heard," Jimmy teased.

"Hey, I can't help it if my British sounds nouveau American," Bernard said, laughing. "My parents didn't name me Bernard Reginald Jefferson III for nothing."

"Where are you from, Bernard? Originally, I mean," I asked.

"North Carolina, but my father moved us to Baltimore for

his work. He's a big wig in the corporate world, but not into the arts at all." *Hmm. Seems to be a theme with our parents.*

After our "informative tour" by Bernard, we considered whether to tackle the actual Arch. Due to the lengthy line and our limited time, we opted not to take the tram to the top of the Arch, instead meandering through the park to the riverside.

"Wait up." We recognized Ted's voice calling out to us.

Once Ted caught up with group, Jimmy asked, "What, no Connie?"

"She wanted to get her nails done or something."

"Looks like you got a 'Free Pass' this morning, my man," Jimmy said.

Ted joined us as we walked through the Gateway Arch National Park to the riverfront. A cool breeze off the Mississippi River provided welcome relief from the June heat. Relaxing on a pier, we spotted a couple of riverboats ambling along the river. Double and triple decker boats, replicas of the nineteenth century paddle wheel-propelled transports, jam-packed with tourists, lazily cruised along. We waved and laughed from the shore like a bunch of dorky nerds. Amy and I broke into a chorus of "Ol' Man River" from *Showboat*, while the guys tried to distance themselves from us.

Our next stop, the Old Courthouse, was within spitting distance of the Gateway Arch. The gorgeous Federal style building housed interesting, yet disturbing information about the city's history concerning slavery. On the one hand, slaves were auctioned from the courthouse steps. And the courthouse was the site for many cases suing for freedom and social justice, including the infamous Dred Scott case. I wondered about other border states, including my own state of Maryland, and the ways our citizens were historically divided about these issues. *During my American History class, we never talked about what it meant to be a border state and the ways that some people stood up for their convictions about freeing slaves, like the Quakers. We didn't have any classroom discussions about slavery or Black soldiers joining the Union Army or the hardships that freed slaves faced after the emancipation or the end of the Civil War or any topics like that. At that time, there were a couple Black students in my American History class. I never thought about how those students must have felt when we were taught about the Civil War. I should have.*

"Hello, Margie! Are you there?" Jimmy jarred me out of my mental fog.

"Sorry, deep in thought for a moment."

"Where to next, boss?" Jimmy asked.

I mentioned the Museum of Westward Expansion, describing some of its exhibits. Sensing divided enthusiasm among the group at the mention of a museum, we decided to split up and meet later for a bite to eat. Jimmy wandered off by himself to have a cigarette. Ted and Amy headed toward the Gateway Arch National Park. Chaz and Bernard saw Ricky approaching from across the park.

"Where have you been?" Bernard shouted out to him.

"Around."

Turning to me, Bernard laughed. "He overslept!"

Damn. Couldn't he have slept until the gig? Every time he's near me, my body goes on high alert. Muscles tensing, breathing struggling. A tiny voice in my head whispers, "Run away. Run away." I can either run away, like I usually do, or deal with it. What to do? Having no desire to hang out in a small group with Ricky, I found an excuse to leave Chaz, Bernard, and Ricky to their own devices.

"This is perfect. I'm going to head over to that Museum

exhibit and then do some shopping at those outdoor kiosks along the riverfront." I said, "I know that would bore you guys to tears, so I'll meet you for lunch later." I scooted away before they had a chance to argue. *Okay, so today I am running away. Tomorrow I'll think of a better strategy!*

The Museum of Westward Expansion's major exhibits consisted of information about the Gateway Arch, the importance of St. Louis as a colonial port for the future development of Manifest Destiny, and St. Louis' role as a border state during the nineteenth century. I thought back to my high school American History class, trying to remember what lessons were taught. Sure, we learned about Harriet Tubman and the Underground Railroad, especially since she was born right in Dorchester County, practically stone skipping distance from my house. And yes, we learned that Fredrick Douglass, a freed Black slave, famed orator, and activist, was from nearby Easton, Maryland. But what about what it meant that Maryland was a border state during the Civil War and how divisive opinions at that time still carried over even in 1978. Like my dad's attitude toward Black people. Dad wouldn't even watch *Roots* with me and Mom last year on TV. *That's how ingrained his prejudice is. How can so much time go by and so little progress be made?*

After the museum I strolled back down to the riverfront where I spied a few colorful kiosks selling purses, peasant blouses, scarves, skirts, halter dresses, and other wares. I hadn't spent money on anything other than food since this tour began, so I thought I'd treat myself to something special. I fell in love with a maxi-length skirt in a flowing fabric. *The aqua and navy swirling print will look totally rad with my white peasant top with blue embroidery. I can even wear it for band set up with dressy sandals. Very practical, Margie!* It was so inexpensive I splurged on a matching scarf for my hair. What the hell! I felt like I needed a pick-me-up after the last few dark days.

A bit later the whole group met up for lunch at a small diner across the street from the Gateway Arch. Amy and I slid into a long booth and checked out my purchases. Once everyone settled, Ted revealed that King had left early in the morning for his business meeting.

"What do you think all this 'family business' is about?" Amy asked. "Seems kinda bananas." I decided not to mention anything about the conversation I had overheard back at the condo. *Silence and redirecting are my specialty.*

"For some reason, King wants Stefano to come back to the band to play drums. At least, that's what Connie says," Ted said.

"Yeah, we've heard it all before." Jimmy seemed disgusted. "King wants to make King Vido's Swing Band bigger and better, flashier and cooler. Not that Stefano and new costumes are the answers."

Trying to diffuse Jimmy's building anger, I redirected the conversation. "Okay, but even if King wants to expand the show by bringing on Stefano and having Enzo sing more, that doesn't explain what all these 'business' meetings are about when we're on the road, does it?"

"She's got a point," Chaz said.

"Connie says King is meeting with financial backers. Some businessmen who want to invest in the band," Ted said.

"That sounds a bit out to lunch to me," Jimmy said. "Plus, anything that's got Stefano's fingerprints on it has gotta be bad news."

"What's your deal with Stefano, Jimmy? Come on, spill it," I said.

Jimmy hesitated. "He's a bad guy, a bad influence. On top of that, he and Simon are like oil and water."

"Uh, okay, but what's *your* deal with him? It sounds like it goes deeper. Am I right?" I knew I was pushing Jimmy. While I wasn't ready to share anything I'd overheard in the condo, I thought I might learn something from Jimmy to confirm my growing suspicions.

"Okay, here's the thing," Jimmy conceded. "Stefano pulled me into this stupid gamblin' scheme he was involved in and I lost a shitload of money. Never was sure if Stefano placed my bet or took my money and pocketed it. Felt like I could never trust the guy again."

Ted nodded in agreement. "Same thing happened to me the first year I toured with the band."

"That's right, man. I remember," Jimmy said. "Stefano was playin' drums back then."

"Right. He talked me into one of those betting schemes of his, took my money, and well...that's the last I heard about it. He made up some cock-and-bull story, but I never saw any proof that the bet was placed or anything."

"You remember that time he showed up at rehearsal all worked over, black and blue, like someone had beat the shit out of him?" Jimmy said, "Pretty sure he cheated the wrong dude that time. Pretty soon after that, King shipped him off to the condo in Omaha."

"King was probably trying to protect him," Ted said.

"Could be, but like I said, trouble always follows Stefano wherever he goes. More likely he goes lookin' for it. What's worse, I think he enjoys it. Kind of a thrill for him...like a high... and he's always lookin' for a better buzz." *Hm. That confirms that Stefano is capable of dabbling in illicit activities. And it sounds like he found some trouble in Omaha. The question remains: What exactly is he involving the band in?*

"You're probably right," Ted said. "And then there's the whole family loyalty thing. They support anything Stefano does. He has a lot of influence with King and the family. Except for Simon that is. Simon sees through him, I think."

"Yep, Simon sure wants out," Chaz said.

"So do I," Ted said glancing over at Amy. "It's not that easy." We all caught his drift. *Being a boyfriend of a Conti sure has its pressures. No wonder he acts like a whipped puppy around Connie all the time. And based on the googly-eyed look he gave Amy, it seems like Ted is beginning to have feelings for her, which could complicate matters.*

• • •

That evening, the band opened on the mainstage of the St. Louis Riverfront Festival for country music artist Waylon Jennings. These festivals all began to blur together. *We set up, perform, breakdown, and hit the road.* Most of the performances fell into certain categories: fairs, outdoor festivals, or indoor events at a club or hotel. But the St. Louis Riverfront Festival became stellar in my mind. After setting up, we had about forty-five minutes to kill before the show began and the coolest thing happened. Jimmy, Chaz, Amy, and I were hanging around near the stage and who did we bump into but Mr. Waylon Jennings himself!

What a cool dude! He wore his signature black cowboy hat, paired with a black leather vest. This, along with his dark beard, moustache, and shaggy collar-length hair, fit the "bad-ass cowboy" image perfectly. He invited us to come inside his grandiose tour bus, handing us each an autographed publicity photo. *Wow, a perfect souvenir for my journal.* Jimmy was all over the poor man, asking questions about how he got started in the music business. Mr. Jennings didn't disappoint as he freely shared his story in his deep voice and Southern accent.

"Well, I ain't proud to say I dropped outta high school to be a musician, but that sure is what happened," he drawled. "Ma first rockabilly band, called The Waylors, played in Scottsdale, Arizona. Once I were lucky enough to start recordin' for RCA records *and* git back creative say-so, ma career started cookin'." Amy and I were more interested in gawking at the amazing interior of his tour bus: wood paneling, cool modern lighting fixtures, beautiful upholstery. Compared to our converted trucks... well, there simply wasn't any comparison.

After our tour of Mr. Jennings' radical ride, we dubbed The Kennel the "Poor Man's Tour Bus" from there on out! For a big celebrity, he sure was down-to-earth and generous with his time, hanging out with nobodies like us. Meeting Waylon Jennings made the St. Louis Riverfront Festival a standout memory for the rest of the tour. I fastened his autographed photo into my journal for safe keeping and took note of my impressions of the tour so far:

> *Touring can be grueling. Driving from gig to gig can be monotonous but the performances are invigorating, energizing, and amazing. Meeting interesting people, seeing new places, and expanding my narrow views of life has been off the hook. Despite all these positives, I still feel the need to catch my breath at times and refocus.*

Re-reading my entry, I reflected on how tiring it was to keep pretending that nothing happened that night with Ricky. *Damn it, I don't want to let it derail me!*

●●●

Heading back to Baltimore for an almost two-week break, my mind swirled with ideas about everything I wanted to do with my precious free time. Jimmy and Chaz promised to take me to a couple Baltimore jazz clubs to continue my "musical education" and I couldn't be more excited. I wanted to squeeze in a visit to Church Creek to see Mom, which surprised the hell out of me. *It was all I could do to run away from my dreary town and my disappointing relationship with David, and now I'm almost eager to go home! Is it because of the Ricky thing? Am I looking for a secure place to run to because I can't freakin' take care of myself? Or is it because I have so much to tell Mom about all these experiences I'm having on the road? The good ones, I mean.* Despite the uncertainty, I envisioned myself sitting by the Choptank River watching the sun reflecting in the river's lazy summer currents. A positive image of me recharging my energy. *I need to fit that in, for sure.*

We hit the road the morning after our St. Louis show and I prayed Jimmy would be driving the equipment truck, but no such luck. Spending the next several hours in a supine position in my bunk watching the miles pass through a tiny window began to wear on me. I tried to use the time constructively by reading, writing in my journal, and working the occasional crossword puzzle. I even purchased the latest issue of *Ms Magazine*, hoping to broaden my feminist horizons, but the hours on the road dragged. A perfect recipe for the doldrums. It dawned on me that we'd been on the road less than three weeks! Even more reason to jump at the opportunity to ride in the cab with Jimmy and Chaz any chance I got.

A few hours into the drive from Missouri to Baltimore, our caravan stopped at a Frisch's Big Boy restaurant for a late lunch. Whenever we entered a restaurant *"en masse,"* it could be a bit overwhelming for the poor hostess or waitress. Eleven of us followed King, our fearless leader, who requested seating "as soon as possible because we're on a very tight schedule." The restaurant wasn't super busy, but only one waitress worked the floor. She sat our group as close together as possible and took our drink orders immediately. As soon as she left to get our drinks, I overheard King making rude and prejudiced remarks.

"Hope she's not one of those typical lazy coloreds," King muttered.

I couldn't believe he said that. Disgraceful memories from Dad flashed into my head, some bubbled up from deep in my subconsciousness where I had shoved them. I recalled that day when I offered Kevin water at the store and Dad reamed me out. I remembered cruel comments Dad made about Black customers after they left the store with their purchases. I recollected statements Dad made at church, denouncing the new Baptist Church down the road because it was "filled with colored folks and we don't want THOSE kind being so close." I didn't want to believe that my father could be so…so prejudiced! *But he is and I know it. His prejudice toward Black people is disgusting to me. And now, here I am with this equally intolerant family.*

King bellowed, "She damned well better make it quick. I made it clear we were on a tight schedule, didn't I?" He looked around for the beverages, even though the waitress had just finished taking our drink orders. As King ranting created tension, the rest of the band members shifted in their seats and tried to continue conversing. Simon tried to defuse the situation, but it did no good. "It looks like she's the only waitress here, so let's change the subject."

"Well, where is she with those drinks?" King asked, looking for a reason to get worked up. At that moment, the frantic waitress came through the kitchen door with a huge tray of drinks and began distributing them. Having worked in a diner myself, I was amazed at how well she remembered which drinks went where. *She must have a system on her tray. Wish I had thought that when I was waiting tables.* As quickly as possible she scribbled our lunch orders on her pad and scooted into the kitchen. *Twelve orders at one time are a lot for any waitress to handle, and she's doing a fine job.* Our group sipped on our drinks, talked, and laughed, as we always did when we stopped at a restaurant. The waitress checked on us, as waitresses always did when we stopped at a restaurant. But King wasn't seeing it that way.

Suddenly, he stood up, banged his hands on the table, and announced, "That's it. I'm not waiting on this server another minute. We're leaving!" The Conti clan all rose, waddling out after him, like obedient goslings following a parent goose. The rest of us, confused and reluctant, stood up and began to shuffle out in shock. *This is so unreasonable. He's blaming the waitress, but she's done nothing wrong. He can't stand that he's being served by a Black waitress. This is beyond rude. It's downright cruel. No payment for the drinks, no tips. He's leaving!* I turned to the kitchen door where the waitress stood, arms crossed, watching this exodus. She appeared deflated and discouraged. Our eyes met and I felt totally helpless. *I should say something. Apologize for King's unreasonable behavior. Let her know I was a waitress too and I thought she was doing great. SAY SOMETHING!* But I didn't. I felt sick to my stomach, put some money on the table to cover my drink and an exorbitant tip, and turned to catch up with the others. Flashes of my father filled my head for the rest of the day. I could see him doing something like this, acting exactly like King. I couldn't shake the shame, guilt, and anger I felt toward King, Dad, and especially myself. *Did I think leaving a tip was going to fix anything? Did it make her feel any better? Or was that to make ME feel better?*

The rest of the drive to Baltimore I stayed to myself. I couldn't shake the restaurant incident and King's treatment of that girl. Even worse than King's prejudice, I was so ashamed of my voicelessness in that situation. *What is wrong with me? Why didn't I speak up and defend her to King? Why didn't I at least encourage her when King walked out? What makes me any different than King or Dad?* Those memory flashes, examples of prejudice I'd witnessed in the past by Dad and others, the ones I shoved down in my psyche, were haunting me.

I feel as if my voice is bubbling at the surface but can't break through.

12

A Visit to Church Creek

Little Italy, Baltimore, Maryland – June, 1978

Arriving back in Baltimore with a two-week break, I kicked off my free time with a trip home to Church Creek. Despite my mixed emotions about visiting home, I decided that in many ways, home was exactly where I needed to go to recharge, find some answers to questions that kept bubbling up, and yes…feel safe and secure for a little while. Plus, I looked forward to sharing my stories with Mom and eating some of her home-cooked meals.

Thrilled that my Gremlin still sat where I left it three weeks earlier and even happier that the engine turned over without a problem, I pulled into the corner gas station, praying for a short line to fill up my tank before heading out of Little Italy on my way home. *Gas prices are up to 72 cents a gallon. Seems like it was only 67 cents a gallon before I left for the tour. Unbelievable!*

I had to admit my emotions were all over the place. Excited to see Mom again, confused about these angry feelings I'd been harboring toward Dad, nervous I might bump into David, and hopeful that my hometown roots might help ground me. I popped the *Chicago IX: Greatest Hits* tape I borrowed from Chaz into my 8-track player and listened to "Feelin' Stronger Every Day." *Not sure if this is a fitting soundtrack for the moment but I'm working on it!* As I approached the Eastern Shore, the magnificent Bay Bridge loomed ahead and any anxious feelings dissipated.

I pulled into the dirt and gravel driveway next to our small house. *There's Mom sitting on our rickety wooden porch, waving. It figures Dad's nowhere to be seen. Probably at the store.* I parked on a sparse strip of lawn along the driveway, leaving plenty of room for Dad to pull in later. *Don't want to cause a "national incident" with him my first few hours home!*

"Margaret, let me look at you, sweetheart," Mom said as she hugged me in a death grip the moment I stepped out of the car. I didn't mind. I hugged her back just as tightly. I'd only been away a total of seven and a half weeks, but it felt like a year.

"Now before you get settled, let me ask. Are you hungry? I made a plate of cheese logs and deviled eggs to nibble on. How about thirsty? I've got a nice cold Tab with your name on it in the frig. *I still laugh at Mom drinking sugar-free Tab when she's the tiniest stick of a woman.*

Once convinced I was neither hungry nor thirsty, she settled into her porch rocker. "Okay, tell me everything." I nestled down near her feet on the top step and began to jabber.

I rambled on about the Conti family, Connie "the drill sergeant," and other band members. I broke down the kinds of venues we played in and listed of all the states we'd toured so far. I explained how we traveled in converted trucks and stayed in motels, skipping the part about sneaking the guys in for showers every few days. Instead, I focused on my new friends – Jimmy, Chaz, and Amy.

I didn't know how to tell her about what happened with Ricky. I was too ashamed. *What if I had somehow brought the whole incident upon myself?* His words plagued me, that I had "asked for it." *I want to push these thoughts down as far as possible, forget the whole thing ever happened.*

No, I didn't mention the Ricky incident to my Mom.

After a moment of silence, Mom said, "The tour sounds a lot different than your life here. How do you feel about that?"

I thought before I answered, although I had already been reflecting on this question in my journal. "I know this tour came to me at the perfect time. I keep saying it was a miracle, but maybe it was simply a chance to run away from David, to avoid seeing him and feeling that pain. You're right. Touring with a band is a lot different than anything I've ever experienced. Different than my life at college or here. But I'm learning a lot about the world. Some of it's interesting and cool, but some of it's hard. I need to do this, Mom."

"I'm not trying to talk you out of it, dear. Checking in, that's all. But I do miss you like crazy!"

"And what does Dad think?" I asked.

"Now Dad is another story. He doesn't understand the whole 'touring around the country with a bunch of hippie musicians!' thing, but don't let him discourage you, Margaret." *Typical Dad. He's never even met the band members and he's already calling them names and deciding they're terrible people. This is exactly the kind of thing that's been bumming me out so much lately. He judges anyone who's different than he is. Different religions, different skin color. And what about Mom? Mom puts up with it. Why? She's smart. Why doesn't she ever say anything?*

Pushing the perimeters of this Mother-Daughter talk, I decided to go for it. "Can I ask you question, Mom?" She nodded. "Has Dad always been like that?"

"How do you mean?"

"Always so intolerant? Like always jumping to label people

he's never met. So bigoted, really." She bowed her head. *I may have hit a nerve but I can tell the answer is "No."*

"When I first met your father, I missed the signs, I'm ashamed to say. Or he hid them better, was on his best behavior. I fell in love, things moved fast, and by the time I moved my life here, settled in, well… he started acting differently. He became more vocal, demonstrative, and less caring about other people. Well, that happens in marriage sometimes, Margaret."

"But he goes to Mass all the time. I don't get it, Mom."

"I guess in his mind he's absolved of any wrong thinking or wrong actions or wrong path he may be taking…by going to church." She seemed sad.

I couldn't wrap my head around this. *Here's a man who freely drinks from a not-so-secret flask every day, berates Black people and any other group of people who are different from himself, regularly gouges his customers with overpriced merchandise, and thinks by going to Mass he's found a work-around for the Catholic Church's principles. Who needs the Pope or those dorky Ten Commandments, anyway?*

"If you know that Dad is saying horrible things about…well, Black people, for instance, even when there are plenty of Black customers who come into the store, how do you deal with that? You're not prejudiced like that, Mom. I know you're not."

"He's my husband, Margaret. I was raised to stand by my husband, support him, and take care of the house and you. That's how I was brought up."

"Hm. That's something else I never understood. You had a teaching career in Virginia, which you've said you loved. But you gave it up to come to this dinky town to help Dad run his barely functioning general store. I understand how powerful falling in love can be, but…I mean… do you ever feel like you gave up a

146

lot?"

"My, you sure are full of a lot of questions. You've never expressed an interest in these things before." She seemed uncomfortable and I felt bad being the cause.

"Hm, well, there are two things to remember, Margaret. In the late 1940s and 1950s, women were still influenced by the philosophy that we had two life choices: Women could choose a profession and lead a solitary life or we could get married and have a family, but rarely both. And, well…women didn't have a lot of choices back in those days when it came to contraceptives or, well…" Her voice trailed off before she jumped in, assuring, "But I've done my best to make a home for my husband and I knew that even though I loved teaching I very much wanted a child. And look what I got…you!"

That stopped me in my tracks. I sat silently for a while, thinking about Mom's story. A pregnancy? *That explains why she gave up her teaching career to live in Church Creek, of all places. Whoa! Not exactly the information I expected.* She interrupted my thoughts.

"Margaret, I want you to know I can see that the world is changing, especially for young women. You don't have to base your life's plan on the path I took. Thank goodness, you have different options in 1978."

"Even though Dad keeps pressuring me to work for him in the store until I find some guy from the Eastern Shore to settle down with?"

Mom got up, sat on the rickety step next to me, and patted my hand. "Look at me and let me say this again. You have different options than I had in the 1950s. I want you to promise me that you will explore them all." *Of course, I did but it's not as easy as I thought. It's like she sees into my soul and can tell I'm floundering.*

Mom gave me a hug and changed the subject. "How long do you see yourself traveling with this band?"

"Not sure yet. I'm kinda up in the air about it." *I don't want to get too detailed about my thinking because then I might have to tell her the whole Ricky thing.* "There are some super cool things about being on the road, like seeing new parts of the country and connecting with the audiences, but there's a lot of...well... drudgery and boredom, too. It's not as glamorous as it sounds, that's for sure." I told her a bit about the long hours on the road and the few opportunities to sightsee because of transportation and time restraints, unless we were booked right in a city, like we were with St. Louis.

"And have you given any thought to what might be next for Margaret Stevens?"

"I'm starting to get an idea. It's not that different from the idea I always had in college before I allowed myself to get distracted with David. I want to do something with writing and music. Have a few things to figure out, first."

"Ah, yes. You always loved to write stories, that's for sure. And you have a wonderful singing voice."

"Right, but I'm thinking about a way to combine my love of both music and writing. I don't know how yet. What is clear is that I need to learn more about both. My musical knowledge is too limited to understand music well and my view of the world is too limited to be a good writer. What's next isn't crystal clear, but it's getting there."

"Ah! That's my Margaret," Mom said, giving me a hug. "Perhaps you weren't running away after all. It may have felt like that at the time, but maybe you were running TOWARD something." I considered Mom's fresh insight for a moment, especially since I was considering "running" back home. *Will she think I'm a failure? Will I think I'm a failure?*

"You might be right, Mom."

"You'll figure it out, sweetheart. You're a very inquisitive and smart young woman." Mom hugged me again and I couldn't help but think how supportive she'd always been despite how sad she might be feeling about her own marriage.

That evening I looked around at the home she had built with fresh eyes. Despite my constant complaining about our rundown house, Mom had created a refuge of warmth, filled with wonderful aromas of fresh baked goodies coming from the kitchen, and cozy handmade quilts on every chair in the living room. *I need to give her more credit.*

• • •

The following day I ventured into Cambridge to say hello to my former workers at Doris Mae's Diner, followed by a planned stroll along the Choptank River. As I opened the familiar red diner door, the wafting odors of frying fish and grilling hamburgers triggered a rush of memories – the first time I laid eyes on David, our first meeting at the cash register, our many intimate meals together in Booth #4 toward the back of the main dining room, his love of tuna sandwiches on rye with extra mayo, his Harley parked on the street out front.

I immediately spotted David sitting at the counter. The possibility of seeing him had lingered in the back of my mind, but I needed to deal with the reality. *Deep breath. Good start.* After greeting Doris Mae and Glenda, her daughter, I walked right over to the counter and said hello. *No sense pretending he's not here. I'm not going to play games.*

"Margie, I saw you come in. I hoped you'd come over."

"Well, sure. How have you been?"

"Same. Living each day in the moment and going with the flow. But what about you? Did I hear you're traveling with some band or something? That's impressive."

He's impressed? Thoughts began to surge. *He never said he was impressed with anything I did in the past. Wow, he looks great with that mid-summer tan and those sun-streaked highlights in his hair. I wonder what's going on with him. Does he still work on the docks? Probably. This is their busiest season. Is he still with the girl? Probably. Should I get involved in a conversation with him or keep it short?*

"Yes," I answered. *Short is better.*

"I'd like to hear about it. You wanna go for a walk over by the river? If you have time, that is?

My heart started beating faster. *A walk. To hear about my touring. He wants to hear about what I'm doing. This seems different.*

"Sure. I was heading over to the river anyway." I shouted my goodbyes to Doris Mae and her daughter as we exited the diner. *So much for keeping it short!*

Strolling to the Choptank riverside, David asked about my time on the road with the band. I provided generic details about touring with King Vido's Swing Band, describing the type of music we performed and places we visited, careful to put a positive spin on the whole experience. He asked questions about the band members and how we traveled, showing genuine interest. In fact, his attentiveness confused me.

"I've got to say, Margie. I'm super impressed that you did this."

"Yes, you said." I began to wonder why he kept saying he was impressed and if he meant it as a compliment. Falling back on my usual strategy when the conversation got too close and personal for me, I pivoted to David's life.

"What's been happening with you? Still working on the docks and planning on buying that sailboat?"

"Still working on it."

"That's great. I know how important a sailboat is to you. You love the– "

"Look Margie, I know you're wondering about Annie. She's gone. And I can't stop thinking about you and how good we were together." *Of course, I was curious about the girl. Annie. Cute name. I wonder why they broke up. Should I ask? No, I'm not going look that interested. But I'm dying to know. No, don't do it, Margie.* I took a moment to shake the dueling "thought demons" from my brain before I spoke.

"Um, I not sure what to...this is kinda sudden. I mean, yeah, we were good together, but..."

"I know. I screwed up. But babe, think about all the great times we had together. I think we can have that again." And then he gazed at me with those gorgeous deep blue eyes, as if he were looking straight into my soul. I felt the same electricity whiz through me as I did when I first met him.

So many thoughts and emotions pulsed through my head at once. A part of my soul sang with excitement: *David wanted me again!* The sensible part of my brain chastised: *He only wants the most available female he can find!* Another part of my head reminded: *You've just started an important personal journey of your own.* The deeply scarred part of my heart warned: *Remember the pain this man has caused you, you idiot.*

Not knowing how to manage this unexpected proposition or the sudden surge of emotions, I did what I always do...I bailed.

"I...I don't know what to say right now, David. Look, I'll be back in town in a few weeks. We'll talk then, okay?" *I'm such a nerd!*

...

In my childhood bedroom that night, sitting on the pink, yellow, and blue granny square quilt Mom crocheted for my high school graduation, I mulled over my confusion about David's sudden interest in me. *Am I simply flattered? Am I that easily distracted? Damn it, I am!* Attempting a short meditation to clear my mind proved utterly useless. Thoughts and emotions flew in and out of my brain like angry wasps swarming a disturbed nest. Instead, I opened *Autobiography of a Yogi*, where a passage by Paramahansa Yogananda reminded me that what we do today affects the outcome of tomorrow. *I have a choice as to how I react to David, to Ricky, to anything. I can pack up my belongings and keep running from uncomfortable situations. Or I can face them today. Right now, I need to figure out what's important for Margie. Can David be giving me the answer I need to avoid having to deal with Ricky and stuffing pain and shame deeper into my gut? Sure. I can come home and be with David. I'd be rid of the Ricky problem, rid of the anxiety issue, away from the intense Conti family, safe and sound. Ah! But then won't I be jumping back into the arms of David and neglecting my own dreams again? Or can I muster up the courage to be true to myself and follow through with seeing where this tour leads me, even if it means facing uncomfortable situations and uncertainties right now?*

I dozed off contemplating these confusing thoughts and felt stronger in the fact that, at the very least, I was not acting impulsively this time.

13

Musical Mentors

Little Italy, Baltimore, Maryland – June, 1978

After my visit home, I convened with my "musical mentors," Jimmy and Chaz, who promised to introduce me to two Baltimore clubs over the weekend. They were intent on "broadening Margie's musical horizons," as Jimmy liked to put it. I could not disagree. I'd already received an entire Music Appreciation course on R&B, funk, soul, blues, rock, early swing, and big band greats… and that was simply by listening to 8–track tapes while driving through the corn fields of America! My college music courses neglected those genres. Sure, ask me anything about the music of Stravinsky or Schubert. I could bore you silly with facts about the genius of Chopin, Mozart, or Beethoven, and regurgitate a wealth of musical knowledge about European and Russian composers! But thanks to Jimmy and Chaz, I realized that the world of music didn't end with Sister Janet's Music Appreciation 101 lectures. *Tonight, we're going to hear some real "Jazz Cats," Jimmy's term for his musician friends. I can't wait for Advanced Music Apprec 201 to commence!*

Saturday night we hit the Café Park Plaza on Charles Street to hear the rhythm section of a band called Pockets. The drum, bass, and guitar players sat in with several musicians from various local bands from D.C. and Baltimore.

"Shit man, I heard Pockets cut another album last year, a kind of funk, jazz, R&B thing with their own sweet vocal groove." Jimmy had the skinny on everyone in the Baltimore music scene. "They're so damn hot right now."

Chaz nodded in agreement. "Yep."

"Hell, they're openin' for Earth Wind and Fire on their summer tour. How freakin' cool is that?" Jimmy waved to several people as we entered the smoky café.

We settled in to enjoy the jam session in the cozy Café Park Plaza. Jimmy knew tons of people, both onstage and off. Even as the musicians were setting up their gear, several caught Jimmy's eye, shouting greetings like "There's the man," or "Hey, Red." Others from the crowd came up to shake his hand or slap him on the back. I felt like I was sitting with a celebrity!

Once the session began, the crowd settled in and focused on the music pouring out from these talented, passionate musicians. R&B, soul, jazz, blues. We heard a bit of everything. Every single player impressed the heck out of me as they traded off solos. The quartet of guitar, electric bass, keyboard, and drums each offered a distinct sound, but combined as if a single unit. The bass player took impressive command of his instrument, helping to drive each number forward. I'd never heard anything like it before. Smooth with a kind of pulsating groove, but at the same time creating a unique sound on its own. Chaz promised to play his Pockets' album, "Come Go with Us," next time we rode in the cab of the truck together so I could hear what the whole group sounded like.

During one of the breaks, Jimmy invited a fellow trumpet player friend over to the table. After introductions all around, Giles Kelley, a Black man in his late fifties, gently teased Jimmy.

"I see ole' King let ya off the road for a spell. Ya gittin' a chance to reconnect with us commoners," Giles said with a deep baritone voice and a resonant laugh. The creases around his eyes showed not only his age but also a lifetime of laughs, tears, smiles, and music. For sure, music. I felt drawn to his warmth.

"You still playin' around, man?" Jimmy asked.

"I'm sittin' in on horn sections here and there, where there's a need. Don't have a cushy tourin' gig like y'all, Red!"

Jimmy chuckled at this gentle teasing. "Hey, Giles, our friend Margie studied vocal music in college, but she's been askin' us to introduce her to more than Beethoven and those dudes. She's super interested in the roots of American music."

"Well, now, Miss Margie. That's quite an interest ya got." Giles looked at me as if sizing me up to see if I was for real or not. *I don't blame him. Why should he waste his breath on some white chick who isn't serious about learning?*

"Let's me and you play a little game. Name a kinda music you been listenin' to, and I'll give its root, okey dokey?" Giles' eyes twinkled as he spoke.

"Okay," I said, searching my brain for a genre. "Um, how about R&B?"

"I love it. R&B. Rooted in Black slave traditions like work songs or protest songs."

"Really? Slave work songs? R&B? I had no idea." That information shocked me. I'd never listened to R&B much before meeting Jimmy and Chaz, let alone thought much about where it came from. Giles captivated me with his game. "Okay, what about swing band music?"

"Came right outta Black instrumental music like ragtime, brass bands, and New Orleans jazz."

"Ragtime...New Orleans...yes. Now that you say it, I can see it, but... that's interesting. Okay, funk?"

"Keep on a-going. Straight outta the R&B tradition and ya got rock and roll, soul, and funk! Ah…and there's some nice sounds coming from our Latin friends, blending into the modern jazz and bop and the funk scene, too. Ya see, most American modern music can be traced to African roots."

"Even rock and roll? Gosh, I sure didn't get any of this in my college classes. I feel so out of the loop. Thanks for the tutorial," I said, as he rose to continue making his rounds.

"Oh, Giles. One question before you go," I blurted out, stopping him in his tracks. "What do you love about playing… music, I mean…What do you love about music?" I stumbled through my question, but Giles' smile told me he understood.

"This. This right here, Margie!" He pointed to himself and me, then paused. "Music expands our understandin' of each other and our worlds." Wow, his words were like a beam of light cutting through the fog. *Of course! Music expands, connects, transcends all people, ages, and cultures. So much wisdom behind those twinkling eyes.*

I watched him move along to greet another group at the next table. *I've got a lot to learn. If I want to do any writing about music in my future, I need to fill this enormous void in my musical knowledge. At the same time, I feel kinda exhilarated, as if I'd been given a key to a secret entryway. What else is there to explore behind this door?*

A second group played later in the evening, featuring five players: a guitarist, drummer, bass, a piano player, and a sax – a pickup band thrown together for the night. The bass player and drummer were from the Annapolis Soul Swayers, and the other musicians all played in multiple bands in the Baltimore area.

"All these cats gotta pick up gigs whenever they can. Plus, they love to play," Jimmy explained.

Such an inspiring night! The smooth music, the genial atmosphere, the stimulating conversations were…wow. The whole experience intoxicated me. Walking past the bar to leave for the night, I snagged a clean swizzle stick with the Café Park Plaza emblem for my journal. I thanked Jimmy and Chaz for taking a novice like me under their wings. As we walked to my car, Jimmy asked, "So what did ya hear tonight?" *My musical mentor is quizzing me, I see!*

"Well, jazz tunes are a lot longer than the typical pop songs you hear on the radio or at a disco, but I like that. You can really let yourself get wrapped up in the music."

Jimmy agreed. "Hell, it's one of the reasons a lot of younger people don't like bebop or jazz. They're spoiled by the three-chord, three-minute blast of music they get with a pop song on the radio."

"I can see that," I reasoned out loud. "Jazz can sound kind of 'out there,' but what I heard tonight had structure, complicated structure, but still…. I heard most numbers start out with a melody that sort of melted away and then returned to a semblance of the original melody. It kept me spellbound, to tell the truth."

"Got a new groupie on our hands," Chaz said.

● ● ●

On Sunday night the Left Bank Jazz Society, a Baltimore organization that promoted jazz musicians, hosted a concert at the Famous Ballroom on North Charles Street. Our little crew of three climbed up three flights of wide stairs and bought tickets for the five-thirty show, which didn't start until six forty-five. I didn't mind though. I spent time taking in the atmosphere at the most amazing, nostalgic ballroom I'd ever experienced. Fronted by a huge dance floor, the wide stage held a grand piano, a drum kit, and a slew of music stands with plenty of room to spare.

Behind the stage hung a blue and white striped curtain with valances and side drapes creating a gentle frame. High above the dance floor, painted fluffy white clouds and stars on the ceiling made the cavernous room feel a bit cozier. Centered over the dance floor hung the obligatory revolving mirrored globe, ready to create its romantic sparkle effect for slow songs. Round tables fitted with six or seven wooden chairs able to accommodate over two hundred attendees surrounded the dance floor.

The crowd began to stream into the space – young, old, Black, White – a diverse mix of music lovers gathered for one purpose, to enjoy a communal musical experience. My eyes scanned the space, looking at old photos gracing the walls, and imagining all the great bands, band leaders, and jazz artists who performed here in the past: Cab Calloway, Eubie Blake, Billie Holiday, Count Basie, Duke Ellington, Charles Mingus, Chet Baker, and even John Coltrane as recently as 1967. *How cool that the Baltimore community was able to embrace these greats right here in this very hall!*

Jimmy gave me the skinny on the group we'd be seeing that night. "Sun Ra's been on the jazz scene since the 1950s with his band Arkestra. He landed in New York in the 60s and now he travels all over the world."

"Arkestra was on 'Saturday Night Live' a couple months ago," Chaz added.

"How rad is that!" I was impressed with both the fact that Arkestra had appeared on SNL and that Chaz offered it up. He didn't seem like a "Saturday Night Live" kind of guy, although the TV show did feature cutting edge musical guests.

"We should warn you, Margie," Jimmy said, "Sun Ra can be a little bizarre. But the music is slammin'."

The house lights dimmed and about twenty musicians and

singers of Arkestra along with Sun Ra himself bolted onto the stage from a side entrance, costumed in silver, gold, and red lamé ponchos with matching futuristic-looking headpieces. *Connie would love all this shine!* The band dove into the first song with a tidal wave of frenetic sound and movement, causing the singers and dancers to jump off the stage platform onto the dance floor at one point.

The music had an improvisational feel, at times emphasizing the keyboard, at other times a specific instrument like a flute or saxophone. The use of alternative percussion instruments like the bongo drum, the tabla, or the conga rather than the standard drum kit gave many tunes an especially strong drive. Every song had a different feel: from boogie woogie to bluesy to Afro-centric to some sounds I didn't know how to even categorize. Seeing the swirling colors of the Arkestra performers, feeling the percussion pulsate throughout my body, hearing the constant frenetic musical variations and modulations – the entire performance was the most unique musical event I'd ever encountered. While I enjoyed every minute of it, I felt exhausted by the end of the evening.

Back in my dorm room in the wee hours of the morning, I gingerly pasted both the Café Park Plaza sizzle stick and the ticket stubs from the Sun Ra show into my journal. See Ya at the Famous! was written in tiny type at the bottom of the ticket stub, referencing The Famous Ballroom. What an amazing couple of nights! I loved spending time with Jimmy and Chaz. I appreciated the way they shared their musical knowledge with me. How inspiring to meet Giles and get a tiny whiff of understanding about African influence on the music I was learning to love.

Something in my spirit felt on fire again, something that had been extinguished for a long time. A shift occurred in me. Words poured out into my journal as I described the music, the musicians, and the crowd's reaction to the distinct, fresh sounds I heard both nights. I'd never written *about* music before, but somehow I began to connect words to music and the overall experience. I liked it. The writing felt inspired and flowed easily. A seed of an idea had been planted and germinated. Energized, I worked most of the night on my first critical music review of the jam session at Café Park Plaza the previous evening.

Could this be what I'm meant to be doing? I have so much to learn, a lot of work ahead of me. It would be a huge challenge. Lao Tzu said, "The journey of a thousand miles begins with one step." *Ah, another great guiding adage presents itself at the perfect moment. With all my confusion about David and running away from the Ricky thing fading into the background for the moment, I'm feeling positive and energized about music and writing right now. Will a future with David fit into this new direction I'm creating for myself? Maybe everything I'm doing now — touring with the swing band, meeting Jimmy, Chaz, and Giles, learning about the roots of American music — is all part of discovering my next steps.*

Not 100% sure if I was exactly where I needed to be, I knew I was living my moment.

14

Westward, Ho! in Gold Lamé

Little Italy, Baltimore, Maryland – June, 1978

Bright and early Monday morning, King summoned the band for an organizational meeting to discuss the second leg of the tour. Connie strutted around the studio, nose and breasts in the air looking oh-so self-important, handing out the latest band schedule of tour dates from June 25th through July 16th.

```
King Vido's Swing Band 1978 Tour Schedule -
Second Leg

Sun 6/25 - Springfield, Illinois - State Fair

Wed 6/28 - Moorhead, Minnesota - Heritage Days

Sat/Sun 7/1 & 2 - Regina, Saskatchewan - Regina
Canada Days

Mon/Tues/Wed/Thurs 7/3, 4, 5 & 6 - Omaha,
Nebraska - No performance

Sat 7/8 - Colorado Springs, Colorado - Country
Club Dinner-Dance

Fri, Sat & Sun 7/14, 15 & 16 - Sacramento,
California - State Fair

7/19 - Return to Baltimore [TBA]
```

I pointed out a couple of dates to Amy as we scanned the schedule together, psyched to see we'd be heading to Canada AND California on this leg of the tour. King stressed that there were three "very important dates" on this leg: Illinois State Fair, Regina Canada Days, and California State Fair. "All headliner events!" Connie said with great emphasis in her usual deference to Daddy fashion. *Oh, brother!*

"King Vido's Swing Band needs to make a huge splash at these bookings, *capisce?*" he said in a booming voice with equally grand hand gestures. We all nodded, although I wondered what we would do differently to make these performances "splashier" than any other performance. King ended his thundering pep talk by calling an early morning rehearsal the following day.

The next morning, Connie made an eye-popping entrance as she strutted into the rehearsal studio modeling our new show costume: a shiny gold lamé halter top jumpsuit with a peek-a-boo cut-out at the waist, extremely form fitting. Of course, a couple of the guys whistled and carried on, which Connie ate up while feigning embarrassment. It was all a bit hard to take first thing in the morning. *This explains how King Vido's Swing Band will be adding "splash" and then some!*

In her conspicuously self-important manner, Connie whisked Amy and me into the storage room adjacent to the studio for our gold jumpsuit fittings. I avoided eye contact with Verna, afraid of laughing out loud. These gold lamé numbers were about the gaudiest things ever. *The only thing worse would be if Connie started bedazzling them with rhinestones!* Before Amy and I exited the fitting room, Connie barked, "You girls need gold heels by Friday!" *Great, another errand to squeeze into our precious personal time!*

Thanks to Ruby's recommendation, Amy and I found a

Kinney Shoe store within walking distance of 323 Albemarle and headed out the following morning. I jumped on the chance to tell her about bumping into David during my visit home.

"Wow, Margie. I don't know whether to say, 'Far out!' or 'Freak me out!' Do you think he's for real with that talk about wanting you to come back and be with him?"

"It sounded like it. He even said he was impressed with me going on this tour. It sounded like he's changed, Amy…like he's not as self-focused anymore."

"Okay, but…"

"But what?"

Amy hesitated. "Look, I don't want to be a bummer or anything, and I get that you're stoked since he *sounds* like he's changed, but what is there for *you* to do, if you go back home, I mean? Sure, you get to be with your old boyfriend, but what else?"

I didn't say anything for a long time. I knew she was right. I'd even started asking myself that same question.

"I hope you don't think I'm a big ole dork. You mad, Margie?"

"No, Amy. I'm glad I have a good friend like you to talk to about stuff like this. I need to think about it for a bit. Now let's find the shiniest damn gold heels we can and knock Connie on her butt!" Out poured that contagious Amy giggle as we entered the shoe store.

• • •

Amy's question whirled through my thoughts all the way to Springfield, Illinois, interrupted only by Connie's constant harping, "This Illinois State Fair is an A-lister, don't forget!"

And what would we be wearing for the Illinois State Fair in Springfield, the first show of the second leg of the tour? The gold lamé, of course. "Girls in the gold halter jumpsuits and guys in the black suits with your new gold ruffled shirts and black bow ties," Connie ordered. Slipping into the golden ensemble, my inner critic gushed. *This outfit is a cross between dazzling and corny, if you ask me, but since no one has, I'll keep my mouth shut. Maybe "dazzling-corny" is exactly what audiences expect of show bands.*

To be fair, the Illinois State Fair *was* a colossal deal in the world of state fairs. Big name acts, tons of vendors, educational exhibits and blah, blah, blah. But overall, the fairs on the circuit began to blur. Whether big or small, they all had the same basic elements. Agricultural exhibits displaying produce of every imaginable garden vegetable and fruit. Cows, sheep, chickens, pigs, and everything in between raised by the diligent 4-H groups. Exhibit halls holding prize-winning cakes, preserves, art and sewing projects, woodworking, photography. The list goes on and on. Earlier in the tour, I enjoyed wandering through the barns and halls, seeking out the blue-ribbon winners. But after the third fair, the exhibits and animals all looked the same. The games and midway rides became indistinct. To paraphrase Gertrude Stein, "A fair is a fair is a fair."

The Illinois State Fair was not only on the ultra-huge end of the spectrum, and it also drew big name entertainment from country, rock and roll, and pop bands to its mainstage, like The Osmonds, Dolly Parton, and Kenny Rogers. *How the heck did a swing band from Baltimore get booked to perform next to these big named artists? And how will the audience receive us if that's the caliber of entertainment they're expecting?* I considered the possibility that King had pulled some strings to get us on that mainstage. Regardless, as it turned out, the audience was there to enjoy themselves and seemed to eat up King Vido's Swing Band. They sang, clapped, snapped, and danced in the aisles, which in turn elated King.

Our next pressure-filled event was Regina Canada Days in the province of Saskatchewan, which took place after a smaller show in Montana on the way north. Amy and I heard from Connie that Canada Days was a prized booking with acts from all over Canada and the U.S. competing for a slot to perform. "Far out!" was Amy's response, of course. I looked forward to catching a few of the other performers, since we were booked at Canada Days for two full days, giving me plenty of time between our shows to explore.

The band arrived in Regina late on the Friday before our performance day. Jimmy, Amy, Bernard, Chaz, and I decided to go to a restaurant nearby. We all downed Molson beers – "A Canadian favorite," Jimmy insisted – before ordering food. Somehow, the beers must have hit me super hard because I don't remember ever eating dinner or how I ended up sleeping in the girls' truck that night, instead of in the motel room I was supposed to share with Amy. All I knew was the next morning we were required to report to the mainstage at nine for a ten o'clock Opening Ceremonies event, a half hour "promo" of our two o'clock afternoon performance. This meant unloading the equipment, setting up, mic check, and singing a couple num- bers in the brightest sunshine, all while experiencing the worse hangover I'd ever experienced. Amy, Jimmy, and Chaz covered for me as best as they could by forcing me to wake up so that I wouldn't report in late, then handing me the lightest duty during setup. They even made sure I was hydrated and found me shade whenever possible. Damn, the sun was bright that morning! Somehow, I got through that promotional performance without suspicion from Connie, who I'm sure would have been delighted to have something to pin on me.

In talking to Jimmy and Chaz later in the day, I shared that I couldn't understand why I had gotten so drunk from only a couple beers. I blamed it on not having eaten enough.

"Could be," Chaz said.

"But probably not," Jimmy added.

"What?" I asked, not sure what they were getting at.

"It's more likely due to the higher percentage of alcohol in Canadian beer compared to American beer," Jimmy said.

"Yep," Chaz confirmed. Well, of course, that made sense. I sure wished they would have warned me the night before!

"I can't remember a freakin' thing after sitting in that restaurant booth. How the heck did I even get to the girls' truck?"

"That'd be me," Chaz piped up, looking a bit shy and flushed.

"Gosh, Chaz. Thank you."

Amy told me later that Chaz had to carry me into the girls' truck in my drunken stupor and was sure to lock me in safely. I appreciated the way he, Jimmy, and Amy pulled together to help me through the morning promotional appearance, especially how they kept Connie from knowing what was going on. *They are my family here on the road, one of the positives of traveling with this band.*

Once the hangover started to wear off, I was able to take in the enormity and beauty of the Canada Days festival. Both Canadian and British flags decorating every craft, game, and food booth along meticulously organized alleys laid out across a vast city park. The mainstage, where we would be performing later in the day, offered the most professional outdoor performance space that we'd seen yet while on tour. The stage, a six-foot high covered platform, surrounded by a scaffolding framework, featured professional lighting and sound equipment with huge speakers on either side of the performing area, including onstage monitors for the performers, manned by an onsite sound team.

In addition to the mainstage, two smaller stages were interspersed around the park featuring a variety of acts. Between our own performances, I had my choice of watching dance troupes in traditional dress from all over Canada and other parts of the world. There were country/folk music groups with little children playing instruments like fiddles and dulcimers, symphonic orchestras, country, pop, folk, and jazz singers, and cultural demonstrations like drum circles formed by Indigenous people. Unless Angelo Conti had some Canadian roots in his heritage, I couldn't help but wonder how King Vido's Swing Band beat out the competition to grab a performance slot. On the other hand, our swing music was representative of a specific American musical genre and we were quite unique compared to anything else I saw on the program. *Hmm. Based on my new understanding about the real roots of swing music, it would be a more truthful representation of this American genre if King Vido's Swing Band was more integrated! But that would never happen with the Conti family in charge!*

King interjected the Broadway and Gospel mini shows between the swing music for our evening show. The audience engaged with this music more actively, clapping and even singing along at times. The Broadway and Gospel mini shows could not have been more diverse in terms of movement (hyper-active choreography in the showtunes versus subtle individualize response) and intent (performing for the audience versus encouraging audience participation with the gospel tunes.) While less demonstrative than other audiences, Canadians received our performances positively. They swayed and smiled, though I saw far less physical participation or clapping in rhythm with the music. *I guess the combo of Swing, Showtunes, and Gospel music has a different effect on our neighbors to the north.* At the end of the evening, after loading up the equipment and pulling out of the city park to head over to the motel, a fireworks display began in the distance. A fitting ending to a long day.

• • •

The band left Canada to spend the July 4th holiday at the condo in Omaha, before heading to a gig in Colorado at the end of the week. Four days at the condo, another four days of awkwardness for me. In my effort to avoid Ricky, I decided to spend as little time at Rosie's Bar and Grille as possible. I avoided situations where he might be drinking and become confrontational. Even the occasional, "Hey, Margie" coming from him as he pretended all was forgiven caused my throat to tighten and my breathing to nearly stop. I so badly wanted to scream at him, "Cut the crap. I'm not your freakin' friend, and I'm sick of pretending you didn't violate me!" But no…those words never came and neither did the courage to say them. Instead, I resorted to the strategy I had perfected over the years – avoid confrontation and shove uncomfortable feelings down deep.

That third night back in Omaha, I bought a soda and a bag of chips from the vending machine and stayed in the condo to read and do some writing while the others went to Rosie's for the evening, as usual. *Okay, you know you're being a dork, Margie. But it's the best way I know to handle Ricky right now other than running away from the band completely. I'm learning to perfect the avoidance strategy.*

I thought I was alone in the condo when I heard the front door open and a couple of people enter. I braced myself for another Conti family argument.

"Listen to me. I'm your papa, Simone."

"No, you're not listening to me but you need to start. You

promised me money to go out on my own. But you keep leading me on. That Conti Cabinet Making sign you put outside the studio was another empty promise. But no more! It's time for me to leave the band, to start my own business and be with Cheryl. I want to help her get ready for the baby. I need to be with my family."

"No, no. This is your family, Simone!" King's voice boomed. "And King Vido's Swing Band is the family business. We all have to pull together now, *capisce*? I need all the money coming in, even what Stefano is bringing in, to put back into the band. Ruby's booking more acts through the Talent Agency, which means more commissions going into the band. No more idle time, the band's got to bring in money every week."

"It's the same thing every year, King." Simon sounded like he was trying to restrain his frustration, speaking in measured tones.

"No, now we must get better bookings, like getting booked solid in Florida over the winter months. The way to do that is get the attention of a big shot manager. We have a chance to audition for the East Coast Music Artists Showcase in November. For that we need better promo materials. An album, flyers, postcards, even the new costumes, yes? We need to look more professional."

"But King, a swing band? Come on?" Simon said, trying to bring King back to earth. But his comment only jacked up King even more.

"I have a vision, si? King Vido's Swing Band can be bigger, better, flashier. That's why I need you to stay, and I need Stefano to come back to play drums. I need Enzo's young voice and energy in the show. With two males, three girls, it's so much better, *capisce*? I can see it. I have a vision in my mind, *capisce*? I can't have you gone! You are family!"

At that point, King was ranting, his voice nearly crazed. Giving up, Simon said, "It's impossible to talk to you when you're like this." I understood why Simon didn't try to argue with him anymore. It would have been futile.

With that King ended the conversation. "That's it. No more talk now. Go to bed. We travel tomorrow." After the sound of the condo door and King's bedroom door closing, it was silent.

• • •

Most of the travel from place to place faded from my mind – hours of cornfields as far as the eye could see, or non-descript Interstate. But one stretch stood out: The grandeur of the Rocky Mountains during the drive to Colorado Springs. The beauty of verdant deciduous trees, winding roads cutting right through mountain rock, brooks of the cleanest water I'd ever seen bubbling over boulders along the road and cascading down the mountainside, ancient fir trees reaching upward, and glimpses of the bluest sky with wisps of white clouds framed by the treetops. This continuous, picture postcard scenery filled me with awe.

Despite the magnificence of the surrounding mountain, I learned very quickly that Colorado held drawbacks. Upon arrival at the motel, I took advantage of the motel pool. But after swimming a few laps, I nearly passed out, feeling as if I was breathing through a tiny straw, sucking in air for dear life! When I got out of the pool, my legs felt like lead and my head like a cotton ball. I realized why King scheduled the band to arrive a full day before the performance. Even with over twenty-four hours to acclimate to the altitude, the horn section struggled through their performance the following evening during the Country Club Dinner-Dance. The girls had it easy since we spent most of the show swaying in our chairs, although King did pull an occasional number from the Pop mini show requiring simultaneous singing and movement, like "Proud Mary" and "Y.M.C.A.." *If I ever come back to the Rocky Mountains, I have to remember to build in enough time to get accustomed to this thin air! No wonder they call it "altitude sickness."*

• • •

Next up, Westward, Ho! California. Even though I hoped my first trip to California would include a glimpse of the Pacific Ocean, it turned out the band only traveled as far as Sacramento. The California State Fair took place at Cal Expo, a huge facility about three miles from Sacramento City Center. For the three-day booking at the California State Fair, we had no transportation between performances to explore Old Sacramento or the Sacramento riverfront. Doubly disappointing: no ocean and no tourist fun. On top of that, a feeling of tension overshadowed the whole booking from the moment we pulled in.

Upon arrival in Sacramento, King gathered the band to announce that a West Coast talent agent would be attending our California State Fair performance to "check out the King Vido Swing Band for future engagements." *Ah! The new gold lamé costumes suddenly make even more sense!* King appeared desperate to impress this agent. He even flew Ruby out to act as his personal assistant. She played the professional role beautifully, although she should have consulted Verna on costuming. *Ruby will definitely impress that talent agent when she makes an entrance in her polyester pantsuit of lime green, tan, and cream Dahlias with a matching lime green scarf in her teased hair. She may not be very West Coast, but Ruby is pure Baltimore!*

At the band meeting, Ruby brought cash for our weekly pay and per diems, which seemed odd but was welcomed since we were all running low on moola. We'd been on the road three weeks, since June 25th, but were already a bit tired and cranky.

Ruby also reported, "Number one, youse all will be paid with cash through the end of July, and number two, youse got three new bookings to add to the schedule before heading back to home base." To a chorus of grumbling complaints from most of the band, she distributed an addendum to the current schedule:

```
Tues 7/1 8 - Durango, CO - Rodeo Days

Wed 7/19 - Armarillo, TX - Rodeo Days

Sat 7/22 - Independence, LA - Sicilian Heritage
Festival
```

Disappointed that the schedule would now be cutting into our free time in Baltimore, I reminded myself that Ruby warned me to be ready for anything. *No short visit to Church Creek for me this break.* On the other hand, I assumed Jimmy and Chaz were thrilled to be playing more. I worried that this schedule seemed tight, especially driving sixteen hours from California to Durango, Colorado in only two days. That meant we'd have to leave early in the morning after the Sacramento job, drive all day, stay over somewhere, and drive all day the following day to make it to Durango in time for our performance on July 17th. *Why would King agree to such a short timetable?*

"What do you think about this schedule change?" I asked Jimmy as we set up on the mainstage for the California State Fair show. "I know you're thrilled to get in some extra playing time, but don't you think King's kinda cramming these gigs close together?"

"Yeah, this schedule seems tighter than normal. Ted said King's grabbin' any gigs he can. Needs all the jobs he can book." *Flimsy excuse, but money issues did make sense, especially based on the conversations I overheard in Omaha.* Again, I opted not to tell Jimmy about the arguments I heard at the condo between Stefano, Simon, and King. I didn't understand enough about what Stefano was saying to make sense of it, so why start rumors?

The talent agent didn't show up the first afternoon of our Sacramento performance, and after several frantic phone calls, Ruby learned the agent cancelled. Of course, the news put King in a foul mood. Ruby took the rental car, whisking Connie off for a dinner, shopping, and movie extravaganza. *What a luxury, having a car and being able to get away from the fairgrounds!* One of the downfalls of touring in huge trucks was having little to no opportunity to explore beyond walking radius of the venue. So, while Connie explored downtown Sacramento, the rest of us scattered, taking in the California State Fair. Amy and Ted went off to check out some of the agriculture exhibits, which seemed odd. Not that cows, sheep, and chickens aren't fun to look at, but we'd seen a whole lot of cows, sheep, and chickens on this tour. Jimmy, Chaz, and I hung out, as usual, looking up the performance schedule for the several smaller stages around the fairgrounds. Bernard and Ricky searched for girls to pick up, the norm for those two, which was fine with me since it meant I could dodge Ricky for yet another day.

• • •

After our noon performance the following day, Jimmy and Chaz went off to score some weed from one of the carnies, so I decided to grab a lemonade and do some journal writing by myself. I noticed Simon walking by with a cheeseburger and Coke, so I asked him if he'd like to join me, a perfect opportunity to get some clarity on his whole band situation.

I figured I'd ease into the conversation. "How's Cheryl doing, Simon?"

"She's good. Complaining about how big she's getting. Gosh,

I miss her."

"Hey, you started to tell me that you might have an idea of how you could be home with her and the baby, once the baby comes, I mean."

"Yeah, but…" He hesitated. I didn't push. "God, King can be so frustrating."

"How so?"

"He doesn't realize that this band is what it is. That's all. Ruby gets us a couple of new bookings and King leaps into these delusions. And then there's Stefano encouraging King for the wrong reasons and King's blind to it."

"Why not walk away?"

"At first I didn't consider it, because…well, family is family, you know? When Mother passed, I felt an obligation. Once I married Cheryl and we traveled together with the band, the steady money was good, or at least that's what I told myself. After Cheryl left the band, there was a promise of startup money for a business. Well, that's a complicated and long story. But now…I don't know. It's a good question. I feel so torn because Cheryl's upset with me. She doesn't trust Stefano. He can do stupid things sometimes. Who knows? She could be right. What I see right now is that Stefano is fueling King's desperation for a grand comeback and manipulating his thinking. King's not a bad man, really. Mostly stubborn and drunk with some crazy idea he has power as leader of this band. He'll never admit that King Vido's Swing Band is a thing of the past."

I didn't speak, letting Simon purge these thoughts, not saying them to me directly but rather to himself. It seemed as if he needed to hear them out loud. When he finished talking, I didn't ask any more questions. We sat in silence.

• • •

Later that evening, Amy dropped a bit of a bombshell back in the motel room. She confessed to me that she and Ted had been seeing each other. Their mutual attraction was obvious to most of us, but Amy revealed that it went deeper than we suspected. I felt more worried than shocked. While Ted had expressed his unhappiness with his relationship with Connie, he also indicated he felt trapped, not ready to make a move.

"It started out chillin' as friends, you know? But he's so funny and nice. It's been hot and heavy whenever we can sneak away together." *Yikes! I hope she and Ted know what they're doing. If Connie finds out, she'll make Amy's life miserable.*

"What's Ted going to do about Connie?"

"He's planning to deal with her and the family, but he's gotta find the right time. Right now, the Conti boys and King are freakin' out about this agent thing and other stuff with the band. King has a few business things lined up in Louisiana and Cleveland that are supposed to help the band, at least that's what Ted can pull out of Connie. After things chill a bit, he plans to break it off with her."

"Amy, you've got to be super careful. If Connie becomes the least bit suspicious, that will be the end for you."

"I hear what you're saying, but even if it came out, I know Ted will stick up for us. I'm sure he loves me."

"Whoa, Amy. Did he tell you he loved you?"

"Well, not exactly. But I told him how I feel, and he hasn't checked out yet. I'm sure he feels the same way."

"Look. It's none of my business, but I've been where you are before and the whole thing went to hell. So be careful, that's all I'm saying."

"Right, and now David is interested in you again. Don't be such a bummer, Margie. It's all going to be fab. He's just gotta find the right time to break up with her, that's all."

She was right about one thing. I shouldn't project my own experiences onto her. As Homer said: "Nothing shall I, while sane, compare with a friend." Yet I couldn't help but see my relationship with David in Amy's revelation. I was so trusting, so sure David felt the same, only to feel broken in the end. *Stop beating yourself up for the past, Margie! But I do see that when I was with David, it was all about David and how I could wedge myself into his future, his passions, his life. I need to remember that I lost myself in him. If I went back to him now, how would that be any different? Can I trust that he's changed?* The time away on the tour – meeting people, having time to reflect on the past and think about the future, even experiencing the pain of Ricky's attack – helped me believe that a unique path was unfolding for me, full of rad music and diverse ways of thinking. *No, Amy's right. Our paths are unique.*

Right now, I needed to pay attention, make good choices, and learn to navigate my own way through tough situations. *And I don't seem to be doing a particularly good job with the navigation part at all!*

15

Touring Monotony

Delta, Utah – July, 1978

After spending the night at the Starlight Motel in Delta, Utah, we woke at the first suggestion of daybreak to process the guys through showers and get on the road ASAP. At least that was the plan. As it had become routine on "shower days," Amy and I sneaked out into the hall to grab extra towels off the maids' carts and stacked them on the beds in our room and Connie's room for the guys. Connie kept watch in the hallway, signaling two of her brothers to rush up the stairwell and into her room for their showers when the maids weren't looking.

Unfortunately, one of the maids caught on and confronted Giorgio and Enzo as they entered Connie's room, causing a huge scene. King heard the commotion and yelled at the maid. The maid threatened to report him to the manager. King ordered everyone to load up and that was the end of that. Totally embarrassing! *This shower farce is beginning to weigh on me. How is it that I'm the only person in the band who feels uncomfortable with the arrangement? King is condoning ripping off the motels on a regular basis and everyone acts like it's business-as-usual. But of course, I say nothing.*

We loaded up in record time and screeched out of the Starlight Motel parking lot, without showers, pushing eastward toward Durango, Colorado. The previous day's travel from Sacramento was a long, hot, dusty drive through the desert of Nevada and western Utah along Route 50. Let's just say, we really needed those showers. The Great Basin Desert felt especially desolate and depressing. We passed through the Confusion and House Mountain ranges in central Utah, but it was nothing compared to the grandeur of the Rockies. The scenery was limited to rock formations with a few distant peaks looking like wannabes yearning to grow into spectacular mountains one day. At least those baby peaks broke up the mile upon mile of dried brush, sand, and dirt. *I'm not a desert-lover. It must have to do with being born under an Astrological water sign or being homesick for aquatic life on the Choptank River and the Chesapeake Bay.*

Having pushed ourselves hard to drive eight hours the day before, we scheduled a leisurely three–hour drive to get to Durango, planning to arrive between one and two o'clock. The outdoor Rodeo Days Festival gig began at five o'clock and we needed at least an hour to set up and change into our costumes. *Despite being exhausted, overheated from crossing the desert in non-air-conditioned trucks, and unable to take showers, this might work after all.* Unbearably hot with hardly a wisp of breeze finding its way into the back windows as we traveled, I thanked God I chose my latest "go-to" truck riding outfit in the early morning motel chaos: cut-off denim shorts topped with a navy-blue tank and easy to slip off clogs.

Then it happened!

Connie, Amy, and I heard a loud squealing noise from the front of our truck. Whoever was driving pulled over to the shoulder. We waited anxiously to hear a report, although we figured it couldn't be good news. The back of the truck became stifling hot in a matter of minutes with no air circulating through the side windows. After about twenty minutes, Connie jumped out to investigate, while Amy and I smashed our faces against the side window over Connie's bunk, trying to see or hear any bits of information. All we could make out was a silhouette of the Conti clan deep in discussion with King.

Thirty minutes later, Connie opened the door and began her favorite thing: screeching out orders. "Quickly change into your dresses for set up. Grab your costumes for tonight. Shoes, rollers, and makeup. We're moving over to The Kennel for the rest of the trip to Durango." Quick as two females desperate to seek moving air in the middle of a desert could hustle, Amy and I jumped to it.

Prior to that moment, I'd never actually set foot into The Kennel. Oh, I'd peeked in to see the layout, but I never had a reason to enter. *I now know how The Kennel got its name. It absolutely smells like a vet's kennel with all those animals!* Once Enzo and Ricky got the "Oo-o, girls in The Kennel" jeers out of the way, Amy and I settled on the edge of Chaz's lower bunk.

Chaz filled us in on what went down with a detailed report: "Broken fan belt." *Well, that's about as detailed as I've come to expect from Chaz.*

Jimmy offered specifics. "King's havin' Antonio stay with the truck to wait for a mechanic and then he'll catch up with us in Durango. We've already lost a shitload time with this stop, add in gas and bathroom breaks, we'll be lucky if we make it by the five o'clock start time."

Jimmy's words turned out to be true. We arrived in Durango, Colorado in the nick of time to set up in front of the waiting crowd, about 45 minutes late. With no showers and traveling in the hot, non-air-conditioned Kennel, any attempt to curl my greasy hair with hot rollers proved futile. Despite the late arrival, the less-than-glamourous singers, and the extreme heat, the audience enjoyed the show, especially the country songs like "Never Ending Song of Love" and "Two Doors Down." It felt as though all these obstacles created a heightened sense of performance electricity within the band. Even Connie's solo, "Stand by Your Man," sounded decent. *And by that I mean on pitch.* It brought cheers and a burst of applause, which pleased "her majesty" to no end. In fact, I took the opportunity to ask Connie for her thoughts about music.

"I know you've been doing this touring thing for a long time, and have tons of professional music experience, so do you mind if I ask you a question?" *Got to butter her up, make her feel like the ultra-pro, as difficult as that is to do with a straight face!*

"Well, that is true. What do you want to know?" *Modest for Connie!*

"What does music mean to you? What I mean is, what makes you get up on that stage night after night, singing your heart out?" *Okay, I'm laying it on a little thick.*

Without giving it a moment's reflection, she blurted out, "For the applause, of course. I do it for the applause." And with that, Connie shouted that break was over and everyone needed to take their positions for the second set. As I scampered to my chair at stage left, I couldn't help but compare her response to that of Jimmy's and Giles'. *There are two breeds of musicians in the world, and I didn't need to think too hard about which path I planned to take.*

During the next break, when I had a moment to stop and take in the scenery, I gasped at the beauty of Durango. The setting sun painted the sky in crimsons and corals as it dipped behind the San Juan Mountains, whose peaks encircled the charming historic railroad town. *I'd love to spend a few days exploring these old buildings, walking the streets, imagining the history of the gold seekers and railroad tycoons of a different age.* Connie interrupted my musings, barking orders to return to the stage for the final set of the night.

Two more tour dates and then back to Baltimore for four glorious days off! The heat of the summer and monotony of the tour began to wear on me. *County Fairs, Cowboy Roundups, Rodeo Days! Just tell me what costume to wear and what time to set up.* I loved the singing and the audience's energy, especially when they were psyched about the music. But life on the road? Not as alluring or even as exciting as I once thought – especially traveling in a converted truck through the West and deep South, as we had been doing this leg of the tour. And with the tight band schedule, we rarely had time to explore any of the cool cities or towns on our tour schedule. It became an "arrive-setup-play-sleep-load-drive-and-repeat" routine, as we crisscrossed the country in the heat of the summer.

• • •

After a performance in Armarillo, Texas for another Rodeo Days event, we landed in Independence, Louisiana for a Sicilian Heritage Festival, an atypical gig compared to the rest of the tour. Ruby had added Independence to the schedule back in California, so this may have been one of those "cash grabs" that Jimmy and Ted talked about. In fact, the whole situation became even stranger when Jimmy, Chaz, and I walked through the event location on Friday, the day before the show. This festival felt like the St. Leo's Crowning of the Blessed Mother event in Baltimore's Little Italy. The same kind of super small, Italian community, parish-related event. *Why is King Vido's Swing Band driving all the way to Louisiana to perform for something this local?*

While we roamed among the festival's crafts booths, games

of chances, and amazing Italian food vendors, something interesting caught my attention. Way off near the entrance gate, I saw two gentlemen wearing leisure jackets over unbuttoned shirts approach King and start what appeared from their body language to be a heated discussion. Wanting a closer look, I told Jimmy and Chaz I needed to use the restroom and I'd catch up with them later. I maneuvered myself to a booth near the entrance and pretended to check out the homemade jams and preserves, keeping one eye on King's meeting and searching this interaction for any information that made sense.

King made some sort of demand, and the two men's body language suggested resistance. I only heard bits of the conversation, which randomly switched between Italian and English. "…a bigger cut…," I heard King say at one point. The larger of the two men shoved King, causing him to reel backward several steps. *Looks like "business" is escalating in intensity!* King raised his hands in concession and the aggressive man backed off. Then all three spoke rapidly in Italian.

Once the men seemed to come to an oral agreement, I heard King say, "We need to have each other's backs, *si?*" and clapped the larger man on the shoulder. At that point, the other man handed King a thick envelope and they both left through the entrance gate. King tucked it awkwardly into the inner pocket of his jacket, looking around briefly. He then walked out through the gate. *What was that all about? Was this booking an excuse for him to connect with these men? A cover? And why? King said he wanted "a bigger cut," but of what? Was the envelope filled with cash?* I remembered the envelope King received at the Wyndhurst Country Club bar before our performance in May. I thought that was payment for our gig that evening, but what if it was part of this same King and Stefano scheme? None of this made any sense to me, and I didn't know what to do about it. *Hm, come to think of it, we did get paid in cash again this evening.*

• • •

After Saturday night's performance in Louisiana, we headed back to Baltimore for a few days off from Monday through Thursday. The mid-week free days left no opportunity for Jimmy, Chaz, and me to catch another jazz performance, since these groups typically performed on weekends. I hoped to run into Giles Kelley again to ask him more about influences on American music, a topic that piqued my interest. Since meeting Giles, the fact that not one of my college Music Appreciation textbooks even approached African or Latin musical roots continued to eat away at me.

Despite the short break in Baltimore, I appreciated the free time to sip cappuccino at Vaccaro's outside café tables, do some journal reflections, and watch the world go by. Moments like those allowed me to visualize what might be next for me. A mental picture began to take shape: I loved writing. I loved music. I wanted to learn more about music. I wanted to connect people to all kinds of music. The same questions kept turning over in my mind: *Is there a way I can build on what I know and love to do? And how can music and writing fulfill a greater purpose? What is that purpose? Still not clear to me.* I did know that I never wanted to lose this feeling, this energy I felt when I connected to music, listened to great music, and expressed myself through my writing. *I don't ever want to let myself get derailed again.*

• • •

We reported to the trucks in front of 324 Albemarle on Friday morning, not knowing where we were heading. Not to worry, though. Connie waved a fistful of schedules "fresh off the mimeograph" and handed them out in her efficient and bossy manner. The third leg of the tour had us hopping all over the map, from North Carolina to Chicago to the Bible Belt and even back to Louisiana! *And on it goes...*

```
King Vido's Swing Band Tour -Third Leg


Sat 7/29 - Raleigh, NC - North Carolina State
Fair


Tues 7/31 - Erie, PA - Moose Club Dinner Dance


Thurs 8/3 - Cleveland, OH - Little Italy Italian
Festival


Sat 8/5 - Chicago, IL - Idlewood Country Club -
Gala dance


Wed 8/9 - LeMars, IA - Regional Fireman's Fair


Thurs - 8/10 Linn, KS - Harvest Days Festival


Fri/Sat/Sun 8/11, 12, 13 - Omaha, NB - No
performance


Mon 8/14 - Des Moines, Iowa - State Fair


Tues/Wed/Thurs 8/15, 16, 17 - Omaha, NB - No
performance


Sat 8/19 - Independence, LA - Night in Little
Italy/Sotto Le Stelle


Thurs 8/24 - Gatlinburg, TN - Outdoors Arts &
Crafts Festival


Sat 8/26 - Return to Baltimore
```

The most exciting thing about this schedule was having one week off in Baltimore at the end of August. *A whole week means I can go home to Church Creek and start to work on my "What's next for Margie" plan!*

The tour dates droned on during the third leg of the tour. The North Carolina State Fair, a high profile booking for King, was well-received as was the Erie, Pennsylvania dinner-dance at the Moose Club. Both the Cleveland and Chicago bookings included time for Conti business meetings. *Hm, I'm beginning to get an idea what that means and I don't feel good about it.* The Italian Festival in Cleveland's Little Italy felt like the St. Leo's Festival for the Crowning of the Blessed Mother, but with larger attendance and layout. *Connie is still trying to figure out my cracks about Cleveland being the city with the burning river. Does she ever read a newspaper?* The dinner-dance at the Idlewood Country Club in Chicago, an "under the stars" event, was cut short because of a thunderstorm threat. The following day, as the rain poured down, we sat around in the motel room while King met with someone on "family business," according to Connie. *Does she have any idea what that term really means or does she repeat that phrase like a mindless robot from the Astro Boy show?*

The ups and downs of tour life continued. Witnessing the beauty of the Rocky Mountains was one of the highlights, while driving through the desert of Nevada and western Utah was one of the bummers. A gig that fell into the "downer" category for the entire band occurred on August 10th in Linn, Kansas, an agricultural town situated northwest of Topeka, population 410. The temperature hovered at around 105 degrees that day, but that wasn't the worst of it. Scheduled during the harvest, only five people attended the show! At least they found a sliver of shade on the outdoor bleachers, while we sweated our asses off playing music, singing, and dancing in the blazing sun. That performance marked the lowest point of the entire tour for me.

To top off the Linn fiasco, we ended up at the condo in Omaha for the following three days, basking in boredom until our next scheduled tour date. I started having the same "Not again" reaction to Omaha as Jimmy's "I just wanna play, man!" – although, my feelings arose from a different place. And though hiding from Ricky was a dumb way to deal with the problem, I mostly avoided hanging out at Rosie's Bar and Grille in the evening. Anything to sidestep Ricky and further "miscommunications." What was super unfair was that Ricky seemed unfazed by what happened outside the condo that night.

A couple times I ventured over to Rosie's for an early dinner with the gang, disappearing once the post-meal drinking began with a feeble excuse like "super tired." Chaz, always the gentleman, offered to walk me back to the condo each time. He often asked, "Somethin' wrong, Margie?" I knew if I allowed the memories to escape from their deep vault, the raw and painful feelings would start all over. A tightening in my throat, a shortness of breath, even nausea. *No! Don't think about that night. Push it all down.* I became an expert at diverting, shoving, and locking away the thoughts, feelings, and shame in a place as far down into my soul as possible.

"Just tired, Chaz," I'd respond. I allowed the monotony of the tour to become a kind of anesthesia, dulling any pain by keeping me focused on the next show, the next break, the next… whatever.

After the Omaha recess, we had a huge booking in Des Moines at the Iowa State Fair. For sure an A-list affair, although we played on a smaller side stage called the Free Stage, not the Grandstand Stage, which hosted headliner acts like The

186

Osmonds, Heart, Anne Murray, and Styx.

Overhearing Amy and I gush about these famous celebrities, Connie seemed perplexed. "Daddy says someday King Vido's Swing Band will be appearing up on that Grandstand Stage!"

We suppressed our giggles while nodding in agreement with Connie's absurd declaration. I did feel a little sorry for her, though. *Is she really that naïve to believe that this band could ever be the caliber of The Osmonds? It'll take a lot more than dazzling gold costumes to make that leap!* Of course, we wore the gold lamé jumpsuits for the show that day.

From Des Moines, we ended up back in Omaha at the condo for three days until our next performance. As usual, the gang all headed over to Rosie's Bar and Grille for the evening. That first night, I opted to spend the evening in the condo bedroom by myself. Amy looked concerned.

"Margie, Chaz and I have been worried about you. Why won't you come out with the group anymore?" she asked. I considered opening up to Amy, but I couldn't bring myself to tell her about Ricky's attack. *What if she agrees with Ricky and thinks I did bring it on myself? What if she thinks I was flirting with him that first night at Rosie's, instead of being my normal, friendly self? What if she thinks I'm being overly sensitive? No, it's better if I try to forget the whole thing ever happened.*

"I still go out places with you and Chaz and Jimmy all the time. I'm kinda tired tonight, that's all," I lied, hoping she'd let it go. Thankfully, she didn't push any further.

I settled into the room, reading my newly purchased book by Thomas Merton, a complete departure from Ram Dass. Merton offered a different view on someone searching for a spiritual path through a fog of doubt. *I can relate. Doubting my own spiritual direction has been bothering me a lot lately. I thought that the whole*

Ram Dass thing was the answer to my resistance to being raised Catholic. But now I see that David's twisted, self-serving interpretation wasn't real. The more philosophies I read, the more questions I have. I'm not sure what I believe anymore.

I continued to dive into Merton's book, when the living room door to the condo opened with a bang and I heard King's voice bellowing.

"And I'm trying to tell *you* that we are so close to having enough money to cut the promo album. This is going to be so big for the band. It's—"

"—Going to take the band to the next level. I know, I know." I recognized Simon's voice, interrupting. "You say that every time. It's always the same. This gig is going to take us to the next level. This tour… this new mini show…these new costumes…"

"But this promotional album will do it. I have a feeling, *capisce?*"

Simon laughed at this idea. "No, King. No, it won't. You might get a few more gigs, but King Vido's Swing Band is never going to make it to the "Big Time." This isn't the 1950s. You're delusional."

"No, you're delusional. Stefano agrees with me."

"Of course, he does. He's using you. I'm telling you the truth. But you don't want to hear it. But you'll let Stefano tell you all kinds of lies. Of course, Stefano will tell you what a great future this band has. Meanwhile, he's pocketing his cut of the illegal money coming in."

"Simone, you've got it all wrong. It's nothing illegal. These investors—"

"They're not investors, King, and you know it. Ogni pazzo vuol dar consiglio. Every fool is ready with advice, si?"

King jumped in. "Stefano is no fool."

"He's worse. He's a con man and you're listening to him for advice. Look, I won't listen to this anymore. I want out after this leg of the tour. You promised me seed money for my carpentry business so I can be home with my wife and baby. You know this is true."

It was quiet for several minutes. Neither King nor Simon said a word, or at least that I could hear. Careful not to draw attention, I opened the bedroom door a sliver. I didn't want to miss anything, especially if Simon said more about the confusing illegal stuff.

Finally, King said, "Simone, I need you to stay through the end of September, eh?

"Agh! It's always the same. 'One more month,' 'One more gig,' 'One more tour.'" Agitation filled Simon's voice.

"Okay, okay, until the end of September. Give me until the end of September to figure out how to replace you? It's two more months. Please, Simone." At this point, he was almost begging, a tone of voice I'd never heard from the domineering King. "Let me figure out how to keep the band moving forward. At least till we finish the promo album in mid-September, eh?"

I could hear Simon's voice soften. "Alright. I'll do the album. But that's it!" Then the door slammed, hard. King muttered to himself in Italian and seemed to be pacing around the living area of the condo.

I felt anxious about what I had overhead. *Stefano has gotten King involved in something illegal, and Simon wants nothing to do with it.* My heart started pounding hard. But worse, I needed to pee badly. *Damn! It's only a few feet to the hall bathroom and I gotta go!* I opened my bedroom door a bit wider and slowly tip-toed out toward the bathroom. *King's still pacing and muttering in the living room, so there's a good chance he won't notice me in the hall. I just won't flush – yuck! – and then I'll quickly tiptoe back to the bedroom.* All went well…that is until I came out of the bathroom and walked smack into King's chest. *Crap!*

"Oh, sorry, King." Acting skills in overdrive, I yawned, stretched, rubbed my eyes, and exclaimed, "I've been sleeping since seven o'clock." I stretched again, for good measure. "What time is it, anyway?"

Although suspicious, he seemed relieved. "Ah, cara. You not feeling well? I thought you'd be out with the others."

"I didn't go to Rosie's. Female problems, you know…It's best to sleep it off." King continued to size me up with a skeptical look. *I don't think he's buying it. I need something more.* "Um, did I hear a door slam? I think it woke me up. Or was I dreaming?" I yawned again, giving him time to take in my performance. "I'll just go back to bed now, okay?" He seemed appeased, or at least he didn't want to talk about the slamming door or my "female problems" anymore. *Close call, though.*

Back behind the safety of the closed bedroom door, I wondered about the illegal dealings Simon talked about. Something sounded fishy, but I had no idea what it could be, or how to put the pieces together. More importantly, what I could I even do about it.

So much tension with this band. I was glad we'd be back in Baltimore in less than two weeks!

16

Amy's Dilemma

Omaha, Nebraska – July, 1978

During load up the following morning, Jimmy and Chaz invited me to ride with them in the truck cab to our next destination: Independence, Louisiana. We settled in for several hours of driving. Once on the highway, Chaz lit up a joint, passed it Jimmy, and turned to me, "Ready for your next Music Appreciation lesson?"

"You bet!" I said.

Chaz said it was time for some funk and bop in my life, which intrigued me. He inserted Earth Wind & Fire's "That's the Way of the World" into the 8-track tape player and introduced me to the world of funk, soul, and R&B. I could hear why Jimmy and Chaz loved Earth Wind & Fire so much. The horns were amazing! So precise, harmonic, and driving. Dovetail the horns with the profound vocal harmonies and the grooving rhythm section...off the hook! I couldn't sit still, bopping my head and body to the rhythm of each song. I especially liked "Shining Star" for its funk style, and the album's title song, "That's the Way of the World" for its vocals.

Next, we listened to a Dizzy Gillespie tape. "One of the greatest jazz trumpeters ever," Jimmy insisted. I was in no position to disagree. He told me that even though Dizzy was most famous in the 1940s as both a bandleader and jazz musician, he had enormous influence on many modern players like Miles Davis, Chuck Mangione, and Arturo Sandoval, and even helped develop jazz genres, like bebop.

"I heard Giles talking about bebop but…what is it?" I asked.

"Yep, you've got a lot to learn, girl, music-wise," Jimmy teased.

Chaz jumped in with the definition. "Okay, bebop is a kinda modern jazz. Usually, fast tempo with complex chord progressions and lots of key changes. Oh, uh, and tons of improvisation that uses harmonic structure and lots of time referring to the melody. Things like that are characteristics of bebop."

I almost fell over in a faint! "Wow, Chaz. You must store up all your talking for your favorite topic!"

"Thank you, Professor Chaz!" Jimmy said, making a dorky face.

Jimmy was right, though. I did have a lot to learn about music. Funk, soul, jazz, bebop, gospel. There was so much more to American music and other world music. While Giles had planted the seed about these musical genres' roots, Jimmy and Chaz continued to introduce me to great new sounds. An energy raced through me, as if the ignition had been turned on, compelling me to want to hear more, learn more. There was also that nagging question about why musicians are so committed to their craft? What do they love about playing? How does that translate to me? *What I'm learning about myself is that even though I enjoy singing and sharing a performance with an audience, I get more jazzed about experiencing the music and writing about it. A fresh discovery about myself!*

Jimmy followed The Kennel and the girls' truck into the town of Independence, Louisiana, circling around the grounds of the

Night in Little Italy festival until he found the driveway to the platform stage. He backed the equipment truck toward the stage like an expert, and we all began unloading and setting up for that evening's performance. I had the cool tune of Dizzy Gillespie's "A Night in Tunisia" on my brain the entire time, making it easy to dismiss Connie's constant, yappy order-barking. Amy, however, seemed out of sorts. She pulled me aside and said she needed to talk to me about "something serious" before the show.

"Sure, Amy. Let's grab dinner at one of the festival vendors before we need to get dressed."

No "Far out!" No "Radical!" A quiet "Thanks" was Amy's response. *Something super big must be wrong.*

With stage set up and sound check completed, Connie announced, "Rainbow jumpsuits. Black suits with yellow ruffled shirts!" *That nasally voice...ew...grating on my last nerve! Deep breath, Margie. Positive thoughts, Margie. Aw, screw it!* When you travel with the same group of people, practically living on top of one another, sometimes it was impossible to maintain the whole "Peace and love" mindset. I continued to avoid Ricky as if he carried an infectious disease, and to be honest, Connie irritated the crap out of me. I counted the minutes until that break next week!

After setting up, Amy and I found a calzones booth and sat down at an out-of-the-way table, hoping none of the other band members would join us. I noticed Amy struggling to get started, her eyes moist with tears.

"What's going on?" I was shocked to see the upbeat Amy so down-in-the-dumps.

"I'm going to come right out with it, but you have to swear on a stack of Holy Bibles this is only between us, okay?" I nodded to reassure her.

Fighting back tears, she blurted out, "I think I'm pregnant.

I'm two weeks late." Remaining silent, I took my time to process this information. During a long pause, Amy's eyes locked uncomfortably onto mine.

"Well, don't you have one of your groovy little quotes to fix this situation, Margie?"

Caught off guard, I grasped for the right words. "Right. I usually fall back on 'go with the flow,' but it doesn't seem to work, does it?" *As much I've been searching for the answers in the inspirational quotes from Hinduism, or Buddhism, or Taoism, the truth is I haven't found a perfect spiritual fit for myself yet. And I certainly flaked on finding the perfect "fix-it" phrase for Amy's situation.*

I could tell she was very emotional so I continued to tread lightly. "So, you're right. I don't have a great pithy quote to help this time. I mean, you kinda need to think about your next steps, don't you?" I asked her how sure she was (Not too sure) and if she had shared this news with Ted (Not yet).

"Well, why don't you come up with a plan for a single, next step, whatever that might be, okay?" I offered. "You don't have to figure everything out right now. Maybe at least confirm that you're pregnant and then go from there."

Together, we devised the following plan: Wait to tell Ted until Amy knew for sure she was pregnant, get an appointment at Planned Parenthood in Baltimore for a pregnancy test during our upcoming ten days off, and then figure out her next couple steps from there. That calmed Amy down a bit. I promised to be by her side. I felt bad for her, but a little mad too. *She should have been more careful. What was she thinking? She should have…* But then I stopped myself.

I thought about the times that David and I weren't "careful." *It could have just as easily been me. Guys don't like to use condoms and it's hard to get birth control pills, expensive too. I know a girl from college who told me she tried to go to her family doctor but all he did was lecture her. She ended up borrowing her married sister's prescription. A gal who was a regular at the diner told me she found a drugstore on the Eastern Shore that sold The Pill without a prescription. But for others, sex turns out to be a game of chance, a crap shoot. I don't have a right to "should" Amy when this could have been me.*

That evening we swayed a little less enthusiastically for the Night in Little Italy audience. I detected that Amy was not her usual energetic self and, despite my reassuring smiles, I struggled with my concern for her.

• • •

After a short, unannounced stop in Arkansas for King's potential partner's meeting, the band arrived in Gatlinburg, Tennessee a day and a half before our appearance, giving us a full day to explore the town and the mammoth Arts and Crafts Festival surrounding the area. Amy, Chaz, Jimmy, and I started the day with a ski lift-type ride into the Smokey Mountains overlooking the town of Gatlinburg, offering amazing views of the gorgeous green-blue mountains. Afterward we walked through the town, taking in each touristy shop, arcade, and food vendor. Gatlinburg provided a refreshing respite for our carnival weary souls. We indulged in silly arcade games, explored the Salt and Pepper Shaker Museum, challenged each other at miniature golf on a beautiful hillside course, and gorged on thick juicy hamburgers at an outside park while listening to a folk duo strum guitars and sing original tunes. We topped off the day with an evening per- formance at the Sweet Fanny Adams Theatre, a vaudeville/musi- cal hall featuring fantastic actors performing original musical comedy. We learned about it from theatre staff, who promoted the evening's show by riding old-fashioned, high wheeler bicycles all around the town during the day. It sure lured us in! But the show was off the hook. I kept the colorful program with the Sweet Fanny Adams logo to glue into my journal as a keepsake.

The following day Amy, Chaz, Jimmy, and I teamed up again to stroll through the Arts and Craft Festival before our four o'clock set up time. We bumped into the Conti boys, Ted, and Connie at various points during our meandering. I watched to see how Amy reacted toward Ted, but she played it cool with a simple, "Hey, Ted." I distracted her by pointing out some nifty macramé purses in an artist's booth, and she seemed fine. *It must be hard to see someone you care about always hanging with another woman, especially under the current circumstances. I know I couldn't handle it with David and what's-her-name. What a mess!*

The Gatlinburg audience and vacationers loved our performance so much they requested two encores. Not only was King glowing, but Connie's head swelled to the size of a watermelon. As we packed up and headed to the motel for the night, she spewed, "King Vido's Swing Band is sure to make it to the big time, now!" I failed to see how two encores equated to "making it to the big time," but I knew better than to argue with Connie… or to discuss anything of substance with her. I did still throw a compliment her way whenever it helped to calm a potential rough sea, even if my hypocrisy made me cringe at times. Ruby's advice that first day *was* spot on. *I'm sure there's a spiritual quote somewhere about not being a fraud, but what can I say? This method makes living with Connie a bit more bearable.*

The Gatlinburg performance behind us, all I wanted to do was get back to Baltimore for ten wonderful days off. Unfortunately, King insisted on two unscheduled stops during this last leg of the tour. Not performances, "investment meetings," as King now called them. After what I had overheard at the condo between Simon and King, I had serious doubts. *I wonder if terms like "family business" and "partner meetings" are really code for King following up on connections that Stefano set up beforehand. Who are these people? While unclear, I'm convinced that something illegal is going on with this band.*

The first stop after our Louisiana gig took us to Little Rock, Arkansas. From there we detoured to Clay County, West Virginia before heading home to Baltimore. Interestingly, both unscheduled stops were prior performance sites for the band. *Could it be that our prior performances did stir up some legitimate investment interest in these towns? Investing in a band like King Vido's Swing Band still seems farfetched to me.* I kept returning to the question: What would investors get in return when they put money into something like a swing band, especially if what Jimmy and Chaz told me about the music industry was accurate? *It's not like King Vido's Swing Band is ever going to cut a top ten album. King must realize that. There's got to be something else.*

I had so many questions. If these meetings were connected to Stefano's side business in some way, are they illegal, as Simon indicated? So vague and confusing. Despite Jimmy's advice, I couldn't stop thinking about these funky band activities. I also had my hands full trying to figure out how to help Amy with her problem. I looked forward to taking a couple days for myself when we got back to Baltimore. *Visit Mom in Church Creek, maybe even see David again and figure out what's going on there. It's time for me to get clear on a plan for my future and connect to a purpose.* As Lao Tzu says: "At the center of your being, you have the answer; you know who you are and you know what you want." I began to believe those words more and more.

I needed to sit still and listen to what my heart was telling me, to connect to what I see for my future. *Right now, all I see is a chaotic mess!*

17

Two Plans in Bloom

Little Italy, Baltimore, Maryland – August, 1978

The trucks pulled into Baltimore late Saturday afternoon, after driving non-stop from West Virginia. Thrilled to be back in Little Italy, I looked forward to an entire week off – no rehearsals, no band meetings, no costume fittings, and no Connie! True, Amy's dilemma required my energy, but I was determined to take time for myself, too. First order of business: Me time!

On Sunday morning, I planned to relax by myself in Little Italy – self-reflecting, writing, mentally sorting out the David thing, and trying to figure out what the heck my post-band future might look like. After a late breakfast at a cute diner around the corner from 324 Albemarle, I realized I'd forgotten my journal so I circled back to the studio to pick it up. As I entered the foyer, I saw Ruby sitting at King's colossal desk. *That's odd. No one dares occupy King's domain.* She was concentrating on an accounting ledger spread out in front of her, so much so that she didn't even hear me come in the office door. I noticed the safe next to King's desk was wide open, a rare occurrence. Inside the vault, placed on top of a small metal box, I spotted five or six thick envelopes, like those I'd seen handed to King on tour. Hunched over the ledger, Ruby deftly punched numbers into an adding machine, pulling back the handle periodically for totals. I watched her for a minute or two before interrupting with my usual "Hey Ruby!" I expected her normal, "Hi, hon. How youse doin' today?" but Ruby's actions and response seemed startled and anxious, almost nervous. She jumped up with the ledger, shoved it into the safe, and slammed the door closed.

Finally, she blurted out, "Oh, hi, I thought youse was out for the day," peering around me to see if anyone else had followed me.

"Yeah, came back for my journal. It's rare to see you in the office on a Sunday."

"Yeah, King asked me to catch up on some accountin' for him, is all. But I got to get goin' soon."

"Ah, well I'll be going back out again in a few. Check ya later." I backed out of the office doorway and headed up the staircase to my dorm room.

"Right, okay then," Ruby said. *A distracted and odd exchange for Ruby, who usually radiates warmth and humor, at least with me.* When I returned to the studio later that afternoon, there was no sign of Ruby. *So strange to see her working on a Sunday.*

• • •

On Monday, I planned to satisfy my craving for Vaccaro's cannoli and buttery mussels from Bertha's! *Wow! Look at me turning into a Baltimore gal!* I squeezed in visits to the restaurants in both the Little Italy and Fells Point neighborhoods, meandering through each street and breathing in the atmosphere, shops, and people. I noted the difference between the two. Both were working-class neighborhoods, of course, but Little Italy concentrated on restaurants, fresh food markets, and the church community, while Fells Point centered on industry, shipping, and the port with a smattering of restaurants and bars catering to those workers. Each neighborhood exuded its own energy, pulsating a unique rhythm generated by the movement of traffic and pedestrians. I loved being both observer and participant in the city's unique choreography. *I could see myself living here one day in my own little sunny apartment, writing about the city's vibe or music scene or whatever...Who knows? Argh! That's the thing I've got to figure out. What does my future look like?*

• • •

I promised to take Amy to her Wednesday appointment at a Planned Parenthood in northern Baltimore. After breakfast at a neighborhood diner, we drove uptown to the Planned Parenthood office. I found a place to park on the street and we inched towards to the office.

"How are you feeling, Amy?"

"Scared and freaked and bummed out. Thanks for coming with me. I'd be a total mess if I had to do this solo."

"It's not a problem. Now look, you're only getting information today, right? You don't have to make any decisions right away. Remember that."

A receptionist at Planned Parenthood took Amy's information and led her to an exam room for a pregnancy test and counseling. She was back there for about two hours, maybe longer. The tiny waiting room felt depressing. *Coming here is scary enough for some of these women. Couldn't they at least paint these ugly taupe walls a bright lemon-yellow or nice teal?* Although I didn't know their individual circumstances, I still felt anxious for all the ladies filling the uncomfortable plastic chairs scattered around. Black, White, Hispanic. Most were my age, in their mid-twenties, but a few were older. One woman even brought along three toddlers under five years old, who sat quietly playing with books or dolls as their feet dangled from the chairs. A mother accompanying a young woman, around 19 or 20, made me think of Amy.

No one seemed to want to make eye contact so I focused on a large wall rack of pamphlets providing information about planning for pregnancy, birth control, adoption agencies, counseling, abortion, and everything in between. "An unexpected child can really rock the cradle" shouted one flyer with a picture of an old-fashioned cradle from the colonial days. The brochure focused on the financial pressures of raising an unplanned baby. *Crap! I'm sure Amy isn't even thinking about that part.* Planned Parenthood's whole deal was wrapped up in the brochure's tagline: Children by choice. Not chance.

Sitting in the waiting room gave me plenty of time to think about Amy's situation and the courage it took for her to even come to the Planned Parenthood clinic to talk to the counselors. My mind wandered to the idea of talking to a professional myself…about what happened with Ricky…not that my situation was in any way like Amy's. *Could I do that? Would I have the courage, like Amy, to talk about something so personal? Anyway, Amy's problem is different. She needs options, suggestions to help her make decisions. What would be the point of me talking to someone? I'd have to dredge up the whole ordeal again. What if, after I laid out the story, the counselor agreed with Ricky and thought I brought it on myself or just didn't believe me? No, I'm not brave enough. I don't have the words. I can't…*

When Amy returned, she looked unhappy but less freaked out. The counselor had confirmed that she was pregnant.

"It's for real now, Margie, to the max. Now what am I going to do?" Amy said, as we walked to the car.

"Was the counselor helpful at all?"

"Yeah, she was. It helped to talk to someone with a lot of experience, but now I gotta face reality. And my parents are gonna kill me." Amy started to sob. I stopped to hug her, letting her cry it out right there on the sidewalk. Once she calmed down a bit, she opened up about the options the counselor discussed with her.

"She talked about me having the baby and raising it either with Ted or as a single mom. Or having the baby and giving it up for adoption. Or having an abortion. And she went into details about each of those plans. It's a lot to take in and really all those options are…" Her voice trailed off into sobs.

"I'm sure this is hard, Amy."

Then she blurted out, "I want to talk to Ted. I'm sure he'll want to do the right thing and marry me." *So much for not making any decisions right away. And as far as Ted's concerned, I hope he feels the same way as Amy does, for her sake.*

• • •

Since Ted was visiting his parent's home in Ocean City for the week, I invited Amy to come to Church Creek with me for a few days as a distraction. She agreed. Most of the time she holed up in our guest room, even for meals, although she didn't eat much. I fibbed and told Mom that Amy had a virus of some sort, stressing how it was great for her to have a quiet place to rest up. Mom made tons of tea for me to take up to her, which gave me plenty of opportunities to check in.

"Teatime for the sickie. Compliments of Mrs. Stevens." I placed a painted tray complete with a baby blue teapot, matching cup and saucer, and freshly baked blueberry muffin on Amy's lap and then plopped myself into the hot pink vinyl bean bag chair next to the bed.

"Good thing I like tea. Your Mom's being so rad, even though I don't actually have a stomach bug. It is nice to chill out, though."

"Have you done anymore thinking? Wanna talk?"

"Nah. I still wanna see what Ted says. That's where I am right now."

"Okay, Amy. You have a plan and, of course, you know I'm always here for you."

With Amy's future semi-rooted, I knew I needed to make headway on my own. Finding a couple opportunities to sit quietly at my favorite spot overlooking the Choptank River, I'd been able to clear my mind, find silence, and look deep into my heart for answers about my next steps. One thought still nagged at me: David. During my last visit home, he seemed so different. His focus on others and the way he was impressed with my decision to travel with the band seemed to show growth. *Had he become less self-focused, more interested in my growing pursuits? Is it possible to have a new relationship with him AND to continue developing my writing and music skills? Could a renewed relationship really work between us?* I needed to stop playing the avoidance game and face him again to find out.

I took a deep breath and drove to the river dock, where I knew David would be finishing work for the day. *The same pier where my heart had been crushed six months ago.* With a clear mind, I walked to the end of the ramp. I mentally surveyed my body and my nerves. *Breathing normal, throat relaxed, legs sturdy. You're doing great!* David waved as soon as he saw me, jogging up the long ramp to meet me.

"Hey, you're back in town."

"Yeah. Been back a few days. I'm here with a bandmate, Amy. We're headed out on tour again soon."

"Still can't get over you in a band, traveling around the country. Blows my mind!"

"Well, I always loved music, David."

"Oh, sure…of course." He quickly changed the subject. "So,

look I wanted to have a chance to talk some more...about us. How long you in town?"

"We're leaving day after tomorrow."

"Ah. That's too bad." *Hm. He seems genuinely disappointed, like he could be for real.*

"Is it? Why?"

"I have something I want to show you. It involves you. It's a surprise. Do you have a few minutes?"

"Involves me? I'm kinda intrigued."

He led me back to the dock, toward the small marina to the left and down a short ramp, stopping in front of a sailboat. I noticed the name painted on the boat's bow: The Flow. David glowed with self-satisfaction.

I simply stared, processing the boat's name. Impatient for my response, David blurted, "She's mine. I got my boat, Margie. She's a bit smaller than I'd hoped for but still perfect for cruising around the Chesapeake and East Coast."

Surprised and a bit confused on how this news involved me in any way, I said, "Good for you, David. I know that owning your own sailboat was your dream. You must feel great."

"Absolutely, Margie. Except..."

"Except what? That's all you talked about when we were together. Your plan to own a sailboat, to feel the Chesapeake breeze in your face, to explore every nook and cranny–"

"–Here's where you come in," David interrupted. "It's not the same without you."

Caught off guard, I concentrated on taking a deep breath before speaking. "I'm not sure what you're saying."

"I want you to come home, Margie. It would be perfect. You'd be the girl in my dreams, sailing by my side." *I can't believe what I'm hearing. Is he messing with my head?*

"It's what we always talked about," he said. "Going with the flow, living in the moment…" His voice faded as he became wrapped up in this mindscape he was painting.

My thoughts reeled. *Is this what I want? It could be the very solution to my Ricky problem. Come back to David and forget that whole episode ever happened. Sail away on the beautiful Chesapeake with…But whoa! What about the other stuff I've been figuring out, my writing and music? And, if I did decide to come back to Cambridge, that means going back to Church Creek, too. Am I doing this on my own terms? Am I moving forward or backward?*

David interrupted my thoughts with his own urgent questions. "Well, what do you think? Perfection, isn't it?"

"Uh, look David. Sailing is wonderful and all, but where do my plans come in? My music and writing?"

Surprised by my question, I noticed him grasping to clear any obstacles in *his* plan. "I don't know. You can pick up some singing jobs whenever we're in port or something. Be spontaneous with it, right? And you can always do your writing stuff on the boat. It's just for fun anyways, isn't it?"

My face and neck flushed as I processed his words. *Just for fun… He doesn't take me seriously. And he was never "impressed" with me touring with the band. Empty words – tools for him to sway me to get his way. "Flow with his flow." And I almost got swept up in it. Again!*

"Look, David. I can't do this right now." I bolted down the pier a few yards, then stopped myself. *Margie, look at you! You're running away. How are you going to feel if you don't face this guy squarely, right now?* Turning around to face him, I searched for the perfect words. I felt so angry. I wanted to cut him with my choice of phrase, to hurt him. But that stupid negative chatterbox persisted: *You suck at speaking your mind. You don't have the courage to tell him what you think of him. You're better off walking away!* Still, I couldn't let myself run away again without taking a stand. Not this time.

After a deep centering breath, I looked directly into his eyes and somehow the words began to flow. "I don't know why you're so surprised about me touring with this band, David. I need to be creative. And, by the way, I'm VERY independent. I can't be with someone who doesn't recognize that. You're going to have to find someone else to be the girl in your sailing dreams."

I began to walk away, but something made me stop. I took another breath and turned to face him once more. "There's something else, David. Music and writing are an essential part of who I am, not some side hobby. Even more than that, in these past few months, I've grown as a person, but apparently you haven't." *Okay, not the most stinging retort but still it felt amazing to say what and who I am out loud. I'm a singer. I'm a writer. I love music and it's an important part of my life. Was this encounter with David some sort of cosmic test to assess my focus and determination?* Regardless, I shut down both that stupid negative chatterbox in my head and David because he didn't say another word. In fact, he looked kinda dumbfounded.

• • •

The following day I drove back to my special spot on the Choptank River to sit and decompress. A few motorboats hurried by creating a gentle wake for waterfowl to playfully navigate. I loved this spot for its tranquility and solitude. This was where my miracle occurred, where I found the audition notice for the King Vido's Swing Band that saved me from my terrible mental downward spiral. Closing the David chapter lifted my mind from its chaotic state and cleared the way to thinking of the future. While my body felt lighter and my heart less wounded, I struggled with other issues weighing on my mind.

Foremost, the Ricky charade. Pretending all was well between us while conjuring ways to avoid him exhausted me. The pretense that the sexual assault was my fault constantly battered my psyche. And while I believed that shoving the whole horrid experience deep down was the best plan, I began to see that the strategy wasn't doing my mental health any favors.

I also struggled with the way most of the band members looked the other way at King's treatment of Black people. But wasn't I just as guilty? My silence made me complicit in his prejudice, a fact that grated on my conscience. *Am I that desperate for a spot in the band, for a weekly paycheck? Or am I intimidated by a loud, aggressive bandleader, and my own father, for that matter? Will I continue to be intimidated by these bigots for the rest of my life?* I needed to decide if I had the courage to take a stand, although I didn't feel very brave.

Overhearing the Conti arguments about Stefano's "business dealings" wasn't helping me feel super comfy about the band experience, either. Instead, discovering bits and pieces about the band's illegal funding activities made me feel like a criminal! While I liked the performing aspect and experiencing the audience's energy, knowing the underlying situation became a dilemma for me.

The problem with all those issues was: I didn't know what to do about them.

I knew I didn't plan to stay in a swing band forever. While I wanted music in my life, I wasn't clear in what capacity? *Do I still want to perform or be involved in some other way? And how does my writing about music fit in? Do I need more education in both music and writing? And the broader question lingered: What will be the purpose of what I do next?* This was all still unclear and messy. The rhythmic sound of gentle waves lapping against the shore near my rocky seat allowed me to quietly ponder these questions over and over until my mind went blank. In the silence, I breathed in the fresh river air and soaked in the August sunshine.

I hoped for a perfect vision solving all my woes to suddenly pop into my head, as divined from above, like a second miracle.

That did not happen.

As Carl Jung said, "Your vision will become clear only when you can look into your heart. Who looks outside, dreams. Who looks inside, awakes."

What I realized in that blissful moment of sunshine and river breeze was something completely surprising.

18

Confronting My Dad

Church Creek, Maryland – August, 1978

I spent the last full day of my Church Creek visit canning tomatoes with Mom. She dragged out the pressure canner from the basement pantry and sanitized a rack of quart jars for the first layer of canning. I oversaw the tomato washing, scoring an X on the bottom, before dipping each group into boiling water to be blanched. Mom moved the tomatoes into a cold-water bath until cooled enough to remove the skins. Then she cooked the skinless tomatoes with a bit of water and filled the sterilized jars with the prepared batches. It was a tedious process, but it gave us time to tell old stories, laugh a lot, and simply be together. And something else.

Between tomato washing and scoring, I surveyed the house. The same house I complained about, mocked, even cringed about so often in my thoughts. The house felt different. The shabby hovel I once criticized now radiated affection, devotion, and love. In the living room, a coordinated Early American, golden harvest print sofa with matching loveseat and side chair was pulled together with a collection of dark wood coffee table and end tables – all painstakingly chosen by Mom years ago. While the olive-green shag carpet was well-worn, I knew Mom had selected it to precisely match the grapevines within the furniture's print.

A labor of love. Blinded to the tenderness behind the selection of each piece to create our cozy home in my self-centered rush to "find myself," I realized I needed a cocoon exactly like this to help me "center myself" now. *Ah, the irony is relentless.*

Amy woke up around noon. I took a lunch tray up to her room, wondering if she'd feel like talking about her situation today. I settled cross-legged on a fuzzy pink throw rug on the floor while she munched on one of Mom's apple fritters and sipped tea. She was all ears as I delivered the update about turning down David's self-serving proposal.

"Look at you," Amy said. "You are totally out of sight!" I sheepishly accepted her praise, not thinking my "David confrontation" was much of a big deal.

"No, for real, Margie. That took courage not to go back to him and then to tell him why. Cool beans for you!" Then Amy got quiet. I wondered if she was thinking about her own situation and having to talk to Ted. *She's gonna need to summon some courage, too.*

"Yay, I guess it did take courage," I said. "I usually shrink from confrontation, and even let people push me around so I can avoid it, but I don't want to be like that anymore. I'm trying to make a change. My next big challenge is trying to have a conversation with my Dad where he will actually listen to me. I might need divine intervention to succeed with that one!" We laughed till our sides ached.

• • •

The following evening after Amy had settled in, Mom, Dad, and I shared a meal of Swanson Fried Chicken TV dinners around the kitchen table. I decided it was time to approach them with my "Margie's Next Steps" plan. I felt nervous, as if making a high school presentation – my heart pounding hard, my breathing rapid. I was surprised when one deep breath was all it took to regain control. I felt grounded.

"Mom, Dad. At the end of September, I will have been with King Vido's Swing Band for five months. I've been doing a lot of thinking about what's next for me, what I want to do with my life, my career."

"Well, ya finally came to your senses," Dad said. "I knew traveling around God knows where with a bunch of hippie musicians was a bad idea." I tried to interrupt but Dad was on a roll. "I told ya, Margaret, ya come work for me at the store and find yourself a husband, settle down." *Here we go. I've got to get him to listen.*

"Ya know, Margaret," he ramped up again. "People like us are set in our ways."

"People like us?"

"Yep, like me and Mother and you. We're set in in our ways. Work hard, don't need fancy things like the arts, or government handouts, or strangers infiltrating the community. Family, faith in the Church, and home. That's all that's important."

I felt as though I'd been crushed by 600-pounds of freshly baled hay. *Other than not being afraid of working hard, I don't believe in anything Dad believes.* I stared at this complete stranger I'd known for over twenty years and felt a new emotion: pity. *What a small world Dad has made for himself and Mom.*

Determined not to be pulled into the vortex of Dad's limited existence, I needed to pivot to my planned approach. I decided my only recourse was to demonstrate that as an adult I have choices for moving forward in my own life. *Of course, it didn't help that I was asking for a place to live for the next few months. Cruel irony!*

Dad jumped into his tirade again, this time raving about the influx of Black families moving into the Church Creek area. "Ya probably ain't aware of this, Margaret, but another colored family just bought a house across the road, 'bout six houses down. Here in Church Creek! Jesus, Mary, and Joseph! What's this world comin' to?"

It's now or never! "Does this family buy items at your general store, Dad?" I thought Mom would choke on her iced tea when that blurted out of my mouth.

"Sure, they do, but that ain't the point," Dad muttered.

"Well, I'm thinking it's exactly the point. This family's money is the same as anybody else's money, wouldn't you agree?"

"But having coloreds living here in Church Creek–"

I interrupted but tried to remain calm and respectful. "That's a different topic. Let's focus on the question of you accepting this family's money. It's the same as anyone's money, right?"

"I suppose so," he agreed reluctantly.

"Well, look at that. There's a starting point for getting along with your new neighbors. Just like the Church encourages us to do every week." *Okay, I might have crossed the line with that Church bit, but Dad did lower his eyes and become thoughtful. Baby steps, Margie.*

Mom broke the silence. "So, Margaret, you started to tell us about your thoughts for September?" *Nifty transition, Mom!*

"Right. So, I was saying, it'll be five months on the road in September and this experience has opened my eyes."

Dad jumped right in again. "I knew it. I was against the idea from the beginnin' but your Mother thought it would be good for ya to see beyond your hometown."

"I'm not saying that it opened my eyes to all horrible things, Dad. I'm saying that it opened my eyes to…well, the world beyond Church Creek and how it operates, and the unique way people think and act and…"

Dad couldn't restrain himself. "That's exactly the kind of dangerous claptrap I'm talkin' about. I don't want it around here. I don't want no diversity and different ways of thinkin' fillin' your head with nonsense, Margaret. For cryin' out loud, I won't have it!" *I need Dad to focus on what I have to say or I'll get nowhere. Calmly take control of this conversation, Margie. Deep breath. Look him in the eye. Say what you believe.*

"Dad, I understand that you felt that way when I was a kid, but I'm an adult now. I've got to start thinking and believing on my own. There may be times you and I won't feel the same, but that's okay."

The room became silent. Out of the corner of my eye, I noticed Mom had the slightest smile forming, though she didn't dare allow it to become apparent. I understood why.

Not wanting to belabor the point about our thinking differences, I decided to let it simmer awhile in Dad's mind. Instead, I plowed forward. "I know this will surprise you as much as it surprises me, but I'd like to come home at the end of September to get my bearings while I explore my options."

"I'm confused. You *want* to come home?" Dad asked. "You sounded like you didn't like anything about home, with your highfalutin–"

"–Dad, I've gotta stop you and allow me to clarify. I'd like to ask you to listen to *my* plan. If afterward, you don't want to help me, well, then…I'll have to figure out something else. Would you be willing to listen?" Mom stifled a laugh as Dad reluctantly agreed.

A little startled at myself for getting this far with Dad, I continued. "What I'm trying to explain is that I've learned so much during this time on the road – about music and traveling and about the country, of course. But I also learned stuff about me...and, well, mostly that I have a lot more to learn." We all laughed at that, which broke the tension a bit. "And yes, Dad, I learned that you and I have differences of opinion. We don't see eye to eye on a lot of philosophical issues. That doesn't mean that I never want to be around you or my home again. In fact, I appreciate Church Creek and Cambridge and the Choptank even more than before. I guess, sometimes you have to go away to realize what you've got."

"What are thinking about doing?" Mom asked.

"Well, that's where my plans are still kinda messy. Maybe grad school, maybe focus on growing up some more, maybe...I'm still not sure." Nobody spoke, but nobody jumped down my throat either, so I took that as a good sign.

"I know I freaked out after the David thing, and I'm sorry if I took it out on you both. I fell apart, but I'm much better now, more focused. For right now, I'm thinking of working a couple part-time jobs. The diner will take me back and Doris Mae told me the Dorchester Center for the Arts is looking for a part-time office girl to help out. I'll even work part time for you, Dad, as long as you understand this is a means to an end."

"Well, I like the sound of that," he said.

"Oh, and you'll need to pay me the same as you pay the male part-time help." This time Mom couldn't stifle her laugh.

"Do you have any specific career thoughts?" Mom asked.

"I've been going around in circles – writing, music, perform-ing. But the most important part, the purpose, was the miss-ing link. But that recently became clear to me. Whatever I do in the future, I want to help people learn through my writing, through music, or through combining the two. I need some time to explore what options are out there. Does that mean graduate school, critiquing, teaching, arts administration? A specific job isn't 100% in focus yet. I know in my heart that I can do something to help people understand music and the world better. I want to help people connect to the music and to each other."

"Hmm" was all Dad could say in response. I could see his wheels turning as he mulled over the idea.

"I must say, I've never seen you so enthused and…well, confident about your future," Mom said. "You do seem to have a sense of purpose; in the way you're describing your ideas and in your whole demeanor."

"I think you're right, Mom. As much as I loved vocal performance before, what I learned these past several months is that I want to help people understand how music inspires and energizes both the musicians and audiences. You know, Albert Einstein said, 'I see my life in terms of music.' I guess I'm starting to see it too."

Dad took it all in, quietly. He finally said, "I think we can make this work, Margaret." *Wow, that's a huge step for him. I was expecting way more push back. Can it be that Dad actually heard me? He even seems kinda interested in my thoughts for a future career. Is there hope for Dad after all? And if I got him to consider equal pay for me at the store, maybe, in time… Can I talk to him about my thoughts on civil rights and tolerance and religion and…? Whoa! Let's focus on one step at a time, Margie. He's as tough as his steel toe boots so maybe baby steps is the way to go.*

"Oh, and Dad. I don't expect you and Mom to house and feed me for free. If you need to charge me for room and board, we can work that out."

Mom jumped in. "If you're trying to save money for graduate school or whatever's next then there's no need to charge for room and board. You'll have enough expenses with gas and car insurance. Your idea sounds like a good start, Margaret." She glanced over to Dad who gave her a subtle nod. "You have our full support."

With my vague plan in place, all I had to do was gather the courage to tell King I'd be leaving the band. I decided to leave at the end of September, which meant I needed to give him two weeks' notice by mid-month. It was one thing to find the words to express myself to David. It was another huge step to confront Dad and get him to listen. But King? Simply thinking about telling King and anticipating his explosive reaction made me start to hyperventilate.

I can do this! Mid-September gives me a couple weeks to compose myself.

19

Recording Studio Drama

Pittsburgh, Pennsylvania – September, 1978

The band's next event wasn't a performance. Instead, we were scheduled to cut a promotional album in a professional recording studio. The whole experience teetered between ultra-cool and ridiculously tense. King initially scheduled Multi-Tracks Recording Studio in Pittsburgh, Pennsylvania for three days but it morphed into five, turning him into a nervous wreck. His constant mantra, "This is costing us time! And time is money!" increased the tension, and became a running joke between Jimmy, Chaz, and me.

It all started with laying down tracks for the first number, "Sentimental Journey," including solos for Simon, Giorgio, and Connie. Every time Connie began playing her violin, the engineer interrupted with "Cut!" The rest of the band knew why: she was overplaying her instrument the same way she over sang! *Poor oblivious Connie!* The same routine occurred with Simon's and Giorgio's solos, who either played flat or missed notes right and left.

"These constant stops are costing me money!" King fumed as he trotted into the booth to discuss the situation with the sound engineer. "Take five but don't stray, *capisce?*"

"This is going to be a long couple days at the rate we're

going," I said to Jimmy and Chaz. "What do you think's going on in there?" nodding toward to the booth.

Jimmy laughed. "Off the top of my head, I'd say the sound engineer is just doin' his job, pointin' out the weaknesses and well…"

"The clams?" I asked.

"You got it!" Chaz beamed.

"We've taught her well, Chaz, my man!" Jimmy slapped him on the back, laughing.

It turned out Jimmy had hit the nail on the proverbial head. The extremely competent sound engineer identified the band's problem right away and knew how to deal with it professionally. The issue pointed to, well… family egos. Giorgio and Simon argued over solos on the trumpet and trombone, Connie insisted on including a number with a violin solo, and Enzo wanted a featured drum solo, even though there wasn't one on the album set list! The bickering wasted a lot of precious studio time and, as King harped, "Time is money!" Adding to the ego competition, the engineer identified certain "musical weaknesses," requiring immediate decisions. King called a meeting with Ted and Jimmy to discuss the sound engineer's suggestions. I'd seen plenty of Conti family meetings, but never a meeting that included Ted and Jimmy. It kinda threw me.

"What's happening?" I asked Chaz and Bernard. "No Conti family pow-wow?"

"I've seen this before when it comes to musical problems. King knows that this promotional album needs to sound as professional as possible," Bernard said.

"Yep, that's true," Chaz said. "And it's costin' him a bundle."

"Right, so he can't screw it up," Bernard said, adjusting his sliding glasses. "He taps his best players who he knows will give it to him straight."

"But we could be fulla cow shit!" *Chaz did have a unique way of laying it out there.*

I watched King's body language as he listened attentively to Jimmy making a comment. Hunched over, weary, looking almost desperate, King appeared defeated. Hardly the ranting Emperor persona he normally radiated. I wondered about Jimmy and Ted's role in this important musical decision-making. *Hm. Ted and Jimmy are in the inner circle when it comes to music and professionalism. Makes sense since they've been with the band the longest. Does Ted think King is grooming him for a position of authority in the band? That could explain his fear of rocking the boat with Connie and the family.*

After the "power meeting," King instructed the band to take a thirty-minute break outside while he talked with the sound engineer. We all filed out, except the Conti family. I figured King was filling them in on the change of plans. The rest of us surrounded Ted and Jimmy, asking for an update.

"I really shouldn't be sharing this information." Ted was suddenly acting authoritative and cocky.

"Cut the bull crap, Ted, and tell us what's going on," Ricky demanded.

"You might as well tell them, because if you don't, I will." Jimmy said, knocking Ted's ego back down to earth.

"Okay, here's the skinny. The sound engineer isolated some solos in the booth for King to review. When King heard Giorgio's and Simon's trumpet and trombone solos, he saw the problems, especially compared to Jimmy or Chaz. And Connie's violin solo…well…a disaster."

"That must have been hard for King to admit," I said, glancing over at Amy, who avoided looking at Ted.

"Right, but that's not all," Jimmy said. "The engineer also pointed out that the entire band sounds thin. He recommended adding a couple of studio musicians to create a fuller sound. So, King agreed to the expense of hiring more players for tomorrow's session. We're pretty much done for today."

"But wait. If this is supposed to be a promotional album representing King Vido's Swing Band, shouldn't it only be the real band members?" I asked.

"King's so desperate for this album to be the answer to his freakin' prayers that he doesn't care if it's honest or not," Jimmy said. "Honesty isn't King's middle name, usually."

"Yep," Chaz said. *I'm starting to believe that more and more.*

"Yeah, Ted. Remember that time Ruby messed up and double booked the band on the same date?" Jimmy said. "Instead of cancelling one of the gigs, King divided us up into two smaller bands: one trumpet, one trombone, and Antonio played some of the guitar parts on organ in my group. Stefano played drums back then, but King brought Enzo in to play with the second group. Shit, Enzo must have just turned 14 or 15. Kid could barely play." The guys laughed, but Amy and I looked shocked. I couldn't imagine how King pulled that scam off and got paid for two appearances.

Ted jumped in. "King's always worried about money. And that's what's driving his thinking about this album, too. I do know he's worried about how much it's going to cost."

"No! You faking me out?" Jimmy's voice oozed with sarcasm. Then he and Chaz chimed in together, "Time is money!" and everyone cracked up. Even Ted joined our smiles and chuckles.

"I know, I know. He's been kind of a grueler. Connie said he's been bumming about finances. All he talks about is moving the band to the "next level," bringing in more money. He's obsessed with the idea of making this an A-list band. And this is strange: She said he's been spouting off about how he wants to stop having to do this 'side business' thing once the band brings in A-list dollars."

Everyone sort of shrugged off the "side business" comment, suggesting that they had no idea what it meant. *Should I tell them what I've overheard in the condo or just keep it to myself?*

"Anything else we should know about the album?" Bernard asked.

"Oh yeah. Get this," Ted said. "The sound engineer also suggested beefing up the rhythm section by adding an electric bass instead of relying on Antonio playing foot pedal bass on the organ *and* replacing the drummer. King would never replace Enzo, so we'll be going with two drummers! I'm totally psyched about playing with a real bass guitar and new drummer!"

"What about solos and licks?" Chaz pressed.

"Right, that was damn big," Jimmy said. "King admitted that Giorgio's and Simon's playing was too weak for the album, so he wants to use me, Chaz, and Bernard for all solos licks. Sorry, Ricky. There aren't any baritone sax solos in the set list."

"Yeah, yeah. Story of my life," Ricky whined.

Jimmy continued, "Of course, King will be featured on alto sax, like all the live gigs. And no ridiculous violin solo by Connie, no drum solo by Enzo either. Shit, this album might sound halfway stellar after all!"

With Connie involved in a marathon family meeting, Amy hijacked Ted for a walk. I knew exactly what she intended to do. It was her only opportunity to have "the talk" with him. Jimmy, Bernard, and Chaz reviewed the latest news, while Ricky bantered with the sound engineer, who took a smoke break. Two things absorbed my thoughts: Amy's situation and having to face

King with my own news about leaving the band. Every time I thought about telling him, facing his potential wrath and aggressive response, my heart raced and my breathing became shallow. *Slow, deep breaths, Margie. Slow, deep breaths. Just because you've seen him fly into a rage when things didn't go his way in the past, doesn't mean he'll act that way when you deliver your news this time. It will all work out...I hope!*

• • •

I didn't chat with Amy again until later that evening, long after the band had been dismissed from the recording studio for the rest of the day, like Jimmy predicted. What a mess! Things did not go well with Ted at all. Between her tears and rage, I tried to figure out what happened.

"Amy, calm down and start at the beginning. You went for a walk and..."

"He said he...he's trying to cope with a lot of...pressure, or expectations, or something, and that he can't deal with this right now."

"What kind of pressure?" I asked, trying to make sense of her words as she sobbed them out.

"Oh, I don't know, something about King counting on him and now he feels pressure to stay with the band, or Connie, or...I don't know..."

"But did you tell him you're counting on him, too?"

"Yeah, yeah. I said all that. About how he told me he didn't care about Connie and that he loved me, and how I believed him. Oh, God. I feel like a complete idiot!"

"You're not an idiot, Amy. Don't say that." Although I tried to comfort her, I remembered exactly how she felt. I related to feeling idiotic, angry, confused, used, heartbroken...the list goes on. That jumble of emotions burned like acid, leaving a searing wound in my heart. I felt her pain. I also knew that time was the only healing salve.

"And then, you know what he said? He said, 'What about another option?' You know what he meant, don't you? That made me so mad. Not that I wasn't considering it, but that he was so quick to jump to it. I said to him: 'Another option? Or do you mean another solution so that you don't have to take any responsibility?' Argh, I could scream."

Then she looked up at me, a complete mess, and began sobbing into her pillow. As I pulled the blankets around her, I suggested she try to get some sleep. "We'll give it a fresh look tomorrow, okay?"

• • •

Walking over to the Multi-Tracks Recording Studio the following day, Amy said she was feeling much better, though I found that hard to believe. She said she realized that "Ted is a big dork" and she didn't need a man. *This emotional pivot seems abrupt but maybe other people get over traumatic issues faster than I do. Am I as overly sensitive as people keep telling me, like David and Dad?* I wondered what Amy planned to do about being pregnant, but at least she was functioning – for the moment.

As Amy and I approached the recording studio, we heard some great sounds coming from inside. *Crisp, clean sounds from the warmup licks they're playing!*

"Do you hear that, Amy? That's got to be the hired session players."

"Cool beans!"

"Man, do they sound great!" I picked up the pace, eager to check out these new musicians.

Once inside the studio, we confirmed the session musicians had already arrived, including an electric bass player and a drummer with his entire drum kit. I thought King and the Conti family were going to pass out! All the players were Black. *How is this going to pan out with King and the Conti boys? Should be interesting.*

Jimmy, Chaz, Bernard, and Ricky were already introducing themselves to the session musicians, which didn't surprise me one bit. But the Conti boys and Connie rebelled, huddling around their father with looks of distress, whispering, and pointing. Amy and I reported to our music stand area and pretended to arrange our music, keeping one eye on the developing drama.

Finally, King's voice rose above his sons' and Connie's protestations. "That's enough. This is what we work with, whether we like it or not. I can't afford to lose another recording day. *Capisce?*" The disgruntled toddlers all trudged off to their designated areas.

The session musicians enhanced every section of the band, even adding the electric bass player rather than using Antonio on organ bass pedals. And much to Enzo's chagrin, by adding a second studio drummer, they set up Enzo's kit in a separate room! I secretly wondered if they had to separate the two drummers because Enzo's rhythm was so bad. *What if they only pretend to record Enzo for his ego's sake? Oh boy!*

"Isn't this hypocritical?" I asked Jimmy and Chaz during a short break when we were alone outside. "I mean the added musicians sound fantastic, but since they aren't part of the real band, it seems dishonest."

"Wouldn't be the first time," Chaz said.

"But what's even sadder is that we could have great musicians like these in the band already, but King's not willing to use the best musicians, no matter who they are," Jimmy said as he lit his cigarette.

"What are you guys saying?" I didn't follow their implications.

"Chaz and I have both recommended guys we've played with to fill spots in the band, and the first question from King is always: 'Are they Negro?'"

"You can't be serious."

"Yep," Chaz said.

I pushed back. "But, Jimmy, you told me King played in integrated bands back in the day, right? Why wouldn't he consider using the best players for his band, whether White or Black or whatever?"

"Beside the fact that he's so freakin' prejudiced?" Jimmy said. "He figured if King Vito's Swing Band was mixed he might miss out on bookings at certain ritzy country clubs. Said it was bad for business. 'Let'em play the Chitlin circuit,' he'd say. So, we just stopped offering up the cats we knew."

What? I'm so disgusted by King, though this shouldn't come as a surprise having seen him in action. His treatment of that waitress still haunts me. And now here we are taking part in King's latest act of degradation: He's willing to use Black musicians on his promotional album to make King Vido's Swing Band sound better for prospective bookings, but he's not willing to hire Black musicians into his band! This is so wrong. At the very least I feel better about my decision to leave this band, but I'm still a coward for continuing to be a part of it, not speaking up, not taking a stand.

Despite my anger knowing about King's deep-seated stupidity in denying himself the opportunity to use the best musicians to fill his band, I continued with the recording schedule without saying a word, of course. The studio musicians played the swing and funk numbers with ease and precision, allowing us to complete the album late Saturday night – an amazing feat considering how far behind we were earlier in the process. King was pleased that he didn't have to pay for an additional day of weekend overtime for the sound engineer and studio. The rest of the band members were thrilled with the idea of heading back to Baltimore. I hadn't told anyone that I planned to give King my notice when we returned. Every time I thought about having to talk to him, about his probable reaction, my heart started palpitating. While I wasn't looking forward to the conversation, more than ever I felt convinced it was the right thing to do.

• • •

The morning after we finished the album, I woke up in the motel room and noticed Amy's bed was empty. A note scribbled on the motel memo pad rested on her pillow.

> *Decided to take bus home. I'm freaking out and broken. Too hard being around Ted. I need help. Say I'm sick or something. Thanks for being my friend.*
> *Amy*

She must have taken a taxi from the motel to the bus station super early in the morning. I never heard her get up or leave the room. Even though Amy acted cool around Ted during the last couple days in the recording studio, I'm sure she was covering. Poor Amy was brokenhearted by Ted's reaction to her news, his minimal support, and lack of backbone. *I've been where you are now, Amy. Well, not the pregnant part, but the heartsick part. I know what "broken" feels like. You will get over Ted and heal and be even stronger.* I didn't know what Amy had decided to do about being pregnant. That was Amy's own difficult choice, of course. At 19, she was so young and whatever she decided would affect her life forever. Abortion? Give the baby up for adoption? Raise the baby herself? And what about Ted's responsibility? Is he out of the picture now? It was so complicated.

My thoughts returned to Mom's words about a woman not being able to have both a career and a family when she was younger. Even though that philosophy had begun to change for us in the 1970s, I still felt bombarded by it. It came from Dad loud and clear. Many of my college classmates jumped right into marriage. Others took jobs as teachers with the intention of leaving their jobs once they married and became pregnant. *What do I want for myself? Right now, having a career seems more important than getting married and having kids. I don't know. But do these have to be "either/or" options foisted on women? I've heard so many reports, tragic stories, about things that happened to women before the Roe versus Wade decision. Like girlfriends pooling their babysitting money to fly a friend to a New York clinic all alone, or women having to find back-alley doctors, some bleeding to death over botched procedures. Thank God and the Supreme Court, we now have a choice if the unthinkable should happen. Like that Planned Parenthood flyer said: "An unexpected child can really rock the cradle." I can't even begin to know the answers at 23 years old. How can Amy at 19?*

Right after cutting the album in Pittsburgh, the band received a bizarre schedule change for the following week including two "non-performance stops" in towns we had recently played. Damn! I wanted to be heading directly back to Baltimore so I could have my exit talk with King sooner rather than later. On the one hand, I understood that the summer fair circuit was ending and bookings would be drying up. But returning to Little Rock, Arkansas and Clay County, West Virginia seemed odd since King's schedule listed these as "overnight stops." *Did these extra stops have anything to do with the "side business" investor thing the family kept mentioning?* I began to connect the dots between the bits of conversation I had overheard and these strange non-booking stops that littered our tour schedule. It wasn't creating a pretty picture.

On the other hand, I felt much more focused since my future plans had begun to crystallize. I'd miss Jimmy and Chaz like crazy, and I owed them both so much. They helped me rediscover my love of music and writing, stirred up an excitement to explore new areas of music, and indirectly got me interested in writing about how music makes me feel and how it connects people. *I'm so grateful for all the experiences I've had on this tour, opportunities to sing and entertain audiences and share that special performance energy.* I scoured my brain for some guiding quote or inspirational words on how to control my anxiety when it came time to tell King that I'd be leaving the band in two weeks! But no adage came to the rescue.

I would have to look deep inside myself to discover personal strength, courage, and calm.

Oh, and remember to breathe.

20

Two Weeks' Notice

Little Italy, Baltimore, MD – September, 1978

King instructed the band to assemble in the studio at ten o'clock sharp on Monday to discuss Amy's sudden departure. I plotted out the best time to corner King for a private conversation. *I hope I can pull him aside before the meeting begins. Sometimes he's up in the office before Ruby arrives. If I miss him there, then I'll grab him during lunch break when most of the other band members are out of the building. "Can I speak with you privately, King? It will only take a few minutes."* I rehearsed my opening lines over and over to build up my confidence and control my anxiety.

I made my way down to the office at nine-thirty. The stars must have aligned because I found King sitting at his imposing desk alone, pouring over paperwork. I took a deep breath and, although my heart pounded, I felt confident. *The words will come, Margie. The words will come.* I repeated this calming mantra.

"King, I'm sorry to interrupt, but I need to talk to you." I positioned myself directly in front of his desk.

"I'm busy, *cara*–" King began without looking up, but I cut him off.

"It will only take a few minutes. It's very important." *Whoa! That's not like me to interrupt someone. Even he looks shocked. But this* is *important*. "What I need to tell you is important because I'm leaving the band at the end of the month so this is my two weeks' notice." I realized that all these words tumbled out in one breath and I needed air. *Take a nice slow breath, Margie.*

There was a long pause. King stared at me with those dark, narrow, piercing eyes. I'd seen him do this with other people when he was angry and about to start yelling, so I braced myself for his reaction.

Strangely, King's facial expression shifted. A slight smile spread across his mouth. He broke into a chuckle as he returned to his papers. Instead of the blast of anger I was prepared for, he ignored and...well, dismissed me! *What do I do now? Allow myself to be disregarded? Walk away? Think, Margie! You're not going to run away from this situation! Find a way to get through to him again.*

I tried to be sympathetic to him as the leader of the band. "Look King, I realize this is not the best timing with Amy's leaving and all, but I'm making plans–"

"–Ah, now I see." King sat back in his chair with his hands clasped over his protruding belly. He looked me over with those squinty eyes. "You aren't making a joke. Ah, of course. With Miss Amy gone, you see a hole in the band and you want to negotiate. Very smart business move, cara. I always thought you were the smart one! Okay, then, what do you want? More duets, solos?"

His response confused me. "No, that's not what I'm–"

"–Well, cara, if it's more money you want, then we have a problem." *Be strong Margie. Lay it out there again!*

"I'm serious about leaving, King. I have a job lined up back home and...I, well...again, I apologize for the timing but I'm giving you the required two-week's notice."

I might have stretched it with the job thing but I thought

that having a rational plan for my life would soften the blow. I couldn't have been more wrong. His eyes narrowed again as he processed that I was serious. After another long, long pause – King blew his top!

"Of course, the timing is bad!" he yelled. "You're only thinking of yourself. And after all my Costanza has done, taking you under her wing and grooming you for greatness in this band! How can you do that to her, to us?" Grabbing his hair in both hands, he rose from his chair. Muttering under his breath, but still audible, he said, "Why is it always the women who cause the problems for this band?"

As King paced behind his desk in anger, I tried to process these comments. *Connie taking me under her wing is laughable. What women causing problems? Does he mean Amy or Evelyn or even Cheryl?*

In a flash, King slammed both fists on the desk, causing me to jump. He leaned forward, blasting out, "I gave you an opportunity that so few singers ever get. To perform with the great King Vido's Swing Band. And now you're throwing that away."

I tried to interject that I was grateful for the opportunity, but King was just getting started, layering on the guilt. "We spent time training you to be part of something huge and this is your thanks. You know that King Vido's Swing Band is going places, heading for the big time, don't you? You're going to miss out, and after all we've done for you."

Not giving in, I tried once more to express my appreciation. "Again, I am grateful and I'm sorry if my leaving causes any problems, but..."

In a last attempt to lay a guilt trip on me, he leaned across the desk and asked, "Why are you trying to ruin my band, Margie?" It was a pitiful tactic, really. I didn't say a word. King looked utterly small and desperate. Not necessarily because I was leaving the band, but maybe because he glimpsed at the windmills he kept trying to fight. The moment didn't last, though.

"How dare you think you can disrupt King Vido's Swing Band!" King's roar erupted from nowhere as he banged on the oak file cabinets like a madman. In a flash, King flew around the side of the desk and grabbed my left arm in an excruciatingly tight grip. "I don't know what you thought you heard at the Omaha condo, but you can't mess around with King Vido, *capisce?*"

"Let go of me, King. You're hurting me."

"Do we have an understanding?" Even though King's grasp was tightening, I was pissed.

"I don't know what you're talking about, but you need to let go of my arm!" I was frightened by the panicked and frenzied look in King's eye and his hot, angry breath. Our eyes locked, his grip continued to tighten. *What the hell? He's freakin' out of his mind!*

As if sent by the angels, Ruby came in the front door to begin her day. She looked into King's office and saw King standing close to me. "What's going on here?"

King immediately backed off, composing himself. "Our Margie has just told me she will be leaving in two weeks. Of course, we don't want a band member traveling with us who doesn't want to be here. I was explaining that if she insists on resigning then I *insist* that she will be the one to tell the rest of the band members at rehearsal this morning, *capisce?*"

"Oh, I see," said Ruby.

King faced me. "How do you think your friends will feel when you tell them that you are letting them down, huh? You'll stand in front of the entire band and make this announcement.

That's it!" King said, as a loud final proclamation. An attempt to regain his "King" status and demonstrate some sort of power over me, I felt sure.

I continued to breathe normally throughout King's ridiculous tirade and accusations – no hyperventilating, no rapid heartbeat! I didn't cry or crumble. In fact, I stood back, watching this man rant and rave. I thought about the many times I'd seen him put people down, model prejudiced behavior, or act with minimal integrity. *This is a man whose past is catching up with him and he's unraveling fast. He's more dangerous than I thought.*

Before I could escape his office, King leaned in and whispered one more parting shot. "I won't let a little girl like you waltz in here and create a problem for my band. I thought you were the quiet, obedient type."

I dug deep into my soul, took a quick breath, and replied, "I guess you were wrong about me."

As apprehensive as I was about facing King, I survived! As I went down the steps to the studio, a sense of calm enveloped me.

While I was sure King believed that forcing me to announce my departure to the entire band would act as some sort of humiliating punishment, I wondered if he had an evil plan. I pictured him calling me up in front of the group but then, at the last minute, firing me. Like he did with Evelyn. *I can't wait till I'm out from under his dysfunctional, and apparently illegal reign. As far as King's threat about my band friends' feelings goes, Jimmy and Chaz are the two remaining band members I care about and they'll understand my decision to try to figure out where my music and writing passions may lead me.*

At nine fifty-five, the band members assembled, without Amy, of course. I hoped she found her way home safely and was getting the support she needed. Glancing around the studio, I noticed Ted seemed a bit out of sorts. *Will he follow up with Amy? Will she reach out to him? Do the other band members suspect why Amy left?* Otherwise, the scene remained normal: the Conti boys warmed up as raucously as ever, Enzo pounded on his drums, Bernard and Ricky talked about girls, and Jimmy and Chaz chatted about something horn related. At ten o'clock sharp, King and Connie made their grand entrance and everyone ceased what they were doing, giving King their undivided attention. King shot me a "death stare" for a couple of seconds before he announced the agenda for the day.

"We have many things to do today, especially working the mini shows around Amy's departure, *capisce?*" King said. Then, with a cruel grin and chest puffed out, he continued, "But before we get started, we have an announcement from one of our own—"

Suddenly, the studio door flew open.

A group of five men stormed in, easily identified by the FBI emblems on their jackets and shirts. Visibly shaken, Ruby entered with a sixth FBI agent and directed him toward King. Everything froze as King bellowed, "What's going on here? What do these men want?" The agent pulled King aside and spoke quietly to him, showing him his badge and a document, while the others scoured the studio, like a pack of hound dogs on the prowl. One agent entered the storage closet, another walked around the perimeter of the rehearsal space, and a third stood erect by the doorway. Ruby held back tears with an occasional whimper. The rest of the band looked confused, except for Simon. I glanced over toward him and noticed his head hung down. *Had he somehow expected this?*

For the next several hours, the FBI agent who seemed to be in charge called each of us upstairs for questioning. During my turn, a serious and direct agent asked a battery of questions, often the same one a slightly different way, taking copious notes as I spoke. At first, the interrogation focused on my background and relationship to the Conti family and the band: How long had I been employed by King Studio & Creative Talent Agency and how long had I known Angelo Conti? How well had I known Stefano Conti? What date had I begun the band tour? How would I describe my relationship with Angelo Conti? On and on…

Once the agent seemed satisfied with my status as a newer member of the band, he began with a specific query about what I may have observed or overheard. I told him everything about the conversations I heard at the Omaha condo those few nights, which interested him. I wondered if I was going to be in major trouble for keeping my mouth shut for so long. *Why didn't I speak up immediately? Because you never do, Margie, that's why. Who would I have told anyway? And I was a wreck that first night. But I didn't completely understand what was going on during that argument between King, Stefano, and Simon.* All I could do was tell the FBI agent the truth. And that's what I did.

The agent followed a line of questioning around the Condo conversation. "Can you recreate that first evening in the condo in Omaha, going back to where you were and where the family members were? What can you tell me about the argument the family was having in the condo in Omaha?" He didn't seem upset that I had kept this information to myself initially, which made me feel a lot better.

The examination continued at a rapid pace. He zeroed in on details about the verbal arguments I'd heard in the condo. I could tell he was attempting to extract any new tidbit of information to help his case. "What exactly did you overhear the family arguing about and how often?"

Moving on, he focused on the other arguments I had overheard as well. "Again, let's recreate the second time you overheard a disagreement at the condo. You were in the bedroom again and who exactly did you hear in the living room? What were they arguing about at that time? Did you hear any names of others mentioned during these verbal clashes, like people outside of the Conti family?"

The agent seemed particularly interested in my observation of envelopes or thick packets being exchanged. He seemed quite intense as he rattled off a list of questions on this topic.

"Who did you see involved in these exchanges?"

"Where were you when you witnessed these exchanges?"

"Besides, Mr. Conti, did you know any of the people involved in the transfers?"

"Can you describe the men involved in these transactions, their ages, height, what they wore, race?"

"Would you be able to recognize any of these people in a photograph?"

His final track of inquiry centered on documentation and the band's spending habits. I felt my nerves fraying but continued to search my memory to be as helpful as possible. Questions flew at me, barely giving me a chance to think.

"Did you ever see any records being kept, either on the road or here in the studio? And if so, where would those records be stored?"

"What about those envelopes or any extra money? Where would that be kept?"

"Are you aware of any recent large expenditures by Mr. Conti, either for the band or personally?"

Despite the influx of questions and my mounting anxiety, I answered them all as truthfully as possible. Of course, I *had* overheard arguments between King, Stefano, and Simon at the condo in Omaha. I *had* seen what I thought was money being exchanged in thick envelopes on two occasions. I *did not know* any other people involved in the transfers. I *had* seen a ledger and similar thick envelopes in the safe behind Ruby's desk. I *had* seen money spent on new costumes and on studio time for the promotional album, and for that matter, for retrofitting the girls' truck. There were many times we had been paid in cash instead of check while on tour.

The agent seemed particularly interested in Stefano, asking me a lot of questions about his comings and goings in Omaha: Had I ever seen him at any of the other cities where we performed, or did he often show up at 324 Albemarle Street? I didn't have much to share about Stefano, since I only saw him in Omaha and overheard him during those few conversations. But I told the agent everything I knew several times. He thanked me and asked for my contact information in case he needed to reach me for further questions. I provided my parents' phone number and address.

The agent looked at me directly in the eye and said, "You may need to come down to the Baltimore FBI office at a later date and repeat this process, for the record, or even testify as a witness in court, if this case gets that far. Do you understand?" I nodded. He also gave me a business card in case I remembered other details that might be helpful.

After questioning the band members, the FBI released all the non-family individuals associated with the company. Ruby told us we were no longer needed. King Vido's Swing Band was "on an extended sabbatical" as of that afternoon. She asked us to gather our belongings from the trucks and return our keys. The suddenness felt surreal. Connie wept in Ted's arms in the side office by King's desk, while Ted looked pale and helpless. I tossed my few dorm room items in a paper grocery bag, then hiked with Jimmy and Chaz to the parking lot where the band vehicles were parked. They offered to help carry my suitcase and other junk from the truck to my car on the next block.

"Did you guys have any idea?" I asked.

"I knew Stefano was trouble, so it didn't surprise me one bit when the agent asked a shitload of questions about him," Jimmy said.

I finally told Jimmy and Chaz about what I had overheard at the condo in Omaha, about how it didn't make sense to me and that was why I never said anything to them. They seemed to understand, nodding as I revealed each new piece of information.

Jimmy shook his head, gazing off in the distance. "Damn, I wondered why the hell the agent asked so many questions about Stefano and past tours with the band when he was involved. I told 'em about some of the towns where he used to meet up with us last year like Cleveland, St. Louis, Clay County, West Virginia. Never did understand why the hell he'd fly out to meet the band when he wasn't playing with us anymore."

Jimmy seemed pissed about the whole affair. "I knew King was desperate and delusional, but it sounds like Stefano dragged him in over his head. Man, King has always been out to lunch when it comes to this band. Not seein' how untalented his kids are, strugglin' to keep up to date, just everything." Jimmy tossed his cigarette and ground it out hard with the heel of his boot. "Who'd ya wanna bet called the Feds on old King and Stefano? I'd sink my last damned dollar on Simon," Jimmy said, lighting up another cigarette.

"Yep, he was gettin' fed up," Chaz said.

"But what about Cheryl?" Jimmy said, contradicting himself.

"She could've called in the Feds easy. Remember how upset she was at the St. Leo's festival when she and Simon were talkin' before the show, Margie?" I nodded.

"Maybe," Chaz said.

"Simon probably told her about the shit that was goin' down and she figured it was her only chance to get him off the road. She knew Simon would never rat on his own family!" Jimmy said.

"Well, I guess we'll never know for sure," I said.

We threw the last of my bags into the back of my Gremlin and slammed the hatch shut, until Chaz broke the silence.

"Kind of ironic."

"How do you mean?" I asked, surprised Chaz was offering up some perspective.

"King spent all that money cuttin' a promotional album and now there's not a band to promote!"

Another sad irony, I thought, as we walked back to 324 Albemarle Street to drop off our truck keys and say goodbye to the others who had gathered on the sidewalk in front of the building. As we approached the studio, I could see Connie and Ted huddled with Bernard and Ricky, their heads shaking, bodies slumped. Leaning on a parked car, apart from the group, Simon stared at the sidewalk in front of him, self-absorbed. Jimmy, Chaz, and I merged into the larger group, joining their postures of disbelief. The door to the studio opened and Enzo popped his head out.

"Costanza, Simone. Dad says we're supposed to stay together in the family quarters until the agents are finished talking with him. Come on." A bit of panic broke through Enzo's cocky veneer.

At the same moment, a voice from the opposite end of

Albemarle Street could be heard. "Simon. Simon." Cheryl waddled her pregnant body down the sidewalk toward Simon. "Oh, Honey. I came as soon as I heard. Are you okay?" Cheryl rambled, breathlessly, as they embraced. "Aw, baby. You look drained. Can you leave? Let's get you home." She locked her arm through his and began to lead him away from the studio.

Connie intervened. "Simone, you're needed with *the family*." He stopped, glaring at the studio door. *Oh God, no, Simon. This is your chance. Make the break and go with your wife.*

Connie's nasally voice pushed through the tension. "Simone, the Conti family needs you, now!"

Deep in thought, he walked with slow, deliberate steps up to the studio door, where Connie stood with that damn smirk on her face. But then, Simon did something amazing. He grabbed hold of the Conti Cabinet Making, LLC sign and with two huge yanks, pulled it off the building. Triumphantly, he tucked it under his arm, hopped down the steps, and joined Cheryl to walk down the street. Connie gasped. I suppressed my urge to shout, "Hooray for Simon!"

"Good job, dude," Jimmy said under his breath. "He's got balls after all."

Connie trained her eyes on Ted next. "Teddy! You coming in?" We turned back to Ted standing in the group huddle. *What's he going to do? This is his chance to break free of the Conti family's seductive web. There's no carrot, no promise of a position of authority with the band. For now, the band is defunct. Who knows what's in store for a future King Vido's Swing Band? A perfect opportunity for a clean start for Ted.*

"Teddy?" Connie beckoned again. We were breathless, watching Ted's face for any indication of what he was thinking.

Connie had enough. "Ted, after all this family has done

for you…you're not deserting us…*deserting me*…in my time of need?"

That was all it took. A well-placed guilt trip – a Conti specialty! Ted turned and slowly mounted the steps to 324 Albemarle. *Wow, like father, like daughter. Was Ted in too deep, or did Connie know how to wrangle the family loyalty angle like an expert? Or was he simply weak and voiceless after all?*

Bernard and Ricky said their goodbyes to Jimmy and Chaz. I gave Bernard a quick hug, but avoided Ricky, par for me. Ricky frowned but turned to walk down the sidewalk.

"Bye, Bernard. Goodbye, Ricky," I called after them. Ricky stopped and turned.

"Well, well. She speaks at last," he said with a sickening edge. I considered walking away, running away. *Why not? I'd never have to see Ricky again, never be reminded of his reeking, greasy, groping self ever again.* But then King's words rang in my ears: "I thought you were the quiet, obedient type." *That's not who I am. That's not who I want to be anymore.*

"Ah, at last she grants her supreme approval and speaks to me. To what do I owe–"

"–Shut it, Ricky!" The words came blasting from my mouth. "I simply said 'Goodbye.' Just because I'm quiet or take time to choose my words, doesn't mean you get to twist them to mean something else." I shocked myself as I let this pent-up anger spill out, but I'd had enough of his game playing. "It's my choice how and when I speak, so no, I don't 'grant my approval' to you for anything. You and I know *exactly* why I don't talk to you. Don't pretend otherwise. Now get over yourself and grow the hell up." *I can't believe I'm speaking these words to Ricky. This is unreal! And I'm breathing normally!*

I braced myself for Ricky to hurl some cruel, hurtful

comeback, but instead his face became bright red. He turned around and hightailed it down the sidewalk. Bernard had to run to catch up with him. *Radical, Margie. That felt amazing!*

Jimmy gave me a bit of the hairy eyeball. "What the hell happened between you and Ricky? Other than he's an asshole."

"You pretty much nailed it," I said, feeling lighter but still not ready to talk about the incident. That story will need to be voiced in my own time frame.

Jimmy, Chaz, and I stood in silence, each waiting for the other to initiate the first goodbye. We'd become so close during the past months, sharing both our love of music and too many laughs to count. *My comrades, my musical inspirations!*

"I'm not that far away, you know. We can still get together for jazz nights sometimes, right?" I asked.

"Yep," was all I got from both Chaz and Jimmy.

"What will I do without my musical mentors? I still have so much to learn about funk and R&B and jazz and bebop."

Jimmy said, "Keep listenin' to the good stuff!"

We exchanged addresses and phone numbers. They promised to let me know when they landed their next band jobs. *Gosh, I hope they get hired by someone soon and can stay afloat.* My eyes filled with tears as we hugged our goodbyes, separating to start our new life journeys.

Driving over the Chesapeake Bay Bridge on my way home to Church Creek, Mom's prophetic words played on a loop in my mind: "Perhaps you weren't running away after all. It may have felt like that at the time, but maybe you were running TOWARD something." Toward new people, new experiences, new skills, new music, new parts of the country. Running away or toward is all a matter of perspective, of being willing to ignore or embrace the people and circumstances that appeared in the moment. I may have thought I needed to hide from the pain of seeing David, and I may have had the urge to run away from Ricky initially but sticking with the tour gave me more than I ever expected – an authentic voice. And when I decided to leave, I did it on my own terms. I no longer wanted to be the girl in gold lamé who sang but never used her voice.

As I continued my trek home, I watched a handful of terns soar playfully overhead. I considered my own feeling of lightness and reflected back on the summer months. *Was the appearance of that audition notice in The Banner a true miracle or merely a coincidence? I still can't say for sure but I do know it became a catalyst for new awareness and growth. And, despite the bad times, the whole summer feels pretty miraculous to me.* For someone who was pretty much an introvert and preferred to avoid the spotlight, I discovered that speaking up took several forms, at least for me. Sometimes I needed to step back, analyze the situation and, if it wasn't right for me, be brave enough to say "No!" Sometimes I needed to speak up in the moment.

And sometimes contacting the legal authorities about potential criminal activity within the King Vido Swing Band and not broadcasting it to the rest of the band members was the right way to use my new-found voice. At first, I wasn't sure if I had the courage or if the tip line folks would even take the information seriously but they did. And I had mixed emotions about the effect an investigation might have on leaving Jimmy and Chaz high and dry if it did lead to shutting down the band. But once I connected the dots about King and Stefano's activities, I had no other ethical choice than to place that anonymous call to the tip line. I did this long before King threatened me in his office, of course, but I wondered how much more desperate and erratic his behavior would have become if left unchecked.

I still had a lot of work to do finding the courage to speak up whenever I saw unjust situations, like the King Vidos of the world berating Black waitresses or Dad speaking ill of "those kind of folks" moving into the neighborhood. The tale of Alfred Wolfsohn, a German voice teacher, popped into my mind. Left traumatized and soulless by the horrors of World War II, he used song to reconnect with his own voice, later helping others to do the same. I loved his quote, "The voice is the muscle of the soul." I knew I needed to keep practicing what I learned this summer and believed I could help others by connecting them to music and writing. My personal and spiritual journey was far from complete.

With the Choptank River in sight, I popped my favorite Earth Wind and Fire tape into the 8-track player and sang along with the lyrics of "That's the Way of the World." In those few short months, I experienced so much about "the way" of my world – some of it new and exciting, some tough and difficult. Taking time to reflect on my past helped to redefine and reconnect me to the soul of who I was and who I'd like to become. Despite knowing I'd only begun to scratch the surface, my healing heart soared with spirit and breath and music.

And finally, a voice to begin to express it all.

Author's Note

Many of my friends and family know that *That Summer She Found Her Voice: A Novel* is based on a conglomerate performing experiences I had as a young woman. I acted professionally in stage musicals and yes, even sang in a couple bands in the 1970s. This naturally leads one to ask: what parts of the story happened in real life and what parts have been fictionalized. So, here's the skinny: The characters in this story are fictionalized, made up of bits and pieces of show biz folk (and even non-show biz folk) I've encountered along my own journey.

While I did use one of my band experiences to construct a made-up tour framework, most of the episodes within the book have all been fictionalized, especially the money laundering sub-plot. I used historical research to fill in details such as the types of costumes worn by show bands in the era, a description of the venues on the fair circuits, the typical set lists that may have been performed to include 1970s pop, gospel, patriotic, and of course big band tunes. The rest of the plot was enhanced by imagination or historical research.

And while Margie's hometown of Church Creek near Cambridge is an actual place on Maryland's beautiful Eastern Shore, her alma mater, St. Angela College in Chestertown, is an invention to fill my need for a Catholic college. (Although there is a wonderful liberal arts college in Chestertown called Washington College.)

Doris Mae's Restaurant, a real establishment, opened in 1979 and was run primarily by Doris Mae and her daughter, Glenda. Regrettably, it's unlikely Margie would have waitressed there in 1978. I loved the history of this downtown diner that catered to a balanced clientele of locals, races, professionals, and "come heres" (a nickname given to folks not originally from Cambridge and the Eastern Shore).

The following is a list of some date-bending I employed between real life and the fictional world of *That Summer She Found Her Voice*. I hope readers will allow me these indulgences in order to make the story flow:

- The Mother's Day Crowning of the Blessed Mother in Little Italy, Baltimore is generally a one-day event, without a prior Saturday neighborhood festival. However, there are several St. Leo Church festivals that do encompass both Saturday and Sunday activities.
- Illinois State Fair generally takes place in August; not in July as depicted here.
- Independence, Louisiana's Sicilian Heritage Festival traditionally occurred in March, not in July as depicted here. The Night in Little Italy Sotto Le Stelle/Under the Stars occurred in September, not in August as depicted.
- Sun Ra's Arkestra performance at the Famous Ballroom took place in 1979, not in 1978 as depicted.
- The Village People's "Y.M.C.A." was not released until October 1978 on the album *Crusin'*.
- The Cleveland Italian Festival in Little Italy is modeled after the Feast of the Assumption Festival. However, this festival

falls on the weekend closest to the 15th of August.

- While the Japanese video game, *Space Invaders,* was released in 1978, it did not reach popularity in the United States until the following year, making it highly improbable that the band members would have been able to play it at the fictional Rosie's Bar and Grille in Omaha in the summer of 1978.

- Wyndhurst Country Club in Roland Park is fictional, however, the issue with the racist sign is not. According to *Members Only: Elite Clubs and the Process of Exclusion* by Diana Elizabeth (Rowman & Littlefield Publishers, 2008), the real Baltimore Country Club in Roland Park had the same sign on its premises through the early 1970s, based on my research. It wasn't until 1995 that the Baltimore County Club accepted its first Black member. (See https://www.baltimoresun.com/news/bs-xpm-1995-02-03-1995034059-story.html)

For those who would like to learn more about the Baltimore music scene, I highly recommend the book compiled, written, and edited by Joe Vaccarino, titled *Baltimore Sounds: An Illustrated Encyclopedia of Baltimore Area Pop Musicians, Bands & Recordings, 1950 – 1980.* This treasure was an indispensable resource for me throughout the research phase of *That Summer She Found Her Voice.* An article on BestRide.com described how Aerosmith converted a 1964 International Harvester Metro for transportation for their early 1970s tour as well as other bands' truck and bus conversions through the years. I also depended on interviews and fact-checking about music venues in Baltimore in the 1970s, particularly concerning the topic of race and the Baltimore music scene. For this, Rodney Kelley, Don McCombie, and Ed Kernan were extremely helpful.

Additional resources about topics in *That Summer She Found Her Voice* include Thomas Vicino's *Transforming Race and Class in Suburbia: Decline in Metropolitan Baltimore*, Debby Irving's *Waking Up White: And Find Myself in the Story of Race*, Suzanna Rosa Molino's *Italians in Baltimore*, Gloria Johnson-Mansfield and A.M. Foley's *Cambridge*. George Mitch Anderson, Administrator and Collections Manager for the Dorchester County Historical Society, was extremely helpful in pointing me in right direction within the collection's wonderful research library. Especially helpful were *Cambridge Past and Present: A Pictorial History* by Donald L. Reid, Roger Guy Webster, and Hubert H. Wright IV, "Cambridge Outdoor Show Program" for 1977 and 1978, and a personal interview Mitch Anderson arranged for me with Historical Society member, Steve Abbott, lifelong Cambridge resident.

Of course, I apologize in advance for any oversights or errors that may be found in my book and claim these as my own.

My hope in writing *That Summer She Found Her Voice* is to restart conversations—some that have gone unspoken from previous decades; some that have resurfaced in the news recently. It's about time, don't you think? Rad, man!

Acknowledgments

I am incredibly fortunate to be surrounded by readers and consultants in a variety of fields, all related to *That Summer She Found Her Voice: A Retro Novel*. Experts in music and the performing arts, mental health, those growing up in the sixties and seventies – who could ask for anything more?

First, I'd like to thank my beta readers. To Carol Cahill, who provided excellent feedback on two early drafts; my dear friend, Ira Domser, who encouraged me to tell this story so often that I finally had to comply; my sister, Mimi Burgess Todd, who bounced around thoughts about mental health, which is her area of expertise, and Sue Hughson, a writer critique partner. Thank you, thank you, thank you! Your input, feedback, and suggestions about characters and plot holes in early drafts proved to be incredibly insightful.

Next, I need to thank Eileen Haavik McIntire, fellow Maryland Writers' Association member and author of several suspense novels and *The 90s Club Cozy Mystery* series published by Amanita Books. Eileen's incredible attention to detail opened my awareness to multiple issues that enabled me to address in the final revision, including a major change to the ending. I thank you, Eileen, for taking the time to share your insights.

My heartfelt thanks goes out to my reader, editor extraordinaire, and wonderful sister, Barbara Burgess-Van Aken, for her contributions to this book and to the process. She is my biggest cheerleader and source of encouragement as well as a fantastic fountain of knowledge about writing. Thank you for allowing me to share this writing journey with you and for your generous feedback and expertise.

I'd like to express my gratitude to the many resource and reference materials I accessed about the music scene in Baltimore. One that must be acknowledged is Baltimore Sounds: An Illustrated Encyclopedia of Baltimore Area Pop Musicians, Bands & Recordings, 1950 – 1980, compiled, written, and edited by Joe Vaccarino. I am deeply indebted to this wonderful guide and highly recommend it to anyone interested in taking a deep dive into this subject.

In addition, my interviews with three fabulous musicians helped to clarify the 1970s Baltimore music scene and climate. First, guitarist Rodney Kelley patiently answered my seemingly never-ending list of questions about the Black experience in Baltimore in the 1970s, about being a Black musician in the Baltimore in the 1970s, and about jazz and music in general. Rodney, you are a gem! Second, bass player Ed Kernan confirmed information about Baltimore clubs and musicians in the late 1970s whenever I was stuck, confused, or in a hole. Thank you, Ed. Finally, keyboardist/organist Don McCombie made himself available to confirm all the musical references throughout the book – both vocal and instrumental. If I had the strangest questions about the composition of a band, the aspect of a particular instrument, voicing, a musical composition, or a genre, he had the answer or pointed me in the right direction for additional research. I am constantly amazed at the breadth of his knowledge and heart in his musical understanding. Thank you, Don, for patiently sharing your talent with me.

I'd also like to thank others who provided, clarified, or confirmed information in the book including Kendra Sweren for her expertise on Baltimore Hons; Barbara Burgess-Van Aken for her knowledge of Italian word usage; and Maryland Center for History and Culture for its amazing online resources during Covid 19 lockdown.

Special thanks are extended to George Mitch Anderson, Administrator and Collections Manager at Dorchester County Historical Society in Cambridge, MD, who was so helpful during my research trips. Mitch went beyond the call of duty when he arranged a personal interview for me with Steve Abbott, a lifelong Cambridge resident, who was able to provide vivid local color for Margie's back story. Sadly, Mitch passed on at age 70 just weeks before I was able to share the good news that this book would be published. I'm sure he would have been pleased.

I would be remiss if I didn't extend a huge thank you to the team of professionals who have taught me so much about the industry in the past few years. To the Maryland Writers' Association, I am filled with gratitude for the many, many workshops and seminars to which I was able to avail myself. To my amazing attorney, Drew Stone, I thank you for sharing your expert advice and knowledge. And to Kevin Atticks and my Apprentice House Press team at Loyola University Maryland, I am forever thankful and appreciative of the professional care I received as we collaborated on my book's journey to publication.

Finally and always, I thank my wonderful husband Don McCombie for believing in me and this project.

Topics for Discussion

1. When we meet Margie, she is at a point of despair. Her heart is broken and she is spiraling into a dark depression. While she does feel anger toward David, why does she blame herself as much as him for her feelings? Why do you think Margie's parents' attempts to help her are futile?

2. Margie is at a transition point in terms of her spirituality. A non-practicing Catholic, she is searching for something that makes sense to her. She admittedly hasn't prayed in a long time. Did Margie's "miracle" seem real to you or simply a coincidence?

3. What may have influenced Margie's turn away from her Catholic upbringing and her subsequent search for some other spiritual guidance?

4. Margie's father impressed her with early messaging about a woman's role, especially concerning parent versus career, and her mother demonstrated similar messages. In what ways do you think Margie's mother was a role model? In what ways was she a negative example for Margie? Have you heard stories from anyone from this era that deliver similar messaging

about gender roles?

5.   Describe how Margie's relationship with her father is different than her relationship with her mother. What do you think contributed to this difference?

6.   When Margie sees blatant examples of prejudice occur during the tour, it starts to eat at her and dredge up memories from her own home life. She wonders why there weren't more conversations in high school about desegregation, tolerance, and communication. Do you get a sense that discussions about racism and racial injustice have improved in schools today? How about in religious settings?

7.   Margie joined King Vido's Swing Band primarily to "heal the gaping hole" in her heart, running away from having to see David around town. Eventually, she realized that the tour offered her insight into what might be next for her. What else might Margie be "running away" from?

8.   How did Margie's reconnection with singing open other possible musical doors for her future? How did touring with the band help reconnect and reignite her passion for both music and writing again?

9.   Margie chose to keep the sexual assault by Ricky hidden, pushing any thoughts of it deep into her psyche. Do you think she had any other options, considering the decade? What might have happened if she reported the assault to King? To her father? To her mother? To Chaz and Jimmy? Where else could she have turned? Are there better outlets for young women today or do you sense that many sexual assault stories are still kept buried?

10. Margie tends to think of herself as one who tries to avoid center stage. In what ways does she shrink from the spotlight? At other times, Margie finds herself smack in the middle of situations. How do you account for this contradiction?

11. What do you think Amy decided to do about her pregnancy? Were the options presented to Amy different from those available today? How have things changed today for someone like Amy? In what ways are they the same?

12. Why do you think Ted decides to go with Connie and the Conti family at the end of the story?

13. The pull of family loyalty kept Simon from leaving King Vido's Swing Band for a long time. What do you think was the final straw for Simon – that final moment when you were sure he would choose Cheryl and his soon-to-be-born baby over King and the band?

14. As you see it, how much did other people's perceptions (her dad, David, her mom, others) influence Margie's perception of herself and contribute to her "voicelessness?" In what ways did other people's perceptions have a positive effect on Margie?

15. At the point that Margie overheard Simon and King arguing about Stefano's illegal activities in the Omaha condo, what did you suspect was going on?

16. We've all encountered a Connie or two in our lifetime. Do you agree with the way Margie decides to handle Connie – "with a combination of kid gloves and avoidance!" Or do you think this was another example of Margie's voicelessness?

17. Where do you see Margie begin to speak up for herself in certain areas of her life as the story unfolds. What aspects of Margie's life may still need work in terms of speaking her truth?

18. The recurring theme, "finding her voice," has a dual meaning. How do you see the dual meaning relate to Margie finding her voice while touring with King Vido's Swing Band?

About the Author

Jean Burgess is a writer, editor, playwright, and workshop presenter. As a former professional stage actor and director, many of her written works relate to the performing arts, including her debut novel, *That Summer She Found Her Voice: A Retro Novel.* Her nonfiction, entitled *Collaborative Stage Directing: A Guide to Creating and Managing a Positive Theatre Environment,* was published by Routledge/Taylor & Francis in 2019. Before diving into a writing career, Jean taught theatre and speech communications on both the secondary and college levels for twenty-three years. She holds an M.A. in Theatre from Northwestern University and a Ph.D. in Educational Theatre from New York University. She lives in Maryland with her husband, Don.

Please visit Jean's website at http://jeanburgessauthor.com and stay up to date with her writing activities by signing up for her monthly newsletter on any webpage.

Apprentice
House Press
Loyola University Maryland

Apprentice House Press is the country's only campus-based, student-staffed book publishing company. Directed by professors and industry professionals, it is a nonprofit activity of the Communication Department at Loyola University Maryland.

Using state-of-the-art technology and an experiential learning model of education, Apprentice House publishes books in untraditional ways. This dual responsibility as publishers and educators creates an unprecedented collaborative environment among faculty and students, while teaching tomorrow's editors, designers, and marketers.

Eclectic and provocative, Apprentice House titles intend to entertain as well as spark dialogue on a variety of topics. Financial contributions to sustain the press's work are welcomed. Contributions are tax deductible to the fullest extent allowed by the IRS.

To learn more about Apprentice House books or to obtain submission guidelines, please visit www.apprenticehouse.com.

Apprentice House Press
Communication Department
Loyola University Maryland
4501 N. Charles Street
Baltimore, MD 21210
Ph: 410-617-5265
info@apprenticehouse.com • www.apprenticehouse.com

Printed in the USA
CPSIA information can be obtained
at www.ICGtesting.com
LVHW022107200324
775041LV00007B/77